HOUSE OF DESTINY

Recent Titles by Anne Worboys from Severn House

HOTEL GIRL
RELATIVE STRANGERS
SEASON OF THE SENSES

HOUSE OF DESTINY

Anne Worboys

The first world edition published in Great Britain 1998 by
SEVERN HOUSE PUBLISHERS LTD of
9–15 High Street, Sutton, Surrey SM1 1DF.
First published in the USA 1998 by
SEVERN HOUSE PUBLISHERS INC., of
595 Madison Avenue, New York, NY 10022.

British Library Cataloguing in Publication Data

Worboys, Anne
    House of destiny
    1.   Love stories
    I.   Title
    823.9'14 [F]

    ISBN 0-7278-5382-1

Typeset by Palimpsest Book Production Ltd.,
Polmont, Stirlingshire, Scotland.
Printed and bound in Great Britain by
MPG Books Ltd, Bodmin, Cornwall.

Chapter One

CASSANDRA Neilson, tall, slender, with a wealth of dark chestnut hair bouncing on her shoulders, marched purposefully out into the Arrivals section at Heathrow. She was tired and disorientated. She hadn't slept since the night before leaving Los Angeles. The man in the adjacent seat on the flight from New York, a salesman selling himself if ever she saw one – dark hair expensively cut, silk shirt open to the lower ribs, uncomfortable and fidgety in tight jeans – had been determined to utilise the flight in getting acquainted.

Goodness knows, she had not dressed to attract. Her skirt was old, deliberately chosen for comfort, as was her navy-blue T-shirt. Her flat-heeled walking shoes were scruffy and did nothing for her ankles. She would have thrown them out when packing but at the last moment decided they would take her round the sights of New York at speed, and in comfort. They had. She had visited the Metropolitan and Frick Museums, the shops of Fifth Avenue; she had seen a unique view of the city from the giddy heights of the Trade Centre; taken in Greenwich Village. All without a single blister.

She retrieved her suitcase and set it on its steady little inset wheels. Looking straight ahead, she strode on past a blur of anxious, waiting faces. Nobody was meeting

1

her, Leila and Gerald being in hospital after the accident.

"Cassandra!" She stopped dead, head thrown back, her bag chuntering untidily with near human surprise. "Cass!" The voice came again, behind her this time, breathless as though the owner was ducking and diving to catch up. She turned. Dark-lashed eyes, blue and deep as a sapphire sea. That lovely, diffident smile. Her heart missed a beat. Jonathan Tarrant! Son and heir of the Earl of Bevington, tall, dark and with a shining lock of hair falling over his high forehead. Seven years slid aside. Emotion no less than shock brought tears to her eyes.

"I – I'm on my way home," she stuttered. "I'm in r–rather a rush." She jerked the handle of her bag. It jumped, dementedly, knocking into the legs of a woman dawdling along in front of them.

The woman turned, outraged. "I'm so sorry," said Jonathan, dexterously taking the offending luggage in hand, apologising in his unique, melting way that always produced forgiveness. The woman smiled in return, saying it was perfectly all right. He bent his head, speaking to Cassie, "I've come to take you home," he said.

"You've got a nerve!" she retorted, her own woman now, practically American, certainly classless, more than grown-up at twenty-five and not about to stand any nonsense from him. "I'm perfectly capable of getting myself there," she said. What are you up to? was what she would have liked to say. She'd been home once a year and he hadn't even been in touch, he who had been the cause of her banishment.

But she was inexorably going with him, hustling along through the crowd, being pulled away from a fat man who

2

wasn't looking where he was going, weaving between a couple of boys wearing baseball hats back to front.

Such power he had.

The innocent friendship of the gardener's granddaughter and the only son of the Earl and Countess of Bevington had begun when Cassie was barely four and Jonathan a little boy. Home from prep school at the beginning of the holidays, he would dash round the brick paths on his bicycle, shouting, 'Cassie! Cassie! Where's Cassie?' She would run from one of the greenhouses where her grandfather had been allowing her to help him and stand shyly waiting, with her long chestnut hair falling on either side of her face, big-eyed, thrilled. A sweet friendship, the grown-ups thought. The son of an earl and the gardener's child. They smiled about it. You were safe when you were barely four.

But she had grown up.

One day when she was seventeen and Jonathan twenty-four he had come upon her stealing lettuces from one of the Bevington Hall greenhouses. Leila had invited visitors for Sunday lunch. The earl's deer had leapt the fence in the night and demolished Gerald's carefully tended garden that adjoined the park. Row upon row of cabbages, trampled and half eaten. Carrot tops gone so that you didn't know where the carrots were.

The grocer in the village, who also kept the paper shop and was therefore open early in the morning, had long since put his greens away and closed his doors. Leila was distressed, her meal ruined. Cassie had taken the matter into her own hands, climbing through the fence and running, running across the park. She knew the layout of the vegetable garden well. Knew exactly where to find carrots, lettuces, beet.

Jonathan, opportunist, privileged scion of the stately hall, had caught her. His arms had gone round her, triumphantly imprisoning her.

'Why, my little Cassie! So you've grown into a thief while my back was turned.'

She gazed up into his dear, laughing face, experiencing ecstasy; and responded, sensuous as a cat, to that first kiss.

After that there were secret meetings in the shadowed part of the gardens. It had not occurred to her until her family so cruelly pointed it out, that his wish for secrecy had a different root cause from hers. He was playing games with the head gardener's granddaughter, they said. Sons of great houses had been seducing servant girls since history began.

'He didn't seduce me!' Defending Jonathan, she realised later, she had not only embarrassed them but damned herself in their eyes. Their high morals were deeply ingrained. People of their generation, expecially those of their class, didn't express love freely until the ring was on the girl's finger. She felt distanced from them. And, 'I am not a servant girl,' she said distinctly. Gerald was a schoolteacher, the first of the family to break away. Leila had come out of service when she married him. But they were stained forever by the past.

'We don't want you to be hurt,' they said, glossing over what could not decently be put into words because times were changing and nobody talked about servants any more. They were supposed to be living in a new classless society, though everyone knew it was not that, never would be. Sure, servants had stopped being servants and become staff, but none the less the sons and daughters of aristocrats did not choose partners from the families who had in the past lived behind their green baize doors.

'You do understand he could never marry you,' they said.

She hadn't thought of marriage.

They didn't tell her whose idea it was that she should be sent to Aunt Elaine in Los Angeles. Was it the earl putting his foot down? Her grandfather, afraid of losing his job? Her parents, because Grandfather's job went with the house where they all lived? Cassie was persuaded it was better that she go. Jonathan had disappeared to London. Willingly? He had a car. He could have come to see her. He could have telephoned. There was no letter. No phone call.

After a while she came to believe what they said. That Jonathan had been playing games. Bitterly hurt, bleeding inside, she was only too pleased, in the end, to run away. A nice long holiday in Los Angeles with Aunt Elaine and Uncle Ben they said encouragingly. Take a job. They were sure Ben would arrange a work permit. It would be good experience.

Were they taken aback when she chose to stay? She read into their silence and their gratitude for her annual visits that they were conscious of having used up their rights.

Jonathan jerked her arm when she would have dived between a man and woman lost in contemplation of the Arrivals board. "I'd prefer not to be escorted like a criminal", she said.

He didn't answer, and he didn't let go.

They reached the moving walkway and were jostled by a party of ebullient youths racing for the exit. "Hold on there," said Jonathan. One of the racing demons paused, looking at him in uncertain surprise. The others telescoped behind. Nobody protested. His authority had a mature quality, now.

She remembered his arrogance that day when her grand-father caught them together, he a privileged youth full of brash confidence, his head gardener looking appalled. 'Get out of here, old man!' Cassie's grandfather had seemed to shrink as he withdrew, the residue of generations of servitude rising automatically. Neilsons had been trained in obedience to their betters. Cassie's great-grandfather had been an apprentice gardener at the Hall in 1856 at the age of fourteen.

They approached the exit. Cars were creeping in to deposit passengers and their baggage. Automatic doors opened. A group of people stood looking curiously at a shining black Rolls Royce that was waiting at the kerb. Cassie recognised with astonishment the Haldane Rolls. And that was Tom Cochrane, his lordship's chauffeur, behind the wheel! He eased himself out of the driver's seat and came round to take her bag.

"Hello, Tommy." She smiled at him, nervously. What was he making of Jonathan's coming to meet her?

"Welcome home, Miss."

She put a hand on his arm and looked beneath the peaked cap into the smooth, kindly face that was on a level with her own. His manner was different. Uncertain. He avoided her eyes, dropped his gaze, picked up her bag. "You used to call me Cassie," she said. Only last June when she visited him in his stable block flat he had called her Cassie. What was going on?

He raised the lid of the boot and put the bag in, then holding the back door open for her smiled as he acknowledged, "So I did."

Cassie waited for him to go on but he wasn't looking at her. She felt shaken. Slighted. Insulted. Confused. Tom

Cochrane was an old friend. She climbed into the car and sat stiffly in the deep comfort of the sprung leather seat. Jonathan slipped in beside her. The chauffeur resumed his place behind the wheel, slid the glass partition across and started the engine. The car moved forward, purring its way down on to the M25.

She glanced at her watch, needing something to do to take her mind off what was happening. "What's the local time?"

Jonathan held out his left wrist so that she could synchronise her watch with his. She adjusted the hands on the modest little timepiece on her wrist.

"Why did you come via New York, Cassie?"

"I'd never been there," she said. "That's all."

It wasn't all. Not by any means. Last moment panic had led her to extend the journey.

She had been coming home next month to fight for the family home, the grace-and-favour head gardener's cottage that the earl considered he had a right to sell, never mind that Gerald had been paying rent for it since his father died. Her mother had written to say his lordship was feeling the pinch. Heavy death duties had had to be paid on the death of the thirteenth earl. The Inland Revenue wanted to take some old masters off the walls in lieu of cash but the Haldanes had refused. By the time everything was settled, the coffers of the fourteenth earl were low.

Estate workers' cottages, built in earlier centuries, brought high prices. City tycoons with money to spend were attracted by their quaintness, their old oak beams, the way their porches leaned drunkenly because the unskilled labourers

7

who built them had not yet learned the art of tying-in. Crabapple Cottage was just such a dwelling.

In Los Angeles Cassie, by turns angry and cynical, had marshalled all her arguments on the rights of the common people. If the earl had offered Gerald the cottage as a sitting tenant when her grandfather died he would have bought it at a fair price. But Lord Haldane had been happy to rent it out – until prices spiralled.

'That's how they got to be rich,' Aunt Elaine had remarked pointedly, she who had escaped in her teens to marry an American. She knew well enough that Leila and Gerald were too immersed in the class system to fight back. 'You go home and put a bomb under your parents, dear,' she said, full of fight still at fifty-four, 'then come back as fast as you can.'

And so she channelled her indignation into her letters. 'His lordship can't put you out!'

Her parents replied that they would never dream of either sitting tight or taking the earl to court. A friendship spanning the generations was not to be ended that way. 'We both feel it's wrong to hold on to something that belongs to someone else,' her father wrote. 'We're grateful his lordship kept the rent reasonable.'

Thereby doing her parents a bad turn, Cassie had said to herself as she reread their letter, angry in their defence. If he had asked rent at a realistic level in the first place they would have been forced to buy elsewhere.

In the end it was the accident that had precipitated her departure. Leila and Gerald had been walking down a lane in the dark. A car hit him. On the telephone Leila had sounded lost and wretched. Gerald had broken bones, she said tearfully. He was badly shocked. She reminded Cassie that he was fifty-eight.

'You're ringing from the hospital?'

'Yes dear.'

Cassie's heart contracted with fear. 'So, what happened to you?'

'I'm all right, dear.' Then she was crying. 'I'm so frightened,' she said.

A nurse came on the line to explain that her mother was very shaken. She hoped Cassie would come.

She recognised that this was the end of the life she had made for herself in the USA.

Now, in the back of the Rolls she sneaked a look at Jonathan. He was gazing straight ahead. If Aunt Elaine had written to Leila telling her of Cassie's intention to take the Haldanes to court over the cottage, then she could see Jonathan might be perturbed enough to meet her and try to talk her out of it. But Elaine was normally discreet. As was Leila. Normally. But there was no knowing what people would do when frightened and alone; who they would talk to; what they would say.

Jonathan turned his head. "I expect you've had breakfast."

"No. I so hate airline food. I'm quite hungry now," she added, not realising she was falling into his hands.

"There's a nice little pub on the river not far from here. Why don't we stop and have a plate of bacon and egg?"

She replied in a rush, fearing too great an intimacy in this going to a pub, hobnobbing over bacon and egg. "No, really, I'm not that hungry. I'd rather get home. I'm anxious about my parents."

"You'll still see them a great deal sooner than if you took public transport."

She acknowledged in her mind that was true. She had expected to get the underground to Piccadilly, and then on to Waterloo where she would take the train to Flyford, then a taxi to the cottage. She had no experience of this complicated journey. Her parents in the past always met her in the Rover. Now she realised it would have taken hours.

She looked down at the clothes she had been wearing since leaving Los Angeles. How long ago was that? She had become lost in the time zones. She ran a palm across her face that hadn't been washed for – how long? Her skin felt dry. With both of her parents at the hospital and Crabapple Cottage empty, would there be any hot water? The immersion heater was slow. She didn't fancy a cold bath.

"All right," she said, though still uncertain. "Perhaps I could have a wash? I wouldn't mind changing my clothes." She guessed the kind of 'nice little pub' an earl's son would choose would have facilities.

"Why not? Though you look fine to me." Jonathan conferred on her one of his approving smiles. She turned her face away, hiding its heightened colour, gazing out over the countryside, seeing nothing at all.

Jonathan did not speak to the chauffeur but all the same the car left the motorway. Cassie knew then that this was not an impulsive idea, this buying her breakfast. Tom already had his instructions. Her nerves tensed.

Jonathan leaned forward and slid the little window aside. "It's the next turning on the right, Tom." And then, a little later, "Next on the right again." Cassie felt trapped. She threw him an apprehensive look. He smiled back. The smile did nothing to reassure her.

She looked out of the window. They were rolling past pretty houses, black and white mock Tudor of the thirties with spring flowers in their gardens. They nosed into a side road, and there was the Thames, grey, energetic this morning with the tide running. A tourist boat throbbed past. A voice over the tannoy slid across the water and stopped somewhere in the air above the railings.

The hotel was a long, low building, all white stucco and Virginia creeper coming into leaf. It would look wonderful in autumn when the leaves turned red, brown and gold. Cassie felt like a tourist at that moment, and then something turned in her mind and the picture became familiar.

Jonathan said, "It's the use of a bathroom you want, isn't it? You'd like a shower?"

"That would be lovely."

"Hang on a moment while I check." He was brisk, businesslike, confident of being able to provide for her.

He came back saying, "It's okay. Tom, would you carry her bag in? Upstairs, directly on the right."

Cassie jumped out and followed the chauffeur through the door. On the landing, out of sight and hearing of Jonathan she opened her mouth to say, 'Tom, what's going on?' but he got in first, "That seems to be the bathroom, Miss," he said, put her bag down, then went off without so much as a glance at her. Cassie's sense of foreboding increased.

She put the bag down on the tiled floor, unlocked it and found clean underwear. It was such bliss under the shower she had to fight a temptation to linger. She dried herself and dug in among her clothes, looking for something to wear. A tangerine tracksuit, a favourite, lay near the top of her bag. She put it on. She was ready to go when a glance in the mirror told her that the bright colours she wore in sunny

California were going to look showy in a sixteenth-century English inn. She grimaced at herself. Oh hell! I'm going to need a whole new wardrobe. She locked her bag, pushed it out onto the landing, and hurried downstairs.

Jonathan was waiting for her in the lounge. She caught her breath. In that all-seeing moment she knew why American males had made so little impression on her. He stood, long legs apart, one hand casually in a pocket; hound's-tooth sports jacket, silk shirt open at the neck with a silk scarf, sand-coloured cords. He might have stepped out of the pages of *Country Life*. He smiled at her. That achingly familiar, gentle, approving smile. "How do you feel now?"

"Better," she said. "Thank you for fixing the shower for me."

"It was a pleasure," he said, mouth tipped up at the corners, blue eyes gentle. She turned away, desperately trying to summon up detachment.

They went into the dining room. There were several groups of tourists, lingering. Outside, through the window, the busy river. Inside, the tinkle of spoons on china, waiters in black trousers and white shirts. It struck her that they matched the ceiling beams and plaster and she nearly laughed. I'm thinking like an American, she said to herself. Why should she not, after seven years? I shall have to learn to think English again. She looked down at the tracksuit and flushed.

They were shown to a white-clothed table. "A full break-fast, sir?" the waiter asked, pencil poised.

"I'll have bacon and egg," she said.

"Two lots of bacon and egg."

"Coffee?" Jonathan asked. She nodded. The waiter went away and he leaned back, tipping the chair, making room for his long legs. The light from the window played on his skin with its even coating of pale tan. The kind of tan young Englishmen acquired playing cricket on a village green in the mild English summer. She remembered the seasons had changed. There were heatwaves in June now where in her childhood she remembered rain. Rain stopping play.

Jonathan had always played cricket for the village. As the son of the local squire, it was expected of him. And the countess, his mother, gave a cake towards the tea. Baked by her cook. Everything the village of Flyford stood for originated with the Haldane family. They had built the church and generously supported it. Over the years, the centuries, their sons had fought and died for England. It was true they were nothing if not responsible and caring – until they needed money. Then they were like everyone else, Cassie thought sourly, they took it – or tried to!

"Cassie! You're miles away. Come back. We need to talk. I—"

She broke in. "Let me say something first. I'm sure you're under the impression I came home because of my father's accident."

Those dark eyebrows rose. The blue eyes looked puzzled. "Yes?"

"That's not the whole of it. I've got to tell you this. I was coming anyway." She drew a long, deep breath and said distinctly, "To fight your father over the cottage."

Jonathan frowned.

She rushed on, "You know very well there's no way my parents can get into the property market at their age. Gerald's fifty-eight. For one thing, he hasn't enough capital to put down as a deposit on the cottage at its present inflated value and for another, he'll soon be retired and wouldn't be able to keep up the payments."

"Cassie . . ."

She held up a hand to stop him. "I'm not as soft as they are, Jonathan. I'm not soft at all. I've been trained in an American school. When Mother wrote that they were going to have to vacate, that's when I decided to come home. To fight you on their behalf."

"Cassie . . ."

She plunged on, "I'm not going to allow you to turf them out of their home."

He didn't answer for a moment. He watched her, as though he knew there would be another outburst. It came, somehow propelled by his air of waiting. "And let me warn you, you're not dealing with the teenage granddaughter of your head gardener now," she said. "And there's something else that might not have occurred to you. I don't give a fig for your—"

She broke off in passionate mid-sentence because the waiter arrived with their breakfasts. She sat in trembling silence, looking down at the cloth while he set out two plates of bacon and egg, a silver toast rack, coffee, cups.

He finished, then lingered, pretending he hadn't heard, looking from one to the other.

"Everything all right sir? Madam?"

"Thank you."

"Were you going to say, my heritage?" Jonathan asked as the man left, which was exactly what she had been going to say. "Heritages are what England is about." He tapped hard with a forefinger on the table, knocking the pepper pot over. He didn't set it right. "I'll make allowances while you scale off that American veneer," he said, smiling kindly.

"You—!"

"Eat up before the egg gets cold." His manner reduced her protest to an irrelevance.

"Why didn't you offer them Crabapple Cottage twenty years ago, when it was worth a fraction of what it's worth now?"

"We did," he said, and waited.

She stared up into his wide-set blue eyes. It was clear he was telling the truth. She had a feeling of the chair having been jerked out from under her. She gathered up her weakened defences. "Have you forgotten that he spent money on improvements to the cottage? You'll benefit," she said. "Do you think that's fair?"

"You're not eating, Cassie. Don't let the food get cold. Your father knew we could have asked for a higher rent. Yes, he did work on the house. It was to his advantage to make it more comfortable. And in the circumstances that he was paying such a low rent it was right that he should do so. Eat up. Come on now. We'll continue when you've cleaned up the plate. You did say you were hungry, didn't you?" Again that charming smile.

She was less hungry, now. She took another forkful of egg, another mouthful of toast, some bacon. A sip of coffee. His plate was clean. She was aware of his waiting. She choked the rest down and pushed her plate away. "When the village raised money to buy the children a minibus so they could have outings at the seaside—"

"Yes, I know. There wasn't quite enough. Your father made it up out of his own pocket. It helped, having a low rent."

She was outraged that he should take the credit. "Altruistic people tend not to concern themselves with building up personal assets. Of course I know my father has been unbusinesslike. You know he works with backward children in his spare time. Such people, such compassionate people, who live for others, easily lose sight of the fact that their dependants need looking after, too."

"More coffee, Madam?" The waiter filled her cup then wandered away slowly, listening.

Jonathan wore an air of patience now, like an adult tolerating the ramblings of a child. "Did they not tell you they are happy to move?"

"Oh yes, after you spelled out your difficulties. They're so loyal." She repeated the words, infusing them with a mixture of bitterness and sarcasm, "After you spelled out your difficulties."

"In the circumstances," said Jonathan, "it would be much better for them to have a smaller place. A flat."

"A flat!" she echoed with disbelief. "You know how Gerald loves his garden."

He picked up a teaspoon, put it down again, frowning. "Are you not aware that your father was quite badly hurt? It's possible he'll never work again. By the time he's recovered anyway, if things don't go really well, he could be pretty close to retirement."

"Isn't that all the more reason why he should have a garden to sit in? If he isn't going to be able to work."

Jonathan set the pepper pot upright again.

"Mother's a keen gardener, too. And full of energy. Why are you looking at me like that?"

"Your mother was – er – involved. Didn't you know?" He looked and sounded uncomfortable.

Cassie's face went still. "What happened? Tell me about this accident."

He didn't answer immediately. There was something in his manner that she couldn't put a finger on. Something more than he was telling her. "She was knocked over, too. You must know all this. That she tried to help your father out of the path of the car."

"Must know?" repeated Cassie numbly, staring at him, tears starting in her eyes. "Must know?"

"You mean they didn't – Didn't you get a letter?"

"Yes, of course. But Mother made light of—" She broke off because her voice was trembling. When she had taken herself in hand she went on. "I should have known it would be worse than she would say. We'll take the motorist to court," she said fiercely. "We'll sue for damages."

He was knocking the pepper pot around again. It lay on its side. Again he set it right. Avoiding her eyes, he said, "You may not do too well in court. Your father was in the wrong. Did they tell you that? The driver was powerless to avoid him. It was dark. He wasn't – neither of them were – wearing reflective clothing. It's not safe to walk along country lanes after dark these days, Cassie. It's foolhardy."

When she did not, could not reply, he abruptly changed the subject. "I agree, they should have a garden to sit in. There's plenty of garden at the Hall. We've offered them rooms on the corner of the west wing, facing south-west. It used to be the old nursery. They'll get all the sun there is. And they'll have the use of that big courtyard with the fountain in the centre. It's very sheltered. Even in winter they'll be able to sit outside."

She knew now, without a shadow of doubt, that she was coming very close to some utterly unacceptable truth. There had to be a very good reason for Jonathan to take such an interest in her parents' troubles; for offering them an apartment in the big house. She lifted her head, looked directly into his eyes and asked her question, knowing the answer, sick with the knowledge. "Were you the driver?"

His face was full of anguish. "Cassie, believe me, he walked right into the car."

"And all this – this – concern, this kindness, this giving them a home – it's your guilty conscience." She pushed her chair back so roughly it teetered on one leg then went over. A waiter rushed forward and picked it up.

Jonathan reached across the table, grasped her wrist as she turned away. "Let me go." She tried to snatch her hand away, but his grip hardened and she winced at the pain. "I'll get my bag and make my own way home. I don't want to be any further in your debt, because that's what it's all about, isn't it? When the case comes to court you'll be seen to be a kind and generous man, doing everything you can to atone. But you're not that. You're just a despicable, smooth talking, no-good, opting out seducer." She rushed on, trying to pretend she hadn't said it. "But you've got a stately home. Oh, I can just see the judge sucking up to you. Of course you know about heritage. You're a representative of it. Of all our heritages, aren't you? No judge would want to topple you. It would make him feel unsafe. Oh, you—"

She flung herself away from the table, wrenching her arm in a futile endeavour to free herself as she twisted round to face the door. All over the room, in all the faces, she read curiosity; amusement. She pulled her arm again and this time Jonathan let her go.

As though nothing at all had happened between them he said briskly to the carefully blank-faced waiter who hovered close by, "The bill, please."

Cassie headed for the door. A young man who was

pretending to reset a table, impassive as the sphinx, stepped aside to allow her to pass. She hurried, tripping and stumbling between the chairs, and then she was out of the door and Tom was standing there in his blue chauffeur's uniform and peaked cap saying kindly, "I've collected your bag, Miss."

She knew then what the 'Miss' was about. His employer had run her parents down driving one of the cars it was Tom's job to look after. You had to be on the side of your employer in this kind of row. She looked at him, at his concerned, gentle face, and recognised that she was on her own.

In that moment she experienced a poignant sense of déjà vu.

Chapter Two

CASSIE gazed out of the window.

"We have nothing to talk about," she retorted in reply to Jonathan's plea, knowing he wouldn't make a scene, the chauffeur having a rear-view mirror at hand.

They sped smoothly south-west along the M3. Hampshire. They took the exit that would lead to Flyford. The so-familiar beech forests were coming into leaf.

"You haven't been home in springtime," Jonathan said. "Remember the daffodils?"

So he did know she came home! Even angry with him as she was, she felt the pain of his not getting in touch. She wanted to say, 'I haven't seen a field of daffodils for seven years and whose fault is that?' but she must not let him see the bitterness. She must be dignified, detached.

Looking for detachment, she gazed out of the window again. The grass was so nearly emerald it took her breath away. The colour of England had never faded from her mind and memory, the billowing beauty of ancient oaks, gardens aflame with colour. Roses everywhere in June, and again in September, a last sweet gift before the snows of winter. She felt a lump in her throat.

They came up the long, slow hill and there on the left was Bevington Hall grandly at one with the landscape. It lay at the end of a long straight drive in a park dotted with oaks and chestnuts. The wrought-iron gates stood open as they always had. Her eyes roved across the Georgian stone façade, the big oblong windows in their white painted frames, the grey slate roofs.

Memories of childhood swarmed in. Christmas Eve in the great hall with the village carol singers standing in the snow, the child Jonathan singing with them, a handsome little boy with snowflakes in his dark hair. At four years old, she remembered being in love. Good King Wenceslas looked out . . . A huge log fire burning. Brightly packaged gifts for the staff.

Bevington Hall wasn't big as stately homes went. A wide façade with Corinthian columns was all one could see from the road. There were two wings but they jutted out behind into the gardens. The great medieval hall was the only part of the original building that had been kept when the old house was torn down in the eighteenth century.

The car took the road round the park. There was the west wing, now coming into view. She eyed the windows behind which lay the rooms Jonathan had offered to Leila and Gerald. The sun shone down on it. Yes, there would be sun. No garden of their own but sun, certainly. The Rolls turned carefully in at the narrow gateway leading to Crabapple Cottage and ran smoothly up to the front door. Sixteenth-century brick and hanging tiles. Wysteria drooping; Virginia creeper where it caught the autumn sun that fired it with reds and golds. A highly desirable country pad for a city man who could afford to do it up.

She asked, her voice bleak, "Are you selling all the cottages?"

"As they become vacant. Yes."

This one hadn't become vacant.

Jonathan jumped out. "You go on home," he said to the chauffeur, then went round to the back and hauled Cassie's luggage out of the boot. The car began to back away.

"You go with Tom," said Cassie, extending a hand to take her bag.

"I'll walk back across the park." He headed for the front door. "Have you got a key?"

"I know where it is."

He looked on sardonically while she felt under the mat.

"I expect it's the safest place, now," she said, defensive on the part of her parents. "No intelligent burglar would expect a key to be under the mat these days." He followed her into the hall. Cassie turned and said, impatiently, "I really don't want to talk to you. Thank you for picking me up. I'm grateful. But I must get up to the hospital. Do you happen to know what the visiting hours are?"

"You can go any time. They're in the private wing." Again, that expression of sheer goodwill that would soften a heart of stone.

"My God!" she said ungratefully, stepping back a pace, looking at him with hostile eyes. If that wasn't admitting culpability! She knew her parents didn't have health insurance. Aloud, she said in a biting voice, "More Brownie points to lay before the judge. You've thought of everything, haven't you?"

Jonathan replied, his voice brisk and full of common sense as though paying other people's expenses was the most normal thing in the world, "The hospital was chock-a-block. Overloaded and understaffed. They would have been sent home. Your father needed nursing and your mother wasn't fit to do it."

So the guilty party stepped in, in the guise of fairy godfather! She wasn't going to let him get away with this. "You've got my nice old-fashioned, unworldly parents exactly where you want them, haven't you?" she flared, feeling cornered by his insidious winning. "You've got possession of their house, and you've persuaded them, with no security of tenure, to take an uncomfortable suite of rooms in your draughty old mausoleum. Oh – you!" She was suddenly close to tears.

He pushed her unceremoniously ahead. "It's up to you to attend to the draughts, if any. And as to security of tenure, that will be attended to. Legally, I mean. They'll have the apartment for their lifetime."

Propelled through the door, she stood looking unhappily round the low-ceilinged room with its enormous inglenook fireplace, its wealth of oak beams, its shabby furniture. What would that comfortable old sofa look like in the grandeur of the Hall? A coffee cup, the dregs long since dried into a brown stain, stood on a low table beside an open magazine. Ashes in the fireplace. Cushions squashed into a body shape and awry. Poignant reminders that the owners had gone for an evening walk from which they had not returned.

He said authoritatively, "Sit down, Cassie."

She looked at the sofa and remained standing.

"Sit down," he commanded again.

She lowered herself onto the sofa's edge, apprehensively impelled to obey, terribly at a disadvantage like this, far below him. Jonathan wandered over to the fireplace. Leaning an arm on the mantelpiece he relaxed, long-legged and easy in his manner now that he had her where he wanted her, saying "I need to explain my circumstances. My father has opted out. He's going to live in the south of France.

23

He's handed over to me. I've had to make a decision. To sell."

Her eyes flew wide.

He continued, diffidently, looking at her with his head on one side, "It's just the kind of house Middle Eastern money could buy. We'd be set for life."

She leapt to her feet, rigid with disbelief. "So all that stuff about heritage was just empty rhetoric! Your family have been here since the fifteenth century – five hundred years! And you're going to hand it over to foreigners because you're strapped for cash!"

"It's an enormous responsibility." He shrugged, carelessly, she thought, conveying the fact that enormous responsibilities were not to his taste. His fingers came in contact with a small ornament on the mantelpiece. A china duck she had bought at a fair when she was small. He frowned at it. "Where would I find an Englishman who could pay the price?"

She was remembering that his ancestors had fought with Henry V at Agincourt. That was when the first house had been built on the site. On King Henry V's bounty. And he was willing to give all that up to an Arab? She couldn't believe it of him. Or of his family, the lordly Haldanes who were so proud of their heritage they had to banish the head gardener's granddaughter lest the heir should fall seriously in love with her!

He turned from contemplation of the duck. "What choice have I?" he asked. He looked suddenly inept. Like a little boy who had lost his way.

She said angrily, "You've got plenty of choice. You could lease out the farms. That would bring in income and save wages. And you could open the house to the public."

"Oh," he said vaguely, "I don't think my parents would like that."

"They're not going to be here. They're running away to the south of France." She considered tact, then decided to dispense with it. "Leaving the sinking ship," she said, enunciating each word cruelly and precisely. "What a despicable lot you are!"

"What would you do?"

She thought he looked frightened. And then she wondered if he was acting. She peered at him through narrowed eyes. "I've already told you. Are you afraid of work?"

"I don't know anything about . . ." He heaved an enormous sigh. "It's a hell of an undertaking. No, I don't think I could contemplate it. I simply wouldn't know where to start. And besides, we haven't got the money to set it up."

So there's no point in suing me. Was that what he was saying? "I could tell you where to start," she said, fired up with anger at his astonishing ineptness. "I have experience of this kind of thing. It's entrepreneurial. It's what I've been doing in America. Organising ice spectaculars, conventions, exhibitions. I've a talent for it. And loads of experience. You know I went to stay with my uncle in the first place?" *When I was thrown out for fancying you.* "Well, he took me into his business. I branched out on my own later. I could translate my expertise to a stately home. I could advise you."

He appeared to be faintly amused. Unable to believe that little Cassie Neilson, being the head gardener's granddaughter, could rise to entrepreneurial heights? Or did he think she had a cheek to tell him what to do?

"I suppose it's an option," he conceded, concentrating on the ornamental duck, frowning at it.

"Think about it. Talk to your parents."

25

He smiled at her, though still with that air of surprise and suspicion, as though waiting to be persuaded; as though it was something so unlikely that he wouldn't attempt to consider it without concrete proof that she could make it work.

It suddenly occurred to her that there could be tremendous advantages to her in persuading Jonathan to open the Hall to the public. She wasn't going to be free to look for work until her parents were on their feet again. She thought about what he had said, that Gerald might not get back to teaching. She saw a job here on her home ground suddenly as very much to her advantage. A gift from the gods. An opportunity to look after her parents and work at the same time. Her mind raced ahead. How long would it take to get the Hall up and running? A year? She could probably do it in a year. She must persuade him.

"Give me a chance," she begged. "Please. Don't sell. It's not right, Jonathan. You must know it's not right."

"I'll have to do some heavy thinking," he said, speaking uncertainly, worriedly. "It's such a complete about-turn. And as you said, I'll have to talk to my parents. They'd have to agree. I think they'd take a lot of persuading, though. You see, they need money to set themselves up abroad."

"I can't believe it," Cassie said. "I simply can't believe it. That you, and your father, who have been born to such privilege and responsibility, should chuck it all away for cash! Is money really so important to you? What are you going to do with it? You can only eat three meals a day and wear a certain number of clothes."

"It might be nice to live in a workable house," he said. "Bevington Hall is bloody expensive to run and extremely uncomfortable."

"But it's yours," she said categorically. She was desperately disappointed, as well as angry. She couldn't believe he had changed so much. He wasn't the man she remembered at all. He didn't look like a wimp, but he was. Only a wimp would run away. "Where's your backbone?" she added for good measure.

He stopped fiddling with the duck and turned to face her, heaving a sharp sigh. "If we accept your offer we would be working together. You and I would have to be friends, Cassie," he said.

"Of course." She looked back at him steadily, aware that he was asking her to forget the past. "Business friends," she said.

"And you'd have to make a definite commitment. You'd have to understand it was your responsibility. You wouldn't be able to skive off halfway through."

"It seems to me," she said, "that the boot's on the other foot. Who's skiving off?" Without waiting for an answer she swung round saying, "I'd better see if the car's going. I must get up to the hospital." She went into the hall and picked up the keys from the ashtray where they were always kept.

Jonathan took them from her. "I'll check that it's going. But first of all I'll take your bag upstairs."

She opened the garage doors, then locked the house while he checked the car and backed it into the drive. He stepped out, saying with a quick smile, "Don't forget to keep to the left." Then he waved, crossed the garden with long strides and climbed the fence.

Cassie slipped behind the wheel but she did not put the car into gear. She was watching Jonathan's erect back as he strode across the park. Something about the way he was walking bothered her. There was a jauntiness in his manner. Yet only moments ago he had appeared lost and in need of help. She frowned. And come to think of it, if he had been seriously considering selling, where did that leave her parents? Hadn't he said categorically that they were to have this apartment for life? He couldn't sell the Hall with a sitting tenant in the nursery wing.

Still watching the back view of him she thoughtfully put the car into gear. At that moment he turned and waved. She didn't wave back. She watched him, distrustfully, then slowly moved forward down the drive.

Cassie was shocked to see how frail her father looked, lying back in his white hospital bed. Leila jumped up from her chair, dropping the book she had been reading to him. It was an emotional meeting. Both women shed tears.

She bent over the bed to kiss her father. "So, here I am," she said cheerfully. "Ready to take over. Who's coming home?"

Gerald said wanly, "Not me, I'm afraid." She stood back, and looking at him, wiped an extra tear away. He appeared shrunken, and dreadfully pale. "So, nobody's told me anything," she said. "What's the damage?"

His ribs were strapped up. Two breaks, he said. And one shin bone was broken just above the ankle.

Leila brushed back the hair at either side of her face, the same thick chestnut Cassie had inherited, though faded now to a light brown. "He's had a lot of pain," she said and bent over to smooth her husband's hand, then looked up at Cassie. "I would like to go home," she said, then addressing Gerald, "Would you mind, dear? We can't put Jonathan to any more expense. He's been so awfully good."

"As well he might be," Cassie retorted, impatient with the

earnest display of gratitude. She lifted a chair and thumped it down beside the bed. "You didn't tell me he was the driver."

"It wasn't his fault." Leila was quick to defend.

Cassie's mouth turned down. "So what happened? Do you expect me to believe you jumped under his car?"

Gerald rubbed a hand across his head. Leila looked distressed. "We were on that first corner in Baker's Lane. You know how narrow it is, with no footpath. And there's quite a deep ditch close to the road, hidden by long grass."

She knew it well. Jonathan was right in saying it was not a place to stroll two abreast now that there were so many cars on the road. In her childhood days all the lanes were safe.

"A driver coming from behind wouldn't see us until he was right on us," Gerald said. "We didn't hear a sound until it was too late."

"Tell me exactly what happened?"

They exchanged quick glances, looking for reassurance in each other that this angry daughter wasn't going to cause trouble. "I jumped aside," Gerald said. "Pushed your mother ahead. Then I remembered the ditch and pulled her back. I must have lost my balance then because the driver of a car coming the other way said I appeared to step right into the road under the wheels of—"

"Jonathan's car," Cassie finished when he seemed loath to say the name himself. "Who witnessed it?"

Again those signs of distress in their faces. "A complete stranger, dear." Leila looked worriedly into her daughter's face. "It's brought you home and we're so pleased about that. You've been away such a long time. Maybe it was meant to be."

"Maybe it was. I think I would have preferred to come

home for something a little less dramatic, though. Anyway, it's all going to work out." Cassie lifted her voice, smiled. "I've got news for you. I've already got a job."

"You've accepted it?" That was Gerald, his eagerness giving the impression of him starting forward.

Cassie froze, yet her mind was whirling with Jonathan's deceit, and obvious manipulation.

"How wonderful!" Leila exclaimed bringing her hands together in a silent clap. They were both looking at her with shining faces. "Jonathan knew all about your work, of course. He's followed your career with interest."

"And how did he know about my career?"

"Of course we talked to him about you, dear. We've seen a lot of him lately, what with these new arrangements for our move to the Hall. He told you about that? That he's arranged for us to have a flat in what was the old nursery wing?"

"Yes. He told me."

"He's been so kind," said Leila warmly. "He's visited us almost every day."

As well he might, Cassie thought cynically. "And it was what you told him about my work that decided him to open the Hall to visitors?"

They looked a little puzzled at her tone. "The fact that you were experienced in setting up large events, yes. Not that he hasn't been considering it for some time. He's been visiting stately homes, seeing how they work. He was going over to see you about it." Leila added apologetically, "He asked us not to tell you. You do understand, don't you, dear?"

"I understand a lot of things – now. I take my hat off to him," she said, but it was without a tone of admiration.

Leila sat with a questioning expression on her face,

waiting for Cassie to explain the anger that must be showing in her face.

"Then this happened," Gerald said, "and you came home anyway."

"I dropped into his lap like a ripe plum. He was born lucky, wasn't he." She was remembering what Jonathan had said. That he would have to talk to his parents. Do some heavy thinking. "I suppose that's how these great families got rich in the first place and hung on to their possessions through the centuries. They were born lucky. And full of tricks," she said bitterly.

"Oh, now, Cassie," Leila demurred. "That's unworthy of you. Wouldn't you like to do this work for him? He's really most anxious to engage you."

"He didn't think of selling the Hall, did he? Like, to one of those oil-rich Middle Eastern potentates?" she asked innocently. "That's what I'd have expected him to do."

Leila's mouth opened in surprise. She thought Gerald's eyebrows would fly away. "Sell it! Sell Bevington Hall? Why on earth would you think that?"

"No, of course. Silly of me." She began to laugh. She laughed until the tears ran down her face. Her parents stared at her with puzzled eyes while she wiped the tears away. "Sorry," she said, "I haven't had much sleep. I'm a bit distraught."

"We'll be awfully pleased to have you in the flat," Leila said when they had settled down again. "After so long away it will be lovely. Jonathan said you'd need to live over the shop, so to speak."

Living over the shop. Living with her parents. Two options she wouldn't have chosen. Still, what would she have chosen out of the day's offerings?

* * *

31

Cassie and Leila stayed at the hospital keeping Gerald company, chatting, until the middle of the afternoon. A nurse brought Cassie tea. Unaccustomed as she was to a bacon and egg breakfast, she had no need for lunch. On the way home they detoured through the town to pick up a Chinese takeaway and some fruit. "I'll stock up in the village in the morning," Cassie said. She always went down to say hello to old friends on her first day at home.

They ate supper at the kitchen table. "I shan't be sorry to leave this place," Leila remarked, looking round the comfortable but shabby room, noting the faded paint on the walls that was shown up by newish curtains. The ancient gas stove had never been updated simply because it worked. The Neilsons were the kind of people who didn't throw adequate possessions out. "It could be made very smart, of course, with some money spent on it," she said wistfully.

"It's always been comfortable," Cassie protested, thinking of the tiny, clinically smart kitchen in her Los Angeles flat, which certainly was not so.

"These tiles were always cold on the feet." Leila looked down at them, tapping them with the toe of one shoe, demonstrating their hardness and their coldness. "The loft needs lagging. We lose more heat through the ceiling than we keep. Last winter we had an awful lot of wind blowing through all the cracks. There were draughts everywhere."

Would there not be draughts in the Hall? Cassie forbore to mention them. She looked out of the window at the sprouting of new leaves. At daffodils already showing a hint of gold. At the fruit trees dotting the lawn. The grass needed mowing. She was thinking of how her grandfather had built up the garden for his own pleasure, working all day at the Hall then

32

in the evenings and weekends at Crabapple Cottage. All he ever did was garden. She remembered helping him, pushing his wheelbarrow, learning the names of plants. How certain ones liked this kind of soil, or that. How this one needed part shade, that one, full sun. "You'll miss the garden. It will be very different, in an apartment – sorry, flat."

Leila recognised that Cassie couldn't let go. She reached out and touched her hand, imposing peace. "I won't. But if I do, goodness knows there's plenty of garden up there. The kitchen window in the flat overlooks the courtyard with the fountain. Remember that?"

What Cassie remembered was the young Jonathan chasing her round the fountain, slapping his hand through the water, batting it onto her hair.

"There's a strip of garden adjacent to the fountain. I dare say I could take that over," Leila said. "And I'm sure the boys will let me have a bit of ground to grow vegetables." The boys were the young gardeners who were in charge now.

Next morning was clear, the air cold. A sharp spring day with a mischievous breeze. Cassie put on a cotton skirt and one of her thin, wholly inadequate, warm climate jumpers. Not only inadequate, but far too bright. Emerald green was fine in the Californian sun, flattering as well as acceptably startling against her chestnut hair, but here, set against the low-key colours of the misty landscape it looked almost as flashy as the tangerine tracksuit. While working at the Hall she was going to have to dress the part of a country girl. Woolly jumpers. Tweed skirts. Low-heeled, sensible shoes. She would have to go into Flyford to do some shopping.

She tied her bright hair up in a pony tail, counted out

her travellers' cheques then opened her wardrobe door and stood looking disapprovingly at the one coat she owned. White leather. Very smart. Very Los Angeles. Very un-Hampshire. She shut the door and went downstairs to get Leila's breakfast.

The curtains in her bedroom were still drawn but Leila was awake. Cassie put the tray down and went to the window. "It's a lovely day," she said, swishing the curtains back, "but cold." The morning sun filtered in through the branches of the budding chestnut tree.

"You'll find a duffle coat behind the door in the cloak-room," said her mother pulling on a bed-jacket, looking happy to be waited on. "Haven't you got anything warmer than that?" She was looking at Cassie's thin skirt.

"No. You saw what I was wearing yesterday. I don't see myself trotting round the village in a tangerine tracksuit. It's a long time since I owned anything suitable for wearing in the English country. Br-r-r." She clasped her arms across her chest. "When I drop you at the hospital I'll run into town and see if I can pick up something to be going on with."

Leila told her there were several shops in Flyford that sold good country clothes.

"Right," said Cassie briskly. "Eat up. I'm off, but I'll be back soon to take you to the hospital."

Down in the village Mrs Oliver who kept the corner store was pleased to see her. "They tell me you're home for good, dear."

"Yes. My parents need me."

"Such bad luck," said Mrs Oliver sympathetically. "But you'll get them on their feet again. You're a good girl." As she walked round the counter to pick up the bread she patted

Cassie's arm, showing her support. Cassie had the notion that Mrs Oliver was expressing in that gesture, and those words, the feeling of the village.

She picked up her basket and went across the road to Pan's Pantry. Mrs Pannington, fiftyish and bustling, came out from behind the counter to give her a hug. "Why, Cassie Neilson! They're saying you're home for good!" She stood back, surveying Cassie approvingly. "It just goes to show, you young ones have what it takes in a crisis. The village is upset about – well – about what happened, if you know what I mean."

Cassie did know what she meant. That the village was upset not solely because her parents had been involved in an accident but because it was a member of the Haldane family who hit them. Hadn't the incumbents of the Hall built their shops? Weren't the shops leased from them? She wondered bleakly if these tenants were now going to be asked to buy their properties so that the lordly coffers might be refilled. She visualised them willingly raising the money; wanting to stay.

How could I have imagined I could sue? she asked herself. There would be no sympathy for her. She would alienate her family. She would be on her own.

"Are you still making your lovely caramel cakes, Mrs Pan?" she asked, smiling brightly over her troubled thoughts.

"Am I what? The day I give up baking I'll shut shop. Fancy you remembering my caramel cake." Mrs Pannington smiled broadly, with pride.

"One caramel cake then, please." She asked about Susan, the daughter; heard she had trained as a caterer and was wanting to start her own business. She tucked the knowledge in the back of her mind. When she visited stately homes with her parents they were always glad of a cup of tea and a piece of home-made cake if it was available. There were outbuildings at the Hall. If the farms, as she had suggested to Jonathan, should all be leased off or sold, the outbuildings would no longer be needed to house farm machinery. Maybe one of them could be appropriated for a tearoom? Her mind was dashing ahead.

She stood in the village High Street shivering in her thin skirt and light shoes. She pulled the duffle coat closely round her, hunching her shoulders. She looked up and down the street, at the Tudor buildings leaning with age, at the mock-Tudor that had been added in the 1890s, complimenting the old; the village pump, requisitioned by the National Trust; Well Cottage where, according to her parents, the locals lined up with their buckets in the '40s when a German bomb fell on the village and the water had been cut off. 'Just like the old days,' Leila had said and Cassie had seen that she was talking about continuity, never mind the discomfort.

On quick trips home she had darted here and there, getting in touch, briefly renewing friendships, dashing off to London. She wasn't thinking of Flyford as her village, then. She was a migrant bird. She felt herself sliding back into place now.

She went to the greengrocer and the butcher.

"Cassie! We're so glad you've come back. For good? Is it true you're back for good?

"We're so sorry about the . . .", the now familiar, telling hesitation before the muted pronunciation of the word, "accident."

She put her purchases in the boot of the car and slid behind the wheel. As she started the engine a long low car swung round into the High Street and parked neatly against the kerb directly in front of her, blocking off her exit. Cassie gasped at his nerve. The driver jumped out, tall, heart-stoppingly handsome, his dark hair shining in the morning sunlight. He strode to her off-side door and as though they were the greatest friends, opened it and slid in.

"For a jet-lagged world traveller, you're up and about early, and looking mighty fresh," Jonathan said breezily. "How did you find your parents?"

"Fine." Cassie switched off the engine again. "Taking all the blame on themselves, of course."

"You've a sharp tongue in that beautiful head of yours. Now tell me, what are your plans for today?"

"I'm taking my mother to the hospital to visit Gerald. After that I'm going into Flyford to do a bit of shopping. Tangerine tracksuits don't seem to be quite right for here."

"I thought it was lovely. And you looked lovely in it. Beautiful. You were always beautiful, Cass." He leaned across and kissed her on the cheek.

"If I'm to work for you I'll construe that kind of thing as sexual harrassment."

"Yes, of course. Why not?" He glanced at that expensive watch. "It's only half past nine. You've plenty of time," he said as though he was in charge of it, measuring it out. "I want you to come up to the Hall to see your parents' flat."

Your parents' flat! He spoke as though it was already theirs, having been bequeathed to them by him.

"You're expected for lunch at the Hall, by the way. I've told my parents your plans."

Her plans! Ignoring his laughing eyes, his teasing, mobile mouth, that enchanting lock of hair that would drop down over his forehead, she said, "Con man of the century, aren't you, Jonathan Tarrant? So you wanted to sell to an Arab! You did a remarkable job of portraying the little boy lost."

He replied disarmingly, "That's not quite fair. It was a test, of a kind. I needed to know how you felt. The depth of your feelings, too, after so long away. The Americanisation of Cassie Neilson was formidable, at first glance. I wasn't to know how paper thin it was until I'd peeled a bit away." He prepared to step out of the car again. "See you about twelve." And then he was gone.

She watched the fast little car as it revved noisily and shot off up the High Street. An arm waved out of the window. She moved off in the direction of Crabapple Cottage, deep in thought.

Chapter Three

THIS morning Gerald's colour was better, though when he took his rimmed glasses off there were dark circles visible beneath his eyes. He put the morning paper aside as Cassie sat down beside him. He smelled of shaving cream and faintly of some hospital scent but perhaps that came from the shining floor.

"How are you, Dad?"

"All the better for your presence." He patted her hand affectionately.

She told him she was to lunch at the Hall. She wondered what they were thinking about that. Neither of them commented. Their faces acquired and maintained for some seconds a careful reserve. "So I'm off into Flyford to get myself something suitable to wear. What, in your opinion, is suitable for lunch at the Hall? A suit?" Not that either of them had ever received an invitation.

Leila said diffidently, "You may not get a suit to your liking in Flyford. What about a jumper and skirt?"

Cassie wondered if she was gently pointing out that a suit denoted a social occasion; an intimacy with her hostess, who might also be wearing a suit. "I'll settle for a sweater and skirt," she said to please them though she was angry that they should assume she had the same attitude to the incumbents of the Hall as had they.

"Jumper," Leila corrected her.

"Yes, of course. I'll try to remember to Anglicise my language."

"Lady Haldane won't notice what you're wearing. She's the worst dresser in the country," Gerald surprised her by saying. "And her daughter runs a pretty close second."

"Oh Gerald!" Leila was faintly shocked.

"It's true, dear."

"You're getting better," said Cassie delightedly. "Getting some of your spirit back. I remember Lady Haldane looking very grand on Christmas Eve. I remember the diamonds. And a long velvet skirt. She was very much the *grande dame* then."

"Always," agreed Leila. "Even in her gardening clothes."

"Don't bother with the warning look," said Cassie. "I'm not about to be intimidated. I'm not seventeen now," she said, trying herself out. And them. Interested to see that her words had sent their glance elsewhere, Gerald fiddling with his bedclothes, Leila straightening her blouse.

She said goodbye and left them, walking briskly down the long, white-painted corridor.

She quickly found a polo-necked sweater – "Jumper, jumper, jumper," she repeated to herself – that was absolutely right for her. Pale peppermint green. And a soft wool skirt, pearl grey with a complementary fleck. She asked the assistant to cut off the tags. "I'm going to wear them. Put my clothes in the bag. I was rather underdressed. The air out there's a bit sharp."

The woman picked up the scissors and snipped the tickets off them, then put the clothes Cassie had discarded into a plastic bag. Outside the sun was shining brightly. The early morning mists had cleared away. She slung the duffle coat round her shoulders and went out onto the pavement, saw herself in a shop window, saw how the coat's shabbiness dragged down the pretty new outfit and slung it over her arm. She thought she would go to London for a jacket. Or a raincoat. She had not owned a raincoat for years.

The cold of the pavement was coming through the thin soles of her pumps. She glanced at her watch. There was just time to get herself a pair of serviceable shoes, if she could find a shoe shop. She discovered one fifty yards away and picked up a pair of shoes that were just right, their sturdiness softened by shiny brown buckles on the toes. She gazed at herself in the full length mirror and marvelled at the English look. Marvelled, also, that she had slipped back into it so comfortably.

She returned to the car park, threw her parcels onto the back seat and sped back the way she had come.

The Hall was somnolent this morning, basking in the spring sunshine. As she came through the wide open wrought-iron gates her confidence began to seep away. Leila was wrong, she thought. I am not in the right clothes. In this jumper and skirt I am presenting myself as the head gardener's granddaughter. If I were invited to lunch as a proper guest, I would be wearing a suit. Of course I would. One did not go to such a grand house for lunch in a jumper and skirt – unless one was the head gardener's granddaughter.

She sat behind the wheel feeling angry with Leila and even more angry with herself for taking her advice. But there was no running away now. She looked down at the new clothes. Hopefully, Cassie said to herself, Lady

Haldane will think that after all those years in America, I'm so unimpressed by her lunch invitation that I didn't bother to dress up. But then again, she might think I've got a nerve. Anyway, it's too late to turn back.

She put the car into gear again and went on. She did not drive right up to the front door. But why should I not, she asked herself. There's no other car there. The Corinthian columns, she remembered, were so spaced as to make sufficient room for a carriage to drive through them to the main entrance. And therefore a car. On the other hand, and perhaps more sensibly, she could park on the gravel just outside.

The car stopped as though of its own accord. "Okay Rover, you know best," she said, patting the steering-wheel. She jumped out and walked the last fifty yards to the main entrance.

The formidable studded doors lay open. There was no one about. She stepped into the hall and stood looking round at the scagliola columns, the floor design of black marble lozenges set in white stone, at the ceiling with its sunken panels, terracotta coloured and enriched with gold leaf. The beautiful Adam fireplace and the magnificent staircase dividing into two flights. The semi-circular windows beneath the dome filled the hall with light. She had forgotten how grand this entrance was. She was overawed now less by its grandeur than by its beauty.

The past came rushing back. She was little Cassie Neilson again, dressed in her party dress, clinging to her grandfather's hand, tremulous with anticipation. In her mind's eye she saw the child she had been approaching the enormous Christmas tree that was laden with gifts for the children and grandchildren of the staff. She saw the lights and the glitter. Lively flames, vermillion and gold, licking the logs in the fireplace. Showers of sparks. Secret, glowing coals. And the presents! One Christmas Eve when she was three, or was it four, Jonathan had sought her out, sliding through the crowd of children, carrying in his hands a dizzyingly beautiful box decorated with ribbons and bells. 'It's the best,' he whispered in her ear. 'It's for you.'

But her grandfather had intervened. 'Father Christmas gives out the presents,' he said, though speaking kindly, and taking it from Cassie slipped it back into the pile.

Her eyes never left that box. She accepted it was hers because Jonathan had said so. When Father Christmas lifted it she automatically stepped forward, eyes shining. But, 'Sophie Flanaghan,' Father Christmas announced, and the cowman's little daughter stepped forward to take the present Jonathan had wanted her to have.

'It was only a teddy bear, and you've already got one of those,' her grandfather had tried to comfort her as they trudged home across the park, ankle deep in snow. 'The panda you got is worth two teddy bears.'

'Jonathan wanted me to have it,' she had sobbed, the sound of her grief smothered by the soft snowflakes that had begun to fall around them. 'It was Jonathan's present to me.'

'No, darling. No, it had nothing to do with him. He'd no right . . .'

She didn't listen to the rest. She felt her heart was broken. The panda slipped out of her fingers. She left it lying in the snow.

"Miss Neilson?"

Cassie started and swung round, feeling guilty, as though she had been caught spying. A butler formally dressed in tailcoat had crossed the marble floor so quietly she had not heard him. She looked at him hard. No, she did not remember him. "Come this way, please," he said and gave her, unexpectedly, a smile.

What did this mean? she wondered, edgy again. It was not the function of a butler to offer a welcome. Had he been told she was the granddaughter of a gardener and therefore his equal? Was that why he felt free to smile? Was he amused at her being asked to lunch? Had he overheard his employers chuckling about it? Or did he think she was wearing the wrong clothes? He, of all people, ushering guests in, would know the correct dress for a luncheon guest. You're getting very mixed up, she said sternly to herself. Stop being touchy. Stop thinking. But she couldn't. Why had Jonathan not come to greet her? She answered her own question. Because one does not keep a dog and then bark oneself. All the same, he might have come.

They went along a wide passage darkly lined with linenfold panelling, round a corner and on past two lots of double doors that were closed. She did not remember ever having been in this part of the house. The man paused at the third pair of doors, straightened, lifted his head as though about to address an assembly, grasped a pair of gilt handles and dexterously swung the doors back. Preceding Cassie, he announced, "Miss Neilson, sir."

"Jesus wept," she muttered to herself, "this isn't the Lord Mayor's dinner."

She had an impression of almost overwhelming grandeur. Of pale blues, greens and white. Plaster decoration in low relief. Classical friezes. Ceiling medallions set dramatically in a cool surround of pale pink and grey. Below the friezes, books, row upon row, shelf upon shelf, all bound in rich red leather. A wonderful carpet glowing in the sun's rays that struck from the big windows.

"Dead on time," said Jonathan. He was leaning against a beautiful antique desk, his long legs casually crossed, arms folded. He swung forward to greet her. The butler receded, walking backwards she noticed and remembered, startled, that was the way one left the queen. Then he, again dexterously, drew the double doors shut.

"So you did go shopping!" Jonathan said, indicating her jumper, running an eye down the skirt, taking in the shining new shoes with an ironical smile. "I liked you in your orange tracksuit."

"I thought this was more suitable for lunch with your parents. I wouldn't think they're into orange tracksuits."

"You may be right. Now, shall we have a sherry?" And without waiting for her to reply, "Then I thought we'd do a quick reconnoitre of the most important rooms. Those that I thought you might consider putting on show to the public." He swung back a double shelf of books revealing a cupboard furnished with bottles and glasses.

"Good lord!"

"None of your flashy cocktail cabinets here."

"No, of course."

"Do sit down. Take that William Kent chair." He pointed and she followed his indicating finger thinking with a touch of apprehension that she knew little about antiques. Was he, being aware of this, giving her her first lesson, employing considerable tact? A picture of a modern apartment in a high rise in Los Angeles leapt into the forefront of her mind. The spare, clean lines of the furniture. The plain walls. Then the picture faded and she felt the warmth of ancient things, hand-made, imbued with the essence and love of their creator. She sat down in the William Kent chair and gazed round the room – at a marble bust glowing in an alcove; at wood polished over the centuries; handwoven wool carpets.

The sherry was too dry for her taste. She sipped it wondering why he had not offered her a choice. Was he telling her something? That it was de rigueur in this kind of house to drink only dry sherry? Would she be flaunting her origins if she asked for sweet? Or even medium? You're letting yourself get touchy again. Stop it! Talk about the past. It might get things into perspective.

"Do you still have Christmas parties for the estate workers' children? A tree in the hall?"

He looked startled. "There are no estate workers to bring their children," he said. "I've divided the land into small farms and leased them out."

Oh really! Already leased out! She gave him a stoney stare but he wasn't looking.

"We don't even know the farmers' families," he said. "Those days are gone."

She swirled the unpalatable sherry round the glass, considering the depth of her entrapment. She had been so sure of herself yesterday, ready for a fight. Now, in his manipulative hands, she felt unsafe.

"There's nothing new about exhibiting one's house you know," Jonathan went on in his easy way. "The populous were welcome here in the past. Anyone could drive up and ask the butler to give them a tour. Our ancestors liked to show off their possessions. It's only recently that we've confined our hospitality to our own kind. I mean, this century."

She sat forward on her seat, interested. "Really? Do you know what they were charged?"

He shrugged. "Nothing. The carriage folk probably tipped the butler and housekeeper, but that was voluntary. My ancestors didn't need to charge them. They had the money to live lavishly. In the shooting season they'd have sixty to eighty people here for weeks on end. Ah well," he said, putting his glass down on the desk, sounding nostalgic, "we could afford to feed them, then. I'd like to have lived in those days. I can see great satisfaction in giving work to literally hundreds of people, which we certainly can't do now. And a home. Take your grandfather. If anyone landed on his feet and lived a completely fulfilled life, he did."

She was touched. "He liked gardening. It was his whole life."

"Oh yes, he did." She was aware that Jonathan was coming closer. His jacket smelled faintly of horse. A kind of panic came over her, a feeling that in stripping away her lost cause he was leaving her naked and terribly vulnerable. He stood in front of her, looking down at her. "Can you imagine a captain of industry leaving a man on the payroll until he was eighty-three just so he could keep his interests and his self-respect? My father did that for your grandfather, Cassie. When the old boy died he went graciously and willingly, recognising he could no longer do what he wanted to do. Such exits aren't given to everyone."

"Yes," she agreed, wanting to jump out of the William Kent chair and run but remaining where she was, under his spell, recognising that there were further truths behind his words: the fact that the earl had allowed her parents to stay on at Crabapple Cottage to which they had no right, for instance, after the old man's death.

"Let's go and see the apartment," she said. "I didn't come here to put the world to rights."

He allowed a brief moment of silence while her ungraciousness hung in the air between them, then glanced at his watch, turned and picked up a bunch of keys that was lying on the desk. "They have a separate entrance," he said. "We'll go out of the main door and round."

She wanted to apologise. She wanted to tell him she was all mixed up. She could blame jet lag. But he wasn't waiting for an apology. He was halfway out of the door. They went back down the passage and through the hall.

"Why did you leave your car away over there?" he asked, looking at her quizzically as they emerged and began to walk towards the corner of the Hall.

Making an effort to match his lightheartedness she replied, "I needed a walk."

"You'll get plenty of that, working here."

They turned left, their feet crunching in the gravel. The creeper-clad wall of the west wing was on their left now. Here was the great orangery jutting out from the main building with its green foliage spread thickly over the inner walls and its fanciful white tracery on the roof, an addition from Edwardian times. Behind it the great hall rose austerely with its arrow slits, a medieval bastion, its enormous dome-shaped doors set with iron studs.

Coming up on their right was the archway leading to the stables and the kitchen gardens. From here she could see the row of horse boxes with their dormer windows above, where the grooms and the chauffeur lived.

Jonathan followed her gaze. "There are no horses there now, so no grooms. And Tom lives in the village."

"Why?"

"His wife prefers it. I dare say he does, too. It was pretty deadly for them here in the evenings with empty flats on either side. By the way," he gave her a teasing look, "it's a flat we're going to look at."

"Sorry. I'm trying to de-Americanise myself. It may take a while."

They turned in round the edifice that was the outer part of the soaring hall and came to a heavy oak door, again decorated with iron studs.

"This is the door that leads to the – flat?" she said and they both laughed. Jonathan jangled the keys, shook one free and thrust it into an enormous keyhole set within an iron frame.

Cassie looked on in amazement. "Do you expect my mother to carry that in her handbag?"

He shrugged.

The door opened. A narrow flight of stairs ran steeply upward. Cassie gazed at them, tight-lipped. "Isn't this just the thing for an elderly lady and a man who has been badly injured!"

Jonathan gripped her elbow and shook it impatiently. "Cassie, give me a break. I'm trying to help."

"Help! You're joking. You expect them to get up that – that – ladder! If you were seriously trying to help we wouldn't be here," she said, turning away. "What's the point in going on? You've made up your mind to turf them out of their home. And they're willing to go. You've mesmerised them into believing its their duty. Let's not waste any more time. Neither of them could use stairs as steep as those. I'll set about finding them a convenient modern flat. Maybe in Flyford. It's only a few miles, anyway. It's not Outer Mongolia. I'm sure they'll adjust."

He gave her an angry little push towards the stairs. "You're going to see these rooms if I have to carry you up and dump you in them. There's no reason why your parents should use this entrance. I brought you here so you'd get a perspective on the flat as you wouldn't if I took you through the house. Of course they can use the front door. They can use any door they like."

Cassie went ahead, propelled by her anger, taking the steep stairs two at a time. At the top there was a landing, or rather a widening of the passage that came from the interior of the house. She guessed it ran down the side of the great hall. Jonathan disentangled another key, a convenient handbag size, and slid it into the keyhole of a plain oak door.

They stepped into a small vestibule. Through an open door she could see a big, graciously proportioned room. She went forward and stood in the doorway, gazing in amazement. There was an exquisite carpet on the floor – Aubusson, she guessed. Elegant and comfortable velvet-covered chairs. An enormous sofa that one could sink into. Some elegant coffee tables, antique. The ceiling was decorated with discreet little plaster cherubs, white as snow. Only the curtains looked out of place. They were faded and in need of a wash or dry clean.

She turned to Jonathan, frowning. "The old nursery? Furnished like this? You're joking. Who lived here?"

"Me, as a child, with the nannies."

"With this furniture?"

He looked vague.

"Anyway," she said crisply, "I don't really think my parents have enough stuff to fill a room this size." She looked up at the plaster cherubs, thinking how incongruous they would look with the shabby old sofas and chairs and tables from Crabapple Cottage.

"This furniture is for their use. Don't you like it?" he asked, looking innocent.

"I like it, of course I do. It's beautiful. But I don't like what it represents."

She could see what had happened. He had rushed in the beautiful carpet and the big chairs from spare rooms when news came of her imminent return. A sprat to catch a mackerel. 'Look what a kind man I am' he was preparing to say to the courtroom. 'I've done all this for the victims of the accident. I've provided them with beautiful furnished rooms in my own home.'

He sighed. "What do you want me to do, Cassie? Chop off my right arm?"

She swallowed. How could she put it? "They need their dignity and their independence, Jonathan."

"They shall have it."

"How can they?" she exploded. "Tricks! It's all tricks, isn't it? Even the separate entrance was a red herring. They will have to use the main entrance and that will embarrass them. You know it will embarrass them."

"As to the front door – haven't we both forgotten the world and his wife will be coming through it two or three times a week?"

Yes. Of course. It was about to lose its identity as a grand private entrance. He seemed to have shot every objection from under her. He came close to her, looked down into her face. "Don't fight me, Cassie," he said. "You won't win."

"As I said, I'll find them a flat locally."

He brought his hands down on her shoulders and shook her. Hard. Her hair streamed away from the band and fell to her shoulders. Before she could gather herself together his arms slid round her waist; he pulled her close against him.

51

She attempted to break away but he kissed the lobe of her ear then rained a shower of little kisses across her neck. Her temples were pounding. There was a wild, plangent beating that might have been his heart or hers. Then he pushed her away.

"You used to like it," he said, taunting her. "You were in love with me, Cassie. Remember that? Remember being in love with me? Perhaps you still are. There hasn't been another man in your life."

She wanted to deny it. Wanted to ask him how he knew, though the answer was already there. 'He has such a way with him,' Leila would say apologetically if Cassie questioned her. What Jonathan wanted to know he found out. She had become defenceless. Tears of fury lay close behind her eyes. She would have liked to say, 'When I was a silly little seventeen year old. Your parents cured that.' She bit the words back, knowing they were dangerous. That they gave her away.

"God! What an opportunist you are," she said, her voice breaking, "It's a game, isn't it? You're playing a game with my parents. And now, with me."

"No," he said. "I always loved you." He could have been sincere, but she was poignantly aware of his not saying, 'And I love you now.' Now was a foreign country. A place that they had to inhabit together.

"You must see the other rooms," he said, back to using his businesslike voice as though the incident of the shaking and the kissing had not happened. "Follow me." He opened a door that led off the vestibule.

"This is the dining room. Not furnished yet. When you're going round the house doing your inventory you can keep an eye out for a suitable table and some chairs your parents might like. Or they can bring their own, if they wish."

She was thinking of Leila and Gerald sitting down to dinner here at their old dining table – made of, what? Chipboard? Hardboard? Something anyway that had to be covered with a cloth. Using the old Windsor chairs. Then after the meal moving into the opulent room next door. She thought, I should laugh. I should be able to make light of it. But she couldn't. Her nerves were tight as violin strings.

"And here's the kitchen," Jonathan opened another door. With startled eyes she took in a deep porcelain sink, cupboards painted in an unattractive beige colour, a brown linoleum seriously worn with cracks across the centre where it had buckled. A small and very ancient looking gas stove, not very clean. A fridge. Jonathan backed away. "I'll show you the bedrooms."

"Just a moment!" She held the door open. "What do you intend to do about this kitchen?"

Jonathan looked blank.

"Don't you know about kitchens?" she asked before realising that of course he would not. A picture came into her mind of the enormous kitchen where she had visited as a child, the great open fireplace into which an Aga had been fitted; the long scrubbed oak table so thick and solid one could dance on it. Even a large adult, if he'd a mind to. Burnished copper pans on the walls. Saucepans suspended from a wrought-iron grill hanging in mid-air from chains attached to the ceiling.

"Something will have to be done about the kitchen," she said.

He looked vague, then shrugged.

"It doesn't exactly compare with the grandeur of the drawing room," she said pointedly.

He seemed puzzled. "One doesn't see them together."

"When was it put in?"

"I don't know. When the nursery was here, I suppose."

"Like, thirty years ago? When you were in the womb?" She conceded it would have been considered good enough for the nursery maids.

Again that uninterested shrug.

"Something will have to be done about this before my parents move in."

"Cassie," he begged, "don't be like that. Don't bully."

"I am not bullying," she said distinctly. "I have to look after my parents' interests. I'd like you to know, Jonathan, I learned to stand on my own feet in America."

"Be sure you're not standing on your parents' feet," he replied, then swung away and headed down a short passage. "Now, let me show you the bedrooms." There was a window at the end shedding sunlight on the carpet. "This is to be your parents' bedroom," he said opening a door on a big airy room with two windows overlooking the park. It was partially furnished with a four-poster bed draped in Colefax and Fowler cotton and an elegant knee-hole dressing table.

"A four-poster has been your mother's, so far unrequited, dream. Did you know that?"

"You seem to know more about her than I do."

He ignored that. "And luckily, it just happened to be here," he went on unconvincingly. His diabolical cleverness frightened her. "And next door, your room." He backed away and opened another door on a smaller room which also overlooked the park. There was no furniture here.

"It might have occurred to you that I don't wish to move back in with my parents," she said.

"Oh yes. Yes, of course. Of course. This is purely temporary. But you have to have somewhere to lay your head while you're getting started. And living with them allows you to juggle the two jobs. I understand you'll want to keep an eye on them." She felt taken over. "What's the matter, Cassie?"

"I have to think," she said. "I have to talk to my parents. I have to think," she repeated. "I'll go away now."

"My parents are expecting you for lunch."

She started, having forgotten. "I'm sorry. I can't stay." That would be to get entangled deeper into the plot they had woven round her family. She had to clear her mind. She was too angry, and at the same time too mesmerised by Jonathan's charm and his awesome, self-seeking wickedness.

She turned her back on him and went to the window. The sky was clear now. A bright sun shone down on the rolling parkland with its great oaks and chestnuts. He came and stood beside her. "Don't fight me, Cassie," he said again. And again, too, "You're not going to win."

No, she felt he had shown her that.

"Come on," he said. He slid an arm through hers and led her out onto the landing then down the steep stairs.

At the bottom she did not break away. Her mind had gone blank with the unreason of what was happening. He turned her towards the back of the building. They rounded the end of the west wing and entered the gardens. Ahead stood a stone arch leading to the little courtyard where the fountain was sited. The little garden was overgrown, the fountain dry. Above them, on the left, a window that she guessed served that sad little kitchen. Ahead the great hall rose sixty feet in the air. Memories crowded in.

A small girl rushing, shrieking. A boy showering her with water. There was a long moment of silence. The tension in the air had an energy of its own. She knew why Jonathan had brought her this way. There was further power in the resurrection of the past.

Footsteps on the stone path. She swung round. Lady Haldane approached through the arch. She was a tall woman, taller than Cassie. She wore a shapeless tweed skirt and very dirty, low-heeled shoes that laced up at the front. Her pullover was frayed at the wrists and her beige cotton tights were darned. Her face still showed signs of prettiness; her eyes, egg-shell blue, were shrewd, and kind. She bore a heart-stopping resemblance to her son.

"Yes, it is you," she said, peering at her. "Cassie Neilson. But my goodness, how you've grown up. You're lunching with us, dear. Where have you been?"

Jonathan said, "I've been showing her the flat."

"Ah, yes." She looked down at the trowel, gave it a shake. Some mud flew off onto the stones. Cassie noticed that her hands had not worn well. "It's going to be comfortable when we've finished, don't you think?" she asked, then without waiting for a reply, "Jonathan has gone to such a lot of trouble. There's so much furniture to choose from. So many unused rooms. You can go through it, anyway. We must be sure your parents are happy."

Cassie tried to think of something gracious to say. Nothing presented itself. "I'm not sure they should be using your lovely furniture," she said ineptly. "You're very kind, but—"

"Why on earth not? They'll keep the moths out. And the dry rot. Vigilance, that's what old houses need," Lady Haldane said robustly. "Tell your mother to whack the chairs and sofa every now and then to make sure the moths don't settle. Jonathan dear, do take Cassie in. I must drop this trowel in the greenhouse and," she looked down at her feet, "get rid of some of the mud off my shoes." She turned and stalked off. "I won't be a tick."

So much for the problem, jumper and skirt versus suit, Cassie thought. She began to laugh.

"What's the joke?" Jonathan turned to look at her.

"I had to choose between laughing and crying," she said.

Chapter Four

THEY crossed the imposing hall and went down the same wide passage where Cassie had gone before in the wake of the butler, their footsteps silent on the Turkish carpet.

"This is Father's snug," said Jonathan opening the first door on the right and entering a beautiful drawing room.

It was considerably smaller than the library where Jonathan had given her a sherry and though no less richly appointed, it lacked the library's grandeur. But snug? No, it was hardly that. Cassie's eyes roved round the room, over elegant, damask-covered chairs with fine, delicate frames; cosy, sprung chairs upholstered in rich velvet. In this room, too, there were books, hundreds of them imprisoned safely behind prettily trellised glass doors decorated with delicate golden keyholes. She guessed the books were never read. A small stack of modern novels stood on a marble-topped table with curved legs stunningly wrought into trailing vines and painted with gold leaf.

She jumped at the sound of a muted, "Hrr-m-p!"

"Ah! There you are," said Jonathan addressing the far corner of the room. He led Cassie forward to where the earl sat, half hidden behind the table with its books.

The earl had changed less than his wife, or so it seemed to Cassie. He was a shortish man – Jonathan had his height from his mother – stocky and slightly bent. He must have taken to using a stick for one lay close at hand, silver topped, against the arm of the gilt chair. He made no attempt to stand. He sat leaning forward, peering at Cassie. The pale eyes still had the piercing quality she remembered.

"Well, Miss, you're back," he said.

His abrupt greeting with its faintly discourteous overtones put Cassie on her mettle. She lifted her head but before she could reply the countess came through the door and they all turned.

Lady Haldane must have paused in some handy cloakroom – yes, Cassie remembered one in the kitchen passageway. She had been taken to it during a Christmas party so that spilt jelly could be sponged off her dress. Her ladyship strode across the room to join them. She had slung an elegant Liberty silk scarf carelessly round her neck. It looked incongruous against the drab oatmeal of her gardening jumper with its frayed wrist bands.

And she had run a comb through her hair, but so carelessly that loose ends had piled up to form a bushy little nest just below the crown. She still wore outdoor shoes but this pair were beautifully polished. An Irish setter with a coat the colour of gingerbread ambled in in her wake and collapsed on the carpet in front of the earl's chair.

"Of course she's back, and it's a jolly good thing for us that she is," said her ladyship, hitching at her scarf. "She's offered to help Jonathan with the house, dear. Now, isn't that kind?" She stood in front of her husband, waiting for his reply.

Jonathan broke in, "It would be more correct to say that I've persuaded her. Treat her with tender loving care or she may yet walk out on us."

Cassie blinked, collected her startled wits and addressed the earl. "I came home to help my parents," she said. "As you know, they're in trouble."

"Yes. A bad business." He spoke as though the accident had nothing at all to do with the Haldanes. It might have been a meteor from outer space that had hurtled in to knock Gerald down instead of Jonathan, his own son, speeding down the lane in his fancy sports car.

"Sit, girl, sit," the earl said, picking up his stick and waving it irritably in front of him, as though her looking down on him showed a want of respect. He pointed the stick at one of the damask-covered chairs. "There, where I can see you." He waited until she had obeyed, then like a headmaster laying down his cane, replaced his stick against his chair arm.

Cassie, faintly unnerved, sat on the edge of her seat.

"America," he said portentously. "My aunt," he looked hard at Cassie with those piercing eyes, "went to America – in the fifties it was – and came back with her face lifted. You never saw such a disaster! She went from here looking like a bloodhound and came back like a pop-eyed peke. Then it all sagged and she went into hiding."

"Oh come, Haldane," protested her ladyship. Her husband grunted, cleared his throat as though for silence and continued, "Nobody saw her again. She even left orders her coffin was to be screwed down immediately she'd snuffed it." He thrust his head forward the better to examine Cassie's face, staring hard as though looking for some sign that she had fallen for the American obsession.

"Sherry?" asked Jonathan, eyes twinkling.

A silver plate on one of the marble-topped cabinets held a decanter of sherry and some glasses. Jonathan filled two,

handed one to Cassie and the other to his father. Cassie took
hers swiftly, nervously, sensing that his lordship should have
had his drink first. That Jonathan was flouting the rules.

"Look at this, my dear. It's a kneeler."

She jumped as her ladyship spoke at her elbow. She was
holding a tapestry frame under Cassie's nose. "The vicar's
bullied us all into embroidering them for the church. The
pelican in its piety. She's pecking blood from her breast to
feed her young." Lady Haldane pointed a finger to an outline
of the breast of a bird embroidered in white. Cassie noted the
dirt embedded beneath the nail. "And that's her beak, or will
be. I've run out of wool. It'll be rather impressive, don't you
think, with scarlet drops of blood falling into the fledglings'
beaks? You'll have seen it in stained glass. And in one of
the stone bosses in Suffolk Cathedral."

"Yes," said Cassie. She felt it was expected of her that she
should have been to Suffolk Cathedral to see the bosses.

"That's fern stitch. Very tricky," Jonathan's mother went
on, "but it makes realistic feathers. If you're not careful,
Andrew – do you know Andrew, he's the vicar and everyone's on christian names here, like it or not. No of course
you wouldn't know him, he wasn't here in your time – if
you're not careful he'll have you making one, too. There's
a range of designs, all taken from the church windows or
the Bible. A clever little girl from the village has drawn
them for us."

"For all you know, Frances, the girl can't sew," his lordship commented cantankerously. Again that piercing look at
Cassie from beneath his heavy brows. "Can you sew? Heh?"

"Of course she can," retorted his wife. She went over to
the table that held the pile of novels and carefully laid the
frame down. "Every girl can sew."

"Then put her to work mending tapestries. Charity begins at home." He turned to Jonathan. "And what does she know about stately homes?" he asked, as though Cassie was absent.

She sipped her sherry and pretended she hadn't heard. By any standards this was a very impressive and beautiful room. The carpet looked as though it had been laid yesterday, though it was 1740 as Jonathan told her later and woven especially at Axminster for this room. Pale walls, painted in a delicate aqua, threw the many paintings into sharp relief. She thought she recognised a Rubens. And surely that horse with its long neck and tiny head had to be painted by Landseer? It occurred to Cassie that she knew rather more about paintings than antiques.

"Everything," said Jonathan carelessly, replying to his father's question.

"Is that what she was doing in New York?"

"She wasn't in New York."

His lordship acknowledged Cassie's presence once again with another hard stare. "So your parents are moving in," he said, as though it was their idea. "They may as well. They can keep an eye on you."

Cassie felt her colour rise. Don't blow it, she begged her grown-up, Americanised self, the part of her that thankfully was refusing to be overawed. He's probably got gout and a bad liver. He's pretending you're little Cassie the gardener's – Stop it! Just keep your cool. You need this job.

"I'm going to sell that cottage, you know," the earl was saying. "Some commuter with money to spare will do it up, I dare say. We don't want these old buildings to fall down, and I can't afford to fix them."

"Living in a draughty old mausoleum isn't everybody's cup of tea, Father," said Jonathan. "They have to decide."

"It's not my cup of tea either," said the earl. He eased himself forward in his chair and picked up the stick again. "If our guest has finished her drink perhaps we can go in to lunch."

Cassie swallowed her indignation along with the dregs of her sherry and stood up abruptly before either the earl or his countess could rise. She went to the door and stood pointedly waiting for them, head lifted. The dog rose too and shambled up to her, nosing at her hand. Cassie smoothed his silky head. "What's his name?" The earl did not bother to reply. She accidentally caught Jonathan's eye. He grinned and gave her a discreet thumbs-up sign. "Spicer," he said.

She went through the door in her hostess's wake, leaving him to follow with his father. The old dog shambled along beside her. She reached down and patted his head again.

The inner wall of the dining room was lined with tall, gilt-framed mirrors, the windows of the outer wall were draped in heavy blue velvet. The table, a magnificent piece of highly polished mahogany on cabriole legs would seat thirty people with ease. Four places were set at the head. Cassie was astonished. Why had the family not found more modest apartments in the building for their own use? There were big chairs with tapestry backs, each with the Bevington coat of arms embroidered into them. On the huge sideboard stood silver that winked and shone in the rays of sunlight coming through the window.

"Where's Zoe?" barked the earl, hesitating behind his chair. "I thought she was coming to lunch." He glared at his wife.

"She's coming to dinner, dear," Lady Haldane replied

patiently, pulling out her own chair at her husband's right, "and I hope staying for the weekend. Sit there dear," she said to Cassie, indicating a place at her host's left.

Jonathan, settling on Cassie's other side, said with an edge to his voice, "You know how busy I'm going to be this weekend. I shan't have time—" He broke off as his mother interposed.

"I shall be only too happy to entertain her. She is, after all, virtually part of the family."

Cassie looked at Jonathan and saw in her mind's eye a badge on his jacket marked 'Reserved'.

Her hostess turned to Cassie, "I don't think you would know Zoe Montcalm, though you've no doubt heard of the family."

Cassie felt she had been accorded her place in her rightful strip of the social strata. That she was acknowledged to be one of those who knew 'of' grand people, without actually knowing them. Fair enough, she said to herself, and by the way, where's your sense of humour? She managed a wooden smile. "I imagine everyone in Hampshire has heard of the Montcalms," she said, deliberately isolating the Haldanes in their privileged position as friends, holding her own, she hoped. She looked down at the highly polished table, not wanting to meet Jonathan's eyes.

The butler came through the door bearing a huge tray of sparkling bowls. Again she thought, what a way to live in the 1990s and felt impatient with them. No wonder the coffers were running dry.

The food was good country fare. Fresh vegetable soup, liquidised, with bits of vegetable floating in it.

"You will remember Cook," said Lady Haldane. "She was here in your time."

Cassie again offered her wooden smile. "Yes, indeed. What a good cook she is. This soup is delicious."

"From vegetables grown in our own gardens."

Cassie's mind flew ahead. Why should they not open a restaurant in the house or in one of the outbuildings? How old would Cook be now? Would she be willing to do the extra work? She couldn't possibly be overstretched, cooking for this tiny family.

The earl drank his soup noisily. When the next course arrived – saddle of lamb, roast potatoes, greens, gravy – Cassie thought again of a restaurant. They might come to an arrangement to get lamb from the farmer who had leased the home farm. She wondered how her hosts with their simple tastes were going to fare in the south of France where it was necessary to serve rich sauces to hide the fact that the meat was inferior.

The butler poured hock into impressive cut crystal glasses. She took one sip, then another. The sharp edges in her began to soften. The conversation was desultory. The earl did not bother to join in. Apple crumble! The children's favourite. She hadn't tasted that since she was about fourteen. She helped herself to a lavish amount of cream.

In a silence broken only by the clink of spoons on fine china Cassie's mind wandered. She thought about the possibility that Mrs Pannington's daughter, who was finishing her training as a caterer, might run the tearoom for her. She wondered if she would be allowed to open a boutique in the house. There was space in plenty just inside the front door.

"Cassie!"

She started. They were all looking at her, the three of them. "I'm sorry," she apologised, flushing. "I was miles away."

"Would you like some coffee?" the countess asked, repeating the question Cassie had not heard, smiling only faintly.

"Thank you."

Jonathan rose. "If you'll excuse us we'll have coffee in the office. We've rather a lot to talk about."

Cassie hid her relief. She walked down the passage at Jonathan's side. His stride was longer, more than half as long again as hers, yet they walked comfortably together. "I felt I had to get you out of that," he said. "Sorry. What's born in the blood . . . He's too old to change. You'll have to be forgiving. And remember, you're employed by me."

She said, knowing she was being intolerant, not caring, "Nobody's too old to change. Especially, it's up to them to realise they're fifty years out of date. And," her voice became unintentionally crisp, "I'd like you to tell your mother she need have no worries on Zoe Montcalm's behalf." She felt a thin, protective skin somewhere inside her creeping out to cover the parts that were too tender, too vulnerable for exposure to the harsh reality of the life she had opted to live.

"I'm sure Zoe's quite capable of looking after herself." He, too, spoke lightly as though he was smiling about his mother, not thinking of the girl at all. "You're going to be good for the place, Cassie."

"Am I?" she asked as they crossed the spacious hall and turned in behind the grand, curving staircase. "I'm not sure my coming here is going to work. I don't think your parents realise that it's seven years since they knew me. And I've grown up."

"Oh yes. They realise that."

"But they don't accept it." She wanted to say, 'They're

scared of me', but that would stir matters better left sleeping. "I'm not a servant," she said distinctly. "That's something you're going to have to explain to them in words of two syllables. You've succeeded in pushing my parents around but I want to be sure you understand you're not going to push me. I'm taking this job on as a professional. Do you understand that, Jonathan?"

They were heading for a door directly in front of them. "Oh yes," he replied carelessly. "This is my office." He reached for the knob.

She went and stood in the open doorway looking in on a tiny room, aware of drabness; of the gritty smell of dust; of papers and files lying askew. There was a threadbare needlecord carpet in an unfortunate shade of brown filmed over with gingery dog hairs. "You work here?" she managed emotionally, meaning, You expect me to work here? All her uncertainties crowded in with a surge of very real anger. "With a hundred rooms to choose from . . . With all that grandeur where you and your family live . . ."

Jonathan looked uncertain. "I suppose it is a bit of a dungeon. But it is only for me," he said apologetically.

There was an unimportant-looking desk of varnished oak and standing on it an ancient typewriter together with a tray overflowing with papers, marked In. Another, empty tray, marked Out. A spike pushed through a pile of bills. Behind the desk, a typist's chair, a filing cabinet.

"It's handy," Jonathan said. Suddenly he looked sheepish as though seeing the room through her eyes. He rallied; became the Honourable Jonathan Tarrant of Bevington Hall. "It's always been the office," he said in a voice that told her she must understand this was the way they did things here.

"You mean, the clerk who worked here didn't count. That's what you mean, isn't it?"

He looked at her uncertainly. Then, "Yes. That's it," he said. "That's how it was. But when I took over it was good enough for me." He seemed to see the look that was spreading from her mind for he added swiftly, "Of course I didn't spend much time here."

She said straightforwardly, "I shall be spending a great deal of time in my office. I'm afraid this is not going to be good enough for me. I am not prepared to work in a dungeon."

He raised one hand and pushed the floppy hair back from his forehead. Moved from one foot to the other. She recognised the Jonathan she used to know and felt herself weakening. But she mustn't. She hardened her heart and without looking at him – for that way lay defeat – said more gently, "We can't hold the reins from here, Jonathan. I shall need a sizeable – and why not attractive? – room, with plenty of light, if possible looking out over the entrance so that I can see the paying public coming in. I shall have to be at the centre of things. I suspect you only nipped in here to pay bills."

"Er – yes, something like that. I've been working in London."

"Are you still working in London?"

"I'll be going up one or two days a week, perhaps. I have to keep things going until we see if this is going to work out."

"It is going to work out," Cassie said categorically. "You hadn't really thought out my part in this, had you?" She could see by the expression on his face that he hadn't.

There was a tap at the door, it opened, and the butler

appeared carrying a silver tray opulently set with a tall
coffee pot, a cream jug, sugar basin and two cups.

Jonathan said sharply, as though the butler was the one
at fault, "Take it to Lady Selena's room, please, Harding."

"Certainly." The man backed out.

Cassie waited until he was beyond earshot. "Don't you
think he might prefer not to be called by his surname?"

"Yes," said Jonathan promptly, though she could see from
the startled expression on his face that it was not something
he had thought of before.

She burst out laughing. "You're not a bad guy," she said.
"You just need bringing up to date."

"I'm not a guy at all." But he said it good-naturedly.

"Sorry. I'm trying to Anglicise myself. You're a chap,
aren't you?"

He grinned. "As you will."

They climbed the impressive staircase and turned right.

Here the passage was well lit from the glass dome in the
hall. The floor was covered with a fine Turkish carpet.

"Why is it called Lady Selena's room?" Cassie asked,
pausing in the doorway looking round, enchanted by the
room's beauty. It had a stuccoed ceiling decorated with
cherubs and grapes. Fructification, she thought. There were
heavy brocade curtains patterned in claret, pink and gold;
lovely portraits of ladies in low-cut, sumptuous gowns; a
decoratively-designed carpet. A polished mahogany bridge
table stood against the wall. An embroidered firescreen
only partially concealed a gleaming steel firebox adorned
with fierce, decorative animal heads. She went forward
tentatively smoothing her fingers across the golden wood
of a spinnet prettily painted with wild flowers.

"It was the withdrawing room of the infamous wife of the

fourth earl," Jonathan said. "No one got around to changing it when she died. That's her over the fireplace."

Cassie looked up and saw an elegant lady in a rich gold frame looking down at her with wide blue eyes and a conspiratorial smile. She had fair hair swept gently back from a porcelain face, a well-shaped, sensuous mouth, puffball bosoms rising out of the daringly low sapphire-blue dress that perfectly matched her eyes, and a tiny waist. She was leaning back against a balustrade, her silken skirts bunched and catching the light. With her head slightly inclined to the side she had a coquettish look.

Jonathan shoved his hands in his pockets, set his feet apart in that way he had and gave her one of those looks that still melted her heart: mouth turned down at one corner, eyes teasing. "She had fifteen children and lived to be eighty. It's rumoured she had lots of lovers, too, though how she fitted them in I cannot imagine for she must have had about a baby a year."

"The answer's obvious," Cassie retorted. "They were what used to be called illegitimate. So you've got bastards in your ancestry! Oh fie, as Lady Selena would no doubt have said."

"It's the working classes who aimed to be moral in those days. Aristos never bothered. At least married couples stayed together, which they don't bother to now." He sounded disapproving. "I suppose with their vast incomes and big houses it was easy enough to support the little cuckoos in the nest. And with so many rooms it would have been easy for husband and wife to avoid each other if they'd a mind to."

"There must be a good many stories about the Hall and its inhabitants. Has anyone been interested enough to put pen to paper?"

"I think you might find my mother could help you there. She's gone into the family's history."

"Perhaps we could put together a little book and sell it to the viewing public as a souvenir of their visit."

"Why not?"

Cassie looked back at Lady Selena, then went to the window and looked at her again. She moved back to the door. "Her eyes seem to follow me."

"Oh yes. They do. I dare say that's why it's still called Lady Selena's room. One gets the feeling she's not only still alive here, but she's making up her own mind about the people who come and go."

"That's a bit daunting. How do I know she's going to approve of me?"

"It'll be interesting to find out," Jonathan replied with a twinkle. "Are you going to pour the coffee? It must be getting cold."

"I could," said Cassie, considering. "But it's not a woman's job any more. You can pour it yourself if you want to."

"Men should be men and women should know their place," said Jonathan as he bent over the tray that the butler had placed on a low table. But he was smiling. "Have you looked out of the window?"

Cassie crossed the room again. Lady Selena's room was almost directly over the front entrance. To the left the drive swept away between chestnut trees to the front gate.

"That's where the visitors will come in," Jonathan said. I suppose you would consider this room suitable for, as you say, holding the reins?"

Cassie waited a moment until her breath came back. Then,

marvelling that he could make such an art of defeat, she said, "It will do very nicely, thank you."

Cassie sped down the drive, turned into the main road that led to Flyford and put her foot down hard. She felt exhilarated, as though she had walked a hundred miles in the dark and emerged in the sunlight. She sped round the perimeter of the estate, glancing aside from time to time, looking at the great house from its various angles, its vine, its red bricks glowing in the rays of the lowering sun. "This," she said to herself with certainty, "is the best day's work you ever did, Cassie Neilson. What an assignment! What a challenge!" Then she let out a whoop of sheer glee.

As she passed the little railway halt where the branch line ended she remembered that the railway had been brought here in the 1860s purely for the convenience of the privileged incumbents of Bevington Hall. No wonder they're having trouble coming down to earth, she thought. The engine raced. The car fled down into Cooper's Dell and up over the Devil's Crossing then joined the main road that would take her to the hospital.

Gerald was dozing. Leila bent over him, kissed him lightly on the forehead, then picked up her bag and tiptoed out of the room. Cassie said as they walked together down the long corridor, "I'm taking the job. You'll be pleased about that."

Leila smiled. "I thought you said that yesterday."

Cassie felt a faint brush of irritation. "There was never any doubt in your mind that I would take it, was there?"

"Why should there be? It seemed so ideal for you." Leila continued happily, "Would you believe it, they've moved the infamous Lady Selena's four-poster bed into the flat!

Jonathan took me to Wallace's in Flyford to select the drapes!"

"Colefax and Fowler. You've got a nerve." Cassie unlocked the car. "Hop in."

"I should have gone for something cheaper, shouldn't I?"

"What can you do with a four-poster but put the most expensive drapes on it? Of course you did the right thing." Cassie was thinking she may as well send everything from Crabapple Cottage to auction. Anything Leila and Gerald owned was going to look sad, not to say ridiculous, in conjunction with the antiques and rich upholstery Jonathan was thrusting upon them. "You're going upmarket, Leila," she said. "Relax and enjoy it."

"You've changed," said Leila critically. "Sometimes I don't understand you."

"Oh yes, I've changed. Seven years is a long time."

"You're not the little Cassie I knew."

"And never will be again. You're all having to get used to it." She softened the words with a laugh.

"All?"

"Everybody, Leila. Everybody."

"Why do you call us by our christian names?" she asked plaintively.

"To help you get used to the fact that I'm not the little Cassie you knew."

Leila patted the hand on the steering-wheel and settled back in her seat, sighing.

Next morning Cassie took her mother up to the Hall. Leila didn't want to use the front door if it could be avoided so they went to the side door to have another look at the stairs.

"I shall be entering by the front door myself," said Cassie briskly. "That's the nearest door to my office. And it's the most convenient method of reaching the apartment – whoops, flat. Come on. I'll hoist you up those stairs."

"Before the accident," said Leila mournfully, reaching for the narrow bannister rail, "I could have run up here just so easily."

"Of course. And no doubt you will again." Cassie took her arm to steady her. "Step carefully. Take them one at a time."

They wandered through the flat. Leila stood at the kitchen window looking down into the small courtyard below. "Oh, what a mess that lovely fountain's in!" she exclaimed in dismay. "I'll clean up the beds round it. It'll be my first job. And my first bit of paying back." She turned to her daughter, hands clasped. "Oh Cassie, do you realise how kind Jonathan has been?"

Cassie thought irrationally she looked as though she was in a state of prayer. She wanted to say, 'Frankly no.' Surplus accommodation and surplus furniture in exchange for a beloved home. Cold cash in Haldane pockets. She decided not to point out the fact that with their home sold and all their furniture and furnishings scrapped her parents were entirely in the hands of the incumbents of the Hall. They seemed to have come too far to think in terms of turning back. But she was afraid. If I don't play my cards right, she said to herself, it's they who'll come a cropper. It was a sobering thought.

"Come a cropper," she said aloud. "Funny how sayings come back. I haven't thought of that phrase for years."

Leila said, "I remember when you were three you came back with Grandad saying, 'I come a cropper off Jonathan's

74

pony.' You were so proud that he had allowed you to ride it. Its name was—"

"Sebastian," said Cassie.

Leila's face glowed. "You do remember! Sebastian put his head down to nibble at the lawn and you went head first over. Grandad said you jumped up and said, 'I meant to do that.'"

Let the memories in, Cassie said to herself thinking of the child she had been. Perhaps they would be therapeutic. But she said merely, "This kitchen!"

Leila surveyed the poor paintwork, the badly worn linoleum, the ill-fitting cupboard doors. "I suppose it's not very—" She broke off.

Cassie thought, This is where Jonathan shows where his heart lies for he has to dip his hand into his pocket. "I'm not going to accept this," she said.

"I hope you won't upset Jonathan."

"Don't worry. I'll deal with it. Now come with me. I want to show you my office. This will surprise you." Maybe it won't, she thought sardonically, considering the implicit faith Leila had in Jonathan's goodwill. They went together along the winding passageways to the front of the house.

Leila gazed around Lady Selena's room. Then she took a long, slow breath and let it out again. "You are so lucky," she said.

Cassie said briskly, "It won't look quite like this by the time it's set up with an executive desk and an array of filing cabinets. And a computer."

Leila's eyes widened. "Is he going to give you a computer?"

"He'd better."

Her mother looked at her uncertainly, then looked away.

75

"Come on then, let's take you home." They went back along the passage. Leila stopped at the top of the stairs looking down at the scagliola columns, the marble floor patterned in black and white squares, then up at the sunken panels in the dome, magnificently painted. She breathed a deep sigh of contentment. Cassie, too, looked round as they came slowly down into the hall, so neither of them saw Jonathan waiting for them.

He came forward as they reached the ground floor. "And how do you like the flat now we've got a few bits of furniture in, Mrs Neilson?"

Leila replied, starry-eyed, "I think it's wonderful."

He rubbed his hands together. "Right! Everyone's happy. Now Cassie, were you thinking of coming back this afternoon?"

"If that's what you want. What time had you in mind?"

"Any time. I'm not going to lunch. I shall have a sandwich sent round to the dungeon. That's where you'll find me."

Leila blinked.

"That's my office, Mrs Neilson," he explained. "I don't aspire to such grandeur as your daughter. I've got a dark little box behind the stairs. We call it the dungeon."

Cassie went swiftly out of the door and stopped dead. The Rover had been brought up the drive and across the portico between the Corinthian columns. She turned. "Thank you," she said politely.

"My pleasure," he replied gravely.

She opened the passenger door and waited for her mother to climb in.

"I'm sorry you're so – so – well, you know, not really comfortable with Jonathan," Leila said as they rolled down the drive. "But if the families get their way," she went on

76

comfortingly, "he'll be married soon and then you'll be on a less personal footing. I'm told he's very close to Zoe Montcalm. You know the Montcalms of Lethbridge Place? I believe they're very rich and clearly the Haldanes could do with an injection of money. That's how the old families have always kept going," added Leila speaking kindly but firmly as though to a small child, "by marrying money. We all know that."

Chapter Five

IT WAS two days later. Cassie was turning left towards the dungeon where she expected to find Jonathan when she heard his voice. It seemed to come from the top of the stairs. She went back round the curving staircase and looked up.

He was standing on the landing with one hand on the bannister. "Come up and see what I've done to your office," he called.

She ran to join him, taking the stairs two at a time.

"It's not that urgent," he told her.

"I need the exercise. Stairs are good for the legs."

"Your legs are okay."

He was Oh, so handsome this morning in a pale denim shirt, chinos and loafers. Though he had a casual look, he wore a businesslike air. As she came abreast of him he turned and walked towards Lady Selena's room. "I hope you're going to like it," he said.

Standing in the doorway she couldn't believe her eyes. The spinnet, the card table, all the pretty fandangles, had gone. In the centre of the room stood an impressive mahogany desk with a green leather top. On either side, their chunky legs tucked into the kneeholes, stood two executive swivel armchairs. Mysteriously, the Georgian elegance of the room had been retained.

"Is this your kind of office now?" Jonathan asked, looking at her with his head on one side.

"Oh yes." She was close to tears. "Every office I've worked in looked just like this. You're really very kind."

"Such a compliment that is, coming from you. You've made my day."

She glanced up into his face then swiftly away. "You certainly move fast," she said.

"If we're to get the house open to paying guests by next summer we're going to have to move fast."

"Quote," she laughed, for that was what she had said to him the day before. "How did you get it here?"

"The gardeners are doubling as furniture removers."

"Did they mind?"

"They've got to adapt, like the rest of us. Try that chair."

She sat down. The chair swung easily in a half circle. She was facing the window with its view of the drive, the view she had asked for. In the distance, through the bare branches of the chestnut trees, she could see the big iron gates through which visitors would enter. She swung round the other way, facing towards the door. "Don't you think we should shut those gates?"

"What for? They haven't been shut for years."

"Security."

"And take on a man to open them?"

"No," she replied, noting with a touch of impatience how he automatically went for the expensive option. "You can take the key if you're coming back late."

"You thought the one we use for the door leading to the flat was over-sized," said Jonathan, amused. "Wait till you see the key to the gate."

"I'm sure there's room for it in your car. Once you start advertising—"

"Not me," he said. "Once *you* start advertising – go on from there."

"We're putting the Hall on the map. People may feel free to wander in. That's the side of the publicity we don't need."

"Publicists," he said with what she thought was a touch of nervousness, "are very expensive."

"I'm the publicist. We haven't talked about my salary, by the way. Why don't you sit down?" She nearly told him he might need to, but stopped herself.

He lowered his long frame into the seat and faced her across the green leather desk top, smiling approvingly. "I must say, you look the part, now."

"Thank you. So, what about my salary?" She braced herself for an argument.

He named a sum generous beyond her wildest dreams.

"Oh come," she protested, taken aback. "That's handsome, but it's the going rate for London."

"For a twenty-four-hour-a-day job, I don't believe it's over-generous."

"Am I to work twenty-four hours?" She frowned.

"Living on the premises means being on call. If we're to get things set up to open next summer I think you'll find you won't have much free time. Perhaps you'd like to start with a month's trial?"

She thought he had found a way to test her. "No," she said, "I wouldn't do the job knowing there was a way out if things got too difficult. I've accepted. That's it. I shall be asking for expenses. As well as the use of a car. Mother will be driving again soon and she'll need the Rover." The shutters had come down. She could see he had not considered transport. She said, "Of course I could run across the park while we're in the cottage. I'm talking about the chores I shall have to do in picking up things and transporting . . ." She leaned forward and looked into his face. "Don't you realise I shall have to run around?"

"Tom could drive you."

"In the Rolls?" They stared at each other and then she burst out laughing.

"Okay," said Jonathan morosely. "You strike a hard bargain."

"You haven't thought this out, have you?"

"No. I suppose not," he admitted, then, "aren't you the one who's thinking things out?"

"The running of the Hall, yes." She waited.

He sighed heavily. "Okay. I'll talk to Tom. I'll get him to look for something suitable."

"Tom? Wouldn't I know what was suitable for me to drive?"

"I don't know. Would you?"

She thought he needed time to come to terms with her unexpected demands. "Let's get on," she said. "What part of the house shall we start on?"

He rose from his chair, pushing himself up with his hands, swinging the chair experimentally with a shove from one knee. "I'll collect the keys from the dungeon. You'll find a pad and pencils in the centre drawer of that desk. And I've got a piece of chalk ready. We'll number the rooms. And by the way, when you find furniture that might suit your parents you can make a note of the room and I'll have it carried over to the flat."

"There's something I'd like to deal with first," she said,

not stirring. "The kitchen. I shall want it attended to before my parents move in."

"Isn't that something that can be left until later?"

"Later than what?" When he seemed uncertain how to reply she said in as firm a voice as she dared use, "My mother won't be using that kitchen." She waited.

"I dare say the estate carpenter could run up some new cupboards," he said vaguely.

"I'll get a kitchen designer to give me a quote." He was looking at her with astonishment. Ignoring his reaction she pushed her chair back and stood up. "Let's go."

They went from room to room. It was not a matter that could be hurried, for the furniture – in rooms that had been shut up for years – was shrouded in dust sheets. They became companionable as time went by. She was surprised by Jonathan's attitude to the family heirlooms. An expression almost of veneration came over his face when he looked at a Regency chair, a Louis Quinze mirror decorated with the extravagances of its time, gold leaves, lush fruit, a Pan. She accepted his offer of dining room furniture for the flat. He was amiable about her choice. She chose an oblong Georgian table with rounded corners and a set of matching chairs, the seats of which were beautifully embroidered in petit point.

"Done by my great-grandmother." He examined the stitching not only with pride, but with interest. "You'd wonder how her eyesight stood up to it, wouldn't you?"

She was smiling, thinking that her parents were going to be living with furniture that would add up to very nearly the value of the house they had lost. Was that a victory of a kind?

They repaired to the library for tea. His parents were

there, the earl asleep, the countess sitting on a sofa with a pile of books on a table in front of her. She looked up as they entered and removed her spectacles.

"Ah! There you are! Harding told me you were upstairs. I'm glad you've come." She glanced across at her supine husband and lifting her voice said, "Wake up, dear. Harding will be bringing tea presently. And Cassie has come to join us."

Jonathan hitched up his trousers at the knees and took his seat. "I've been talking to Edward Harding. He would prefer to be called Edward."

The earl, coming to a sitting position, blinked. The countess stared.

"We're having to move with the times," Jonathan told them.

"Times! What times?" barked the earl. "He's never objected to being called Harding."

"Did you ever ask him?"

The earl said in a puzzled voice, "We've always called butlers by their surnames." He turned to Cassie, "Your grandfather, young lady—"

"A long time ago," said Jonathan cutting him off. "Two generations away."

The earl regarded him suspiciously.

"You put me in charge, remember, Father. You put me in a position to make the rules."

"Well I'm blessed." In the silence the door opened and the butler came in carrying tea on a silver tray. No one addressed him by name. The earl and countess looked at him curiously, as though searching for signs that he had changed.

After tea Lady Haldane put her cup down on the tray and said, "Jonathan has told me you're interested in getting out a little book about the house. Do you think you're going to have time?"

"I don't intend to start immediately. Besides, I don't know anything about the family, and very little about the house, yet. But I intend to make notes, and if, when there's less work to do, I've got enough facts, yes, I would like to put them together. Perhaps you could help me."

"What do you want? Scandalous tales? Or—" She rose, went to the marble-topped table and came back with two books. "I've got here a diary written by Lady Alicia, wife of the seventh earl, and some account books." She sat down with the books on her knee. Cassie saw that one of them was a ledger. "The prices of goods, and the amounts ordered are very interesting to me."

"Then I'm sure they would be interesting to the visitors," Cassie said. "And as for scandalous tales, why not? It's scandal that sells papers, is it not?"

She nodded vaguely. "This is what interests me. The prices are beyond belief." Lady Haldane leafed through the pages. "And the amounts of food ordered. Listen to this recipe for mincemeat." She read the ingredient list aloud: "28 lb raisins, 28 lb currants, 28 lb moist sugar, 2 lb mixed peel, 1 lb of mixed spice and a good many apples." She pushed her glasses down her nose and looked up. "What do you suppose is 'a good many apples'?" They shook their heads, smiling. "Then, 4 bottles of brandy, 4 bottles of sherry, 2 bottles of rum. Your ancestors certainly did themselves well, Haldane. This is a list of the housekeeper's daily needs: 6 dozen short gooseberry corks. Now my dear, what on earth is a gooseberry cork?"

They all laughed.

"Four quarts of groats," went on the countess. "Six hair

brooms. Now I do wonder how they could wear out six brooms in one day. Two spitting pots. How disgusting! But people did spit in those days. One must be grateful that they've given it up. Now," she placed a finger firmly in the centre of the page, "what on earth is a flint crewet?" None of them knew so she closed the book and put it back on the table. "I think, Haldane," she said to her husband, "you could tell Cassie something about the portraits in this room. They're quite an interesting lot."

"After I've finished me tea. After I've finished me tea." It was clear the earl did not allow anyone to push him around.

"I'm sorry, my dear. I thought you had finished."

She turned back to Cassie. "I dare say you find this room over-grand, my dear. I know I did when I first stayed here as a girl. I was nervous as a cat, thinking I'd spill tea on that." She indicated the fine carpet with its magnificent colours, deep purple reds, grey and blue on a pale ground. "The Haldanes had all their floor coverings specially woven for them by the best companies, as often as not in France. My family, the Aynsleys, you've no doubt heard of them, were poor as church mice. Our castle in Argyll was bleak in the extreme. We used to freeze in winter. In summer, sometimes, too. Our money – what there was of it – came from Ireland. We were absentee landlords," she said.

"I wouldn't admit it if I were you," Jonathan said, smiling his teasing smile.

She shrugged. "I cannot alter history."

The earl put his cup down and addressed Cassie, "See that old boy in the portrait over the fireplace? He got into trouble at the time of Mary, Queen of Scots and nearly had himself decapitated in the Tower. He was always at logger-heads with Elizabeth so to spite her he entertained Spanish Catholics during the time the queen had Mary incarcerated and consequently he landed up on the suspicious list. But they pardoned him in the end."

"What a pity!" Jonathan put in.

"What do you mean, boy?" The earl looked at his son from beneath lowered brows.

"A pardoned ancestor is a lot less colourful than one who lost his head. Didn't some ancient Haldane get involved in that plot against James I to set his cousin Arabella Stuart on the English throne?"

His mother replied, "His portrait is in the long gallery. And there's a portrait of another ancestor, one William Tarrant, on the main staircase, who was burnt as a heretic during Mary Tudor's reign. Rather a dull little picture, but the story's worth recording."

Cassie was looking from one to the other, marvelling that they had come so far in only a few days.

"Here's something you might not know," put in the earl leaning forward, hands on his knees, frowning at her. "They were playing cricket on the green here in the early 1600s."

Cassie sat up, straight as a ramrod, her brain racing. "I've got an idea. Why don't we open the Hall with a cricket match? And dress the players in Elizabethan costumes."

"Who's going to make a damn fool of himself, dressing up in doublet and hose?" growled the earl but his lady looked at Cassie with immense respect.

Jonathan said, "I would, for a start. And I'll bet the village team would fall for it. Remember that team I made up of old boys from school, years ago?"

Cassie saw those strong fingers gripping a cricket bat.

Hitting boundaries.

"On your twenty-first birthday."

"That's right. I'll have a go at tracing them. We could kill two birds with one stone – have a reunion at the same time. They're a jolly bunch. I'll bet they'd be willing to dress up."

Cassie was remembering. There had been a glittering ball at Bevington Hall, preceded by the cricket. Jonathan's school friends versus the village. She remembered the excitement in the local shops. She had stood in the High Street watching while mountains of bread sticks were packed into a van outside the baker's. She remembered the butcher proudly showing the locals sucking pigs with an apple in each wide open mouth. The Haldanes had always been exemplary about employing local people, though it would have been rather less trouble to call in a caterer.

That night she had hidden in a big rhododendron bush on the edge of the drive so that she would see the glamorous young people stepping out of their cars. She saw them now in her mind's eye, tall young men in black ties, lovely slender girls in shining silk gowns and dainty high-heeled shoes. How she had envied them, and not least for their privilege in dancing with Jonathan.

She sensed, or heard, a waiting silence and looked up, startled out of her reverie. "You were a long way away," said Jonathan.

She flushed. "I was, indeed." They waited for her to explain. She said, "So what do you think about a cricket match for the opening?"

They were indulgent. "If you had been listening you'd have heard me say I think we were bang-on when we decided to offer you the job," said Jonathan.

*   *   *

87

That evening Cassie carried Lady Alicia's diary and the rest of the books Jonathan's mother had found back to Crabapple Cottage. She was feeling light-hearted, even excited. Since the suggestion of the cricket match there had been a shift of feeling. In some way the entire atmosphere had subtly changed. She sensed that they saw her now as a person in her own right, someone whose ideas the family were prepared to treat with respect. She walked tall, with new confidence.

That evening she sat up late. She could not have said exactly what she hoped to glean from the household accounts and Lady Alicia's diary, but they were giving her the feel of the old house. In the small hours of the morning she came half awake, thinking about the stables, that long, low building with flats above the stalls where the grooms had lived in the past. Could they be converted into shops? What about a craft workshop, with a craftsman living on the premises? But the flats might have been in disuse for a long time. They might be in a sad state of disrepair. It would mean spending money. A long-term plan, then.

Now, what of immediate matters? The opening of the house was the first priority. She reached for a pad and pen that she had left on her bedside table. Would she look for guides in the village? There must be women who would like a part-time job in summer. Or would she make tapes and supply headphones, charging a rental fee? Or would she put a typed list of the more interesting details of each room on walls allowing the visitors to roam in their own time?

In spite of her broken sleep Cassie was at Bevington Hall

at a quarter to nine. The butler let her in. His eyes were shining. "I believe I have to thank you for—"

She waved his thanks aside. "I'm trying to bring the Hall up to date. You've been here only a short time. What made you agree to be called Harding?"

He shrugged. "The earl interviewed me. I could see he's of the old school. And I desperately wanted the job."

"You were finding it hard to get work?"

"No. I wanted to work here. I like beautiful things." He turned to gaze at the sweeping staircase, his eyes roving over the gilt-framed portraits on the landing. "I've never been around the kind of stuff they have here."

"Not many of us have," replied Cassie wryly. "Has it done anything for you?"

"Oh yes, Miss Neilson. I've never been so happy."

She smiled at him. My name is Cassie. And I shall be calling you Edward."

He looked delighted. "You're a breath of fresh air, and no mistake."

So, nobody had told him not to call her by her christian name! What did this mean? That the staff didn't gossip these days? Everyone, in her experience, gossiped. Unless they were ordered not to. She was thoughtful as she went about her work.

In a drawer of her desk she found a telephone directory and a Yellow Pages. There was one kitchen specialist with showrooms in Flyford. She wrote the address down in her notebook, which would have to be all-functional until she could find the time to drive into town and buy a proper working diary. Then she went down to the dungeon to look for stationery.

Jonathan's office, that never saw the sun, was dark

89

and gloomy. She turned on the light and looked round. She wanted paper but hesitated to open the desk drawers without his permission, so she would have to come back. She lifted the ancient typewriter in her arms and turned towards the door.

"Hey!" protested Jonathan, striding along the passage at that moment and swiftly taking the machine from her. "We've got a lot of strong men round here. I hope you're not one of those people whose motto is 'If you want a thing done, do it yourself'." He put the typewriter back on the desk.

"As a matter of fact, that is my motto," Cassie retorted in the new brisk style she had adopted. "The reason I was carrying the typewriter was because, apart from Edward, I haven't seen a soul this morning. And frankly, it didn't occur to me to ask him. You didn't mind my coming here, did you? I needed some stationery."

Jonathan said, "Help yourself to anything you want." He looked round critically, shoved his hands in his pockets and said, "Yes, I do see what you mean. It is pretty awful."

She sat down in the chair behind the desk. "Tell me," she said, remembering that he had apparently not been at home when she was making her annual visit to her parents, "do you commute to London?"

"I've got a flat at the Barbican."

"You've given up your London job? You're going to be here all the time, now?"

"I've kept a few interests. I'll be going up one or two days a week, I dare say. Why?"

She thought a flat at the Barbican would not be cheap. And what about his 'few interests'? Were they money-spinners? Or would he be better employed at the Hall? That's delicate ground, she said to herself. There's plenty of time. Aloud, she told him, "I'm just getting the picture."

"By the way, I ought to introduce you to the staff. Goodness knows," Jonathan said, "there aren't many now. Two jobbing gardeners and one full-time. One cook – er – one live-in maid," he hesitated and added vaguely, "and a handful of dailies from the village. I think that's all."

"Just introduce me to the two jobbing gardeners. I'd like them to find me some boxes. We need to transfer these files upstairs." She indicated the pile that were lying haphazardly on a shelf. "I'd like to get my office straight."

When he had gone she blew the dust off the files and laid them on the desk, then took a pile of headed paper from the drawer and some plain A4. In the centre drawer she found an untidy collection of typewriter ribbons, cork mats bearing coffee stains, a calculator, pen refills. She fingered through, putting aside anything she thought might be useful, tossing rubbish into the capacious wastepaper basket that looked as though it hadn't been emptied for some time.

There were footsteps in the hall. A stocky, brown-haired man in early middle age swung through the doorway wearing a wide smile on his weatherbeaten face and balancing a column of cardboard boxes in his arms. "Hello," he greeted her, then "Whoops!" as the boxes overbalanced and scattered across the floor. "I'm told you need some help." He grinned as she went to help him pick the boxes up. "I'm Eddie. You won't remember me, but I remember you when you were small. I worked here with your grandfather."

Cassie put the last box on top of the pile then held out her hand, smiling. "I do remember you."

They talked about old times. "Your grandfather taught me all I know about gardening. He taught me to love living things," Eddie told her. "I've always been grateful to him. I wasn't here when he died. I believe he went very suddenly. I'm glad. A good way for a good man."

They talked, too, about the Italian garden he had created round a collection of Florentine statues that Jonathan's grandfather, the thirteenth earl, had brought back with him from his Grand Tour.

"It's still there," Eddie said. "Hidden, of course, by the tall yews. I hope you're going to arrange for the visitors to see it."

"I dare say. We haven't got to thinking about the gardens yet."

"We take cuttings each year from the original white roses your grandfather planted because they must be replaced from time to time. So it's still his garden," Eddie continued. "It's quite a shock, coming through the green gap in the hedge in June, and seeing the blaze of white flowers and the elegant white statues on their plinths above them. We'd be pleased if you'd let the visitors in to see it."

Cassie agreed. "Okay. Why don't you take responsibility of getting it into order? And plot a path for the visitors to follow. Perhaps you could list the plants on the route, and put down anything of special interest about them. I don't know. I'm going to leave this in your hands. Perhaps you'd like to reshape the lot? I'll provide you with a notebook and pens."

"That's what I'd like to do. I have got a kind of plan." Eddie rubbed his hands together. "Right! Now, what do you want moved?"

Cassie was busy at her desk when there was a knock at the door. A plump woman appeared wearing a crossover floral apron. She had ruddy cheeks and untidy wisps of

greying hair curling on her forehead. In her hands she held
a wooden tray with two mugs. She came forward and placed
it on the corner of the desk. "Here's your coffee, dear," she
said. "Remember me?" She stood beaming down on Cassie,
waiting.

"Mrs Bachelor!" She jumped up and held out her hand.

Mrs Bachelor regarded her gravely. "I'm so glad you've
come home, dear. We was all very upset about your parents'
accident. I think everyone'll be pleased about you working here."

"Everyone?"

"The village, dear. There's always been such good feeling
between the village and the Hall. Young Mr Jonathan
couldn't help what happened. Your parents was right in
his path," she said. "He couldn't avoid the accident."

Cassie felt she was waiting for an answer. And not
just an answer. She wanted agreement. She took a deep
breath. "No," she said, "I dare say he couldn't." Then
quickly changing the subject she added, "You've brought
two mugs."

"Mr Jonathan said to bring one up for him. He'll be along
in a moment. I'll be on my way now." She paused in the
doorway, turning back, smiling. "How pretty you've grown,
dear." Then, before Cassie could reply Jonathan appeared.

"Thanks, Mrs B." He crossed the room, handed one mug
to Cassie and took the other himself. "Now, what about these
pictures?" He glanced round the walls.

"I'd like them to stay, if that's all right with you."

"You're accustomed to having your office decorated with
old masters of course." He took a sip of his coffee, looking
at her over the rim.

"I could very easily accustom myself to it."

93

"Right. When you've slurped that down we'll have a go at sorting out a trail for the public to follow. Have you got your notebook and pen?"

She nodded.

"We'll head back first along the servants' corridor."

"Staff corridor."

He looked wry. "Of course."

As they went down the staircase he said, "Some of the trail will be obvious. The long gallery upstairs, for instance. It runs across the building, north to south. That must go to the top of the list. And the chapel on the first floor. And the great hall. Some of the furniture that used to be in large reception rooms has been spread around a bit. Some of it's under dust sheets. With nobody coming up here . . ." His voice trailed off. "I'm hoping I'll remember where it belongs. If I don't, Mother will."

"Have you an inventory?"

"Not that I'm aware of."

"Honestly!" Cassie was exasperated.

"Okay, we've been a bit lax," he admitted. "All that's changed, now we've got you. You shall do an inventory." He said the last with the air of one bequeathing a great honour.

"We'll do it together," Cassie retorted. "All I know about antiques at the moment, as you well know, could go on one side of an A4 sheet."

"But you'll learn. Won't you?"

"Of course."

The door opened silently. They both looked up, then down. His lordship's dog came strolling in. He looked at Jonathan, then made his way round the desk, laid his chin on Cassie's thigh and gazed up into her face.

"Spicer!" exclaimed Jonathan, pretending to be stern. "What are you doing here?"

The dog politely acknowledged his presence with a glance then returned his attention to Cassie. "Dogs know when you like them," said Cassie smoothing his head affectionately.

"Remember that cross you had when you were about six? Half Welsh sheepdog, half terrier? Do you remember how he used to try to get down rabbit holes?"

"Once he got stuck—"

"And you had to pull him out by the back legs." Jonathan chuckled. "What happened to him?"

"He died of old age. What a lovely fellow he was. One day I must get a dog. They're such good company." She waited to see if he would suggest she bring one to work but he didn't.

"You won't need company," he said. "There's almost too much of it round here these days."

Chapter Six

THERE was a butler's pantry and a flower room with big cupboards leading off the hall. "You'll find all kinds of useless stuff here," said Jonathan. He was businesslike, pulling out drawers, picking up small trophies. "That's no use. Throw this out. And this."

"What's this enormous key for?" Cassie held it up, a great black iron thing, beautifully wrought.

"Ah! That's the key I told you about. It's for locking the main gates, though it hasn't been used since heaven-knows-when." He took it from her, dropped it into the drawer and pushed the drawer shut. "Let's get on." They went back into the passage, heading towards the back of the house.

"There's nothing of note here. Storerooms. You can investigate them in your own time. Here are some larders, sculleries, maids' sitting rooms, servants' – sorry, staff – dining room, housekeeper's room, still room. All virtually unused now." He opened a door and strode into a dark little passageway. There was a bathroom to their right. Ahead lay a shabby living room and beyond that a tiny room furnished with a cooker, and a bench on which stood a plastic basin. Above it, sticking out from the wall, was a cold tap.

Cassie said, "I'm keeping an eye out for something for myself. Who used these rooms?"

"Goodness knows." Jonathan looked vague. "But it wouldn't do for you. You'll be all right in the flat."

"Jonathan," she said distinctly, "I do not intend to live with my parents."

"No. Of course not. But you'll be all right for a while." He marched off along the passage and she followed, conceding there was no point in showing annoyance. Her accommodation was not a priority in the scheme of things.

They reached the end of the passage. A small staircase ran up on their right. "Let's take this," Jonathan suggested. "It'll lead us into the rooms of the north wing. They've all been shut off. Everything there will be under dustsheets, but there's a lot of good stuff worth cataloguing."

The passage was dark here, the morning sun blocked off by the great bulk of the house, the panelling darkly shadowed. They climbed the narrow oak staircase. Ahead of them now stood a heavy Gothic door. Jonathan lifted the draw-bar and it swung inwards. "The family chapel," he said.

The interior was grey stone; ancient, brooding, silent in its shadows. An arched ceiling, embroidered kneelers, brass rails, dark wooden pews. Cassie gazed at it in absorbed admiration. "Is it ever used?"

Jonathan's eyes roved round the chapel, to the silver and gold altar cloth, the wall plaques, the narrow stained-glass windows. "I don't believe it's been used in my lifetime, except for my christening."

"Did nobody get married here?" Cassie visualised a bride in white with her family closely gathered round. How wonderfully romantic it was, how ancient and all-enduring, with the gilt coat of arms over the altar and the little brass portraits of long-dead ancestors.

"In the past. Yes, of course. There's a register somewhere. When you've got time you could look it up for your book. But it's a bit small for a modern wedding. Where would we put the guests?"

She thought of Zoe Montcalm wanting a thousand people to witness the fact that she had snared the handsome inheritor of Bevington Hall.

Jonathan was standing close beside her. He bent his head. She caught her breath and stepped aside. Jonathan laughed softly. "I'll try to remember you've been hired for your businesslike qualities. But there are some times, when you look like that, wistful, like the Cassie I used to know, when I have trouble containing myself." He lifted his hands and rested them on her shoulders. "Couldn't we go back?"

"No," she said and made for the door, heart hammering. Don't forget, never allow yourself to forget, she reminded herself, that the Jonathan Tarrants of this world are programmed to marry the Zoe Montcalms. Don't forget, either, you can never be more to him than a bit on the side. She strode along the passage and stopped at the next door, keeping her back turned. She heard his footsteps behind her, watched his hands as they put the key in the lock. Think of the humiliation if you started an affair then he went off and married Zoe. Worse, if he came back from the honeymoon and expected to carry on with you under the dustsheets. And his lordship found out! And my parents found out! And Zoe!

She pushed the door open and stalked into the room, head high, cheeks flaming. There was an Adam fireplace, a pretty Chinese screen and some stiff little chairs upholstered in silk. She took out her notebook and began to write. "I may find a place for that screen," she said busily. "And I'll make a note of the table. What is it?"

"Chippendale," Jonathan said, also pretending that nothing had happened. "I'll find you some reference books. I think there are some in the dungeon. There's bound to be something in the library, too."

They went through the rooms immediately below the old nursery then turned the corner and entered the anteroom that led into the great hall. Cassie stood looking at the arched ceiling high above her head, and then down at the huge slabs of stone that formed the floor, seeing herself as a small, plump child, chasing the leggy Jonathan who was pretending to run away. Over in the centre the ancient medieval firebox still lay directly beneath the grey smoke stains on the ceiling. How full of memories was this old house!

"Those suits of armour standing on either side of the fireplace are medieval. They date from 1550."

"Do you remember measuring yourself against them?" Cassie asked.

"I remember the day I discovered I was tall enough to fit them. I wanted to try one on, but I wasn't allowed. I was twelve, and the same size as a full-grown medieval knight."

She learned a great deal that morning.

"Louis the fifteenth," said Jonathan, holding up a dust sheet in another room, exposing an elegant gilt wood sofa with two chairs. "And that love seat also came from France. It's said to be originally from the Palace of Versailles. That pair of tapestries on the wall are Flemish."

An enormous portrait of the countess dominated one of the disused rooms. "Why is this here?" Cassie looked at it admiringly, thinking how beautiful Jonathan's mother had been as a young woman, and how much he resembled her.

"It used to be in the long gallery," he said. "As to why it's here, I don't honestly know."

"Could we put it back?"

"You'd better ask her ladyship."

Cassie made a note to do so.

They went up another short flight of stairs and he opened a pair of panelled double doors. Cassie found herself looking into a great windowed gallery with a high barrel ceiling. The blood-red silk that lined the walls was a magnificent backdrop to the vast array of pictures. "Our most valuable paintings are here," said Jonathan at her side. "That is a Jacob Bogdani. He was a Hungarian who came to work at the court of Queen Anne. And that's a Van Gogh; that a Rubens. Two Constables over there, and over the fireplace a Rembrandt. The tenth earl made a lot of money gambling and spent most of it on art. There's a story that the Van Gogh was won from his weekend host, Lord Ellesmere, after he'd taken all the poor fellow's cash."

"What a scandalous lot you were!"

"You wouldn't get a book out of a boring family."

"Well, no."

They walked side by side through the gallery. "I remember what was here," Jonathan said. "Half a dozen quite elegant sofas and some side tables, or card tables. I'll recognise them when we come across them. I suppose we'll have to put little ropes across the sofas, or notices telling people not to sit. Some of these portraits need cleaning," he went on, examining first one then another with a critical eye.

"We could set up a fund for that as soon as the house begins to pay." Cassie felt the tentacles of the job spreading around her, pushing the last vestiges of uncertainty away.

This is the job of a lifetime, she said to herself, and I am going to make the greatest success of it.

They emerged from a door at the opposite end of the gallery. A flight of stone steps rose on the left. "There's a lookout here from the south-western tower. You might like to include this on your route."

She paused with one foot on the first step. "My route? You're the one who's familiar with the territory."

He laid a hand on her arm. "I trust you to see with a visitor's eye. Didn't I say that?"

If he had she had not been ready to take it seriously. Now she could see his point. "I shall expect you – and your parents – to make the final decision, though."

"Very well."

They went up the steps and entered the tower by an oak door. Sunlight shafted in from the mullioned windows, falling across a large octagonal table decorated with inlaid brass and painted nymphs. There were no chairs in the room. No other furniture.

"Oh!" exclaimed Cassie delightedly. "How beautiful!"

"It was used by the twelfth earl as an intimate banqueting room. I imagine the food must have been pretty cold by the time it arrived up here, but no doubt the view was worth it." Jonathan proceeded round the octagonal room, opening the windows one after another. Cassie remained by the table. She wanted to push a stop button inside her; to hold this moment for eternity. She felt she had never seen Hampshire before now when it was magically laid out before her in the sunlight; the big bunchy chestnuts coming into spring leaf, the soft green of the grass, the little hump-backed bridges, their stone whitened by the light. Words burst passionately out of her, falling one over the other.

"I hated LA," she said. "I hated America. The newness. The hardness. The man-madeness. I loathed it. It was bad, what brought me home – the accident, I mean – but I'm glad, so very glad, I'm here." She felt forgiveness pouring out of her. Cathartic relief.

He laid a hand on her shoulder and looked into her eyes. "Why did you go to the States? I couldn't understand why you went without even leaving a note for me."

Time seemed to stand still. She looked at him mutely, helplessly.

"They didn't discuss it with you?"

He shook his head.

Relief and anger surged through her in equal parts. "It must have been your parents' idea. They must have put it to my grandfather." He who had a lifetime behind him of obedience; whose entire existence was given over to the good of the Haldane family and all it represented. "Maybe they paid," Cassie said. He did not answer and she took his silence for agreement. She thought he was going to take her in his arms. She moved instinctively away. But he, too, seemed to understand there was too much between them now. That what had been broken could not be mended with a kiss.

Jonathan went round closing the windows. She began to descend the little staircase.

He did not attempt to catch her up, though she could hear his footsteps behind her all the way to the front of the house. As they entered the hall and Cassie stepped onto the main stairs she saw the figure of a girl silhouetted in the front doorway. For a moment, with the light behind her, her features were invisible, then she came forward across the marble floor, looking up.

She was not as tall as Cassie and her eyes, large and widely set in an oval face, were a very light green, startling against a mane of dark, glossy hair. She was dressed similarly to Cassie though her jumper was cashmere in a beautiful shade of rose pink. Her Gucci shoes tapped lightly on the marble floor. She wore a woollen skirt of the same colour as her jumper and with it a pretty waistcoat. Over her shoulder she had slung a flamboyant bucket bag made of crocodile skin.

Even before Jonathan's voice behind her said, "Hello, Zoe," Cassie knew with a sickening jolt who it was. The girl wore an air of being very much at home and very sure of her welcome.

"I'm sorry I'm late," she said breathlessly, not as though she was out of breath but as though she had cultivated this type of greeting.

"Zoe," said Jonathan passing Cassie and greeting the visitor with a light kiss on the cheek, "I'd like you to meet Cassie Neilson who is our new—"

"I know. Comptroller," said the girl in that same breathless voice. "Your mother told me about her," she said. Then she turned to Cassie, looking her over coolly from head to toe. "I believe your father was a gardener here," she commented, faintly amused.

"Grandfather," said Jonathan urbanely. "He was head gardener. A very responsible and much loved retainer."

Zoe gazed into Cassie's face. Looking for – what? Don't let her get under your skin, she said to herself. Don't be vulnerable. You're in charge here. Don't forget. In that moment she realised how shaky her confidence was, after all.

"Wonderful that you're available, Miss Neilson." Zoe's

voice was only faintly patronising. The voice one might use when addressing the granddaughter of a gardener. Or somebody equally unfortunate, like the disabled.

"I'm sure she'd like you to call her Cassie. We're all on christian name terms here," Jonathan said.

"But of course. Cassie," Zoe said thoughtfully, turning the name over her tongue. Considering it. Cassie waited, without hope, for permission to call her Zoe. It did not come.

Zoe turned to Jonathan. "You seemed surprised to see me. Didn't you know I was coming to lunch?"

Jonathan slipped an arm through hers. "I'll take you to find Mother," he said. Over his shoulder he remarked, "See you later, Cassie."

She stood looking after them as they went down the passage that led to the library. Then she went to Lady Selena's room, took her sandwiches out of her briefcase and made her way back to the tower. She opened all the windows and leaning against a sill closed her eyes. She felt the warm spring breeze lifting the tendrils from her forehead, moving soothingly across her skin, comforting her. She didn't want to think. Was afraid to. This is my room, she said to herself. The public will never come here. I will keep it for myself, for licking wounds. I shall come here to be replenished by the beauty of it, and of the view, when the gut has been torn out of me and the past is poisoning me. I cannot shake off what has been. I have to live with the indignity of it, and that's a fact.

There was no further sign of Zoe that day. Jonathan came to Cassie's office in the late afternoon. "I'm off to London tomorrow," he said. "When you're properly settled in I'll go up a couple of days a week. I don't want to give up the City entirely. Not until . . ." He broke off but Cassie knew

what he had been going to say. Not until we're certain the
Hall is going to pay. Then he added, "I think I've filled your
head with enough random ideas. It's a good moment to leave
you on your own. Now you know the layout of the place you
might like to concentrate your attention on the visitors' trail.
Without me to refer to you can sort things out your way."

Cassie nodded. "And have I your permission to look out
for accommodation for myself?"

He looked genuinely surprised. "I thought that was settled."

She heaved a sigh. "I'll take the best of the staff quarters,"
she said. "I could furnish with some of the stuff from the
cottage. Otherwise it's only going to be thrown out."

"The old staff quarters as you call them – we called them
the maids' rooms – are up in the attics," he said, as though
that put them right out of bounds.

"I've got strong legs. And I might be glad to get right
away in my time off." She glanced at her watch. "I think
I'll pre-empt the tea lady. I want to have a look at the
kitchens, anyway. Has anything been done to them in the
last few years?"

"Nothing."

"I remember copper pots hanging on the walls. And
enormous ladles. And there was a spit for roasting an ox.
I dare say that's gone."

"I don't think you'll find too much brass and copper."

"You haven't disposed of it?" She was immediately
dismayed.

"No. I really don't know where it all is. Maybe dumped
into cupboards out of sight. But it's a working kitchen, you
know. We can't have visitors trailing round while the staff
are having tea or Cook's preparing meals."

"Not trailing round. No. But the door could be left open. That is, if there's a good view from the doorway. We could put a cord across." She rose. "I'd better go before Mrs Bachelor starts making her way up to Lady Selena's room."

"I'll go with you." The passage leading to the kitchens lay behind and beyond the great staircase. They walked side by side, their footsteps silent on the needlecord. Lively chatter filtered out of an open door. They stood in the doorway, unnoticed for a moment. Half a dozen people were seated on forms at either side of a huge slab table. An enamel teapot stood in the centre. There was a pile of bread and butter, scones, a big fruit cake. They moved forward into the room. The chatter faded and they all looked up.

"Sorry to disturb you," Jonathan apologised. "Don't get up. I want to introduce my new comptroller to those who don't already know her."

There was Mrs Strong, the cook. Two dailies, Mrs Chadwick and Mrs Grainger. They all remembered her as a child. Bart and Sid, the jobbing gardeners. The butler. They greeted her with warm and friendly murmurings. "I'll go back," said Jonathan, "and leave you to get acquainted." They made a place for her on the form. Cook poured her a cup of tea and cut a slab of the rich, dark fruit cake for her.

Tom passed her bread and butter and a bowl of strawberry jam. "I've been asked to help you choose a car, Miss," he said.

She frowned. "Cassie," she said impatiently. "You've been calling me Cassie since you first knew me."

Mrs Bachelor tapped her spoon consideringly on the table and keeping her eyes down said quietly, "It's been decided we should call you Miss Neilson, dear. So, if you don't mind – not that we wouldn't ra – I mean, some of us that knew you—"

Cassie spared her discomfort by breaking in, "Miss Neilson it is." She heaved a sigh. "Well, that's businesslike, anyway. She noted that Edward was looking at her with startled eyes, he who was new and had agreed to call her Cassie. She smiled at him warmly. Jonathan should not separate her from the rest of the staff in this way. And why amend his instructions to Tom with regard to her transport? She dragged her mind back to the immediate present. She told them about the marks on the doors. "I hope you won't be over zealous with your dusters. Leave me the chalk numbers just until I've made my inventory and got my bearings."

They cheerfully agreed. They plied her with scones, with fruit cake and buttered bread. Cook suggested she drink up and have another cup of tea.

She looked round the big room, at the enormous Aga cooker that had been brought in in her time; the vast open fireplace where the roasting spit still hung. She made a note to have some logs brought in, and perhaps a box of ashes to give the spit an air of being in working order. Her eyes roved round the bare walls. "Didn't you have copper pots and pans hanging there?"

They exchanged dismayed glances. Mrs Bachelor asked apprehensively, "You'll not be wanting them back?"

"Well, yes, but you won't be expected to do any polishing. I'll get them professionally buffed up and coated with something that'll protect the shine."

They allowed themselves little puffs of relief. "Folks aren't so keen on the elbow grease these days," explained Mrs Chadwick.

"No, of course. I quite understand."

"Have one of these, dear," said Cook offering the scones.

Cassie helped herself saying, "Next week this will stop. I've only just bought a new skirt. I don't want to bulge out of it. Just don't offer me any more fruit cake. Do you know, I haven't tasted fruit cake for years. It's not around in the States."

They went silent and she recognised her being in the States was a subject they did not know how to deal with. She came hurriedly back to the safer topic of the Hall. "I'd like to have that spit blackened and a pile of logs brought in."

Bart and Eddie agreed to deal with the logs. "I'll look out some stove black," offered Mrs Grainger.

"I'll look out the copper and brass," offered Mrs Chadwick. "I'm the one who knows where it is because I packed it away."

Cassie made notes. "I need to write down who's doing what. I'm not trusting to my memory."

"Very wise of you," they said.

Tom added in his quiet way, "We're real pleased about all this. We've been in the doldrums for years." He looked round the table for agreement from his fellow staff. "The place was running down. Nobody seemed to care. We heard these rumours about his lordship wanting to go abroad to live. And Jonathan was up in the City, not interested."

Cassie's mind flashed off the subject to make a puzzled note of the fact that Tom called the heir Jonathan while she was to be called Miss Neilson. "He's very interested now," she said. "He's most anxious to make a success of it."

They expressed themselves glad.

"There's people in the village been talking about volunteering to be guides," offered Bart tentatively. "Mrs Wild and Mrs Duncan both asked me. Are you going to want guides?"

"Possibly. I think very probably. Especially if there are enough people offering."

"The village would like to be involved," said Mrs Grainger.

"That's good." Cassie felt the warmth of their goodwill spreading round her. She asked them if they would mind the kitchen being on view.

"Wandering in while I'm cooking?" Cook looked doubtful.

"No, no." She told them she would merely want the door kept open. "And I'd provide a cord to fence it off so no one could wander in. "I don't see why you shouldn't carry on as usual. A lived-in kitchen is three times as interesting as a stone cold empty one."

"We'll get used to it," Cook decided.

Cassie eyed the fruit cake again. "If I were to get a shop going," she said, addressing the cook, "would you be willing to make those by the dozen? We could sell them in tins with a picture of the Hall on the lid?"

Cook wriggled like a pleased puppy.

"I'd give you a credit, of course, something like 'Made by Mrs Strong, cook at Bevington Hall.'"

Somebody clapped. They all looked delighted for her.

"There's Flora Barnard from the village," offered Tom. "Remember her?"

"I was at school with her."

"She's got a little shop selling hand-made chocolates, in Flyford. Perhaps you could persuade her to make you up boxes to sell."

"Now, that's a splendid idea." Cassie's eyes shone. "We

could have some little gold tabs carrying the family coat of arms and stick them on the boxes. I'll go and see her. Thanks for the tip." She made more notes in her book then closed it. "I'd better be off now."

Later, back in Lady Selena's room she went to the window and stood looking out. Jonathan's BMW came slowly round the corner of the house and pulled up at the front door. Tom got out. Jonathan strode across the gravel, took the keys from him and threw an overnight bag into the back. From the shelter of the portico Zoe appeared, walking side by side with Lady Haldane. Jonathan opened the passenger door. Her ladyship kissed Zoe. She slid into the passenger seat.

So Jonathan was going to spend tomorrow in the City. Cassie sat down in her chair, facing the desk. It is none of your business, she rebuked herself; *this* is your business. She rolled a sheet of paper into the awful typewriter. Zoe Montcalm is not your affair. But come to think of it, a computer is. She would have to tackle Jonathan about more modern equipment, she thought, as with every thump, thump, thump of her fingers on the ancient keys, her spirits sank lower. After a while, when the errors were mounting, she snatched the paper out, threw it into the wastepaper basket, and made her way down to the dungeon in search of the books on antiques that Jonathan had said might be found there. As she crossed the hall Lady Haldane came back inside. Cassie smiled at her and her ladyship smiled back. As she came closer Cassie saw that she, too, was wearing a beautiful cashmere jumper and she remembered that day *she* came to lunch, when Jonathan's mother hadn't even bothered to change out of her gardening clothes.

She went into the dungeon feeling cast down. But why should it bother me, she asked herself sternly. I'm an

110

employee – never mind the gardener's granddaughter stuff. Why shouldn't Lady Haldane dress casually for – oh, shut up. Stop justifying. She slumped down in the chair behind the battered desk and stared into space.

The door opened silently and Spicer padded across to her, put his chin on her thigh in that way he had and gazed up into her eyes. "Hello, old boy." She leaned down and put both arms round him. "You're a great comfort," she said. "Thanks for coming."

Chapter Seven

IN JONATHAN'S office, denuded now of all but the desk, an ugly lamp and an assortment of books, Cassie found some volumes devoted to period furniture. She took them home to study them. She had a good memory for shape and form. She soon learned to recognise the changing trends; the cabriole form of the feet in the early Georgian period, the ball and claw of Queen Anne's reign, the veneered marquetry of the William and Mary years. She memorised the unfamiliar. An apron piece on a bureau bookcase; a break-front; Gothic glazing bars. The chairs were easier. She could run her eye over an Adam armchair, a Sheraton, a Hepplewhite and immediately place them. She loved to caress the silky surfaces of the furniture, each piece glowing with the patina bestowed on it over hundreds of years of loving care.

In one of the locked rooms she found some chair seats in need of mending. She went through the Yellow Pages and made a note of the names of upholsterers in Flyford. Taking with her the dimensions of the kitchen in what was destined to be her parents' accommodation, she drove into town, parked the car and called on the kitchen specialist whose address she had noted earlier. There were several exhibits set up in the showroom. She chose one made in honey-coloured wood and invited their designer out to quote for the job. What would Jonathan say? She told herself this was one battle she intended to win.

She talked to upholsterers. One of them was experienced in working with old furnishings. She said she would bring the chairs in. "As soon as I get a suitable vehicle to transport them in," she said. It occurred to her that she was going to need some sort of pick-up truck. A van, in English terms. Time to speak to Tom.

She wandered on. There was a well-cut cotton skirt on a model standing in the window of a boutique. And a T-shirt with a squirrel on the front. She looked at it with interest, entranced by the squirrel. I'm not going to get up to London, she thought. There isn't going to be time. She decided to come back on Saturday morning and buy one or two mix'n' match outfits for the summer.

Jeans, she knew instinctively, were out. Perhaps the squirrel on the T-shirt was out too. Too frivolous for the comptroller of a stately home? She recognised a very real desire to fit in and was momentarily amused at herself. What would the elegant Lady Selena, looking down at her from the wall of her office, think of a squirrel? What would she think of tight jeans? She's not in a position to pass judgement, Cassie decided, thinking of the raw flesh Lady Selena exposed above her tightly fitting bodice.

On the way back to collect the car from the car park she noticed a sign elegantly and discreetly painted in enamel. 'Colin Darcy. Ceramics'. Ceramics! Ah! She followed the direction of a small arrow painted underneath the sign and found herself in a mews. Directly ahead lay a glass-fronted showroom. She stood in front of it, looking in. In one corner pots and plates, all in their original white and apparently awaiting decoration, were piled up on the floor. A table in the centre held painted vases. A potter's wheel stood on a sturdy table. She went inside. There was no one about. She picked up a vase from the table and examined it closely. The lines were elegant, the object supremely tactile. She held it, sensuously, between her palms. The design, in rich reds, dark blues and a shimmering gold, was strange and very beautiful. Looking at it from one angle it appeared to portray cloud effects, windswept trees, misty mountains. She held it at another angle, narrowed her eyes and thought she saw biblical figures in flowing robes.

"Hello," said a voice behind her.

Cassie spun round. A young man stood in a doorway she had not noticed at the back of the showroom. He was tall and slender, a Renaissance man with a pale oval face and longish fair hair. He was dressed in very old, torn jeans; his shirt had tiny bits of plaster or clay sticking to the cloth. "Are you the proprietor?" she asked, carefully putting the vase down.

He nodded. "Colin Darcy. Can I help?"

"You're new here?" Everything about the showroom was new. The clean plaster of ceiling and walls. The wood door frames. Two elegant modern chairs standing on either side of a small bleached oak table.

"Very new," he said. "I've scarcely got started. There's more to look at in the room behind. Would you like to have a browse around?"

She nodded eagerly. "Yes. I would."

In the room behind he had set up display cases. He took a key from a drawer, opened a glass-fronted case, reached in and brought out a bowl decorated with those swirling lines and strange effects that had so intrigued her on the vase. Faces dimly perceived. A hint of movement. More than a hint of movement. The patterns seemed to merge and re-form. It was archaic, yet modern. Ancient precepts in a modern form.

She said spontaneously, "Would you be interested in holding an exhibition next summer?"

"I intend to hold an exhibition next summer," he said. "The question is, where to hold it. I've got the premises here but I'm too hidden away."

"I've a proposition," said Cassie, eyes shining. "Have you got a minute to talk?"

"Sit down." He pulled out one of the two chairs for her and took the other himself. They sat down facing each other across the narrow table.

Cassie told him who she was and what she was doing. "I can't of course make a commitment at the moment, but I'm fascinated by your designs and I'd love to sell your stuff." She outlined her plans. "We've got empty stables where you could set up a workshop if you wanted to. I don't mean you should move from here, but would you be interested in working there on open days? It could be lucrative. People going to look at the gardens will have to pass the stables. We could put up signs. In fact," she suddenly decided, "we could divert them through the pottery on their way to the gardens."

His face, serene and almost sad in repose, took on an absorbed look. "Why don't we talk about this? Let's go down to the pub."

She glanced at her watch, then remembered she had to pick her mother up from the hospital.

"I'll tell you what," Colin Darcy said, "you deal with your mother, then come back. I live here in a flat upstairs. I'll rustle around and get a meal while you're gone. I was going to stir-fry some chicken for tonight. Do you like wok cooking? Good," he responded to Cassie's nod. "I'll lock the studio. The entrance to my flat is next door. Go up the stairs and you're there."

"Right." She ran back to the car and sped off to the hospital.

"Having dinner with a stranger?" Leila asked in consternation as she climbed into the passenger seat. "Really, Cassie!"

"He could be a great asset to me." She recognised in that moment why she had known instinctively she had to set up separate accommodation for herself. She was too old now, to be a daughter. Too accustomed to independence.

She dropped Leila off at Crabapple Cottage, drove back to Flyford and put the car in the car park. As she drove in she noticed that directly behind, there was a lane that ran in the direction of the studio. She went through the turnstile into the lane and there it was, not a hundred yards away. The door was locked but one close by stood ajar. She pushed it open and walked up a flight of narrow, steep stairs to the first floor. The door on the landing also stood ajar.

"Hi!" she called as she pushed it wide.

Colin appeared from the kitchen with an apron draped across his front. "You made good time."

"I put my foot down. It's not easy driving on the wrong side of the road."

"What?"

"I've been living in California for years."

"You must tell me about it."

"Not now. I'm here to talk about your work." She was standing in an L-shaped living room with a dining table at one end already set with table mats, cutlery and glasses. She glanced down at the table mats then up at her host.

"You designed them?" They were decorated with the same swirling graceful lines as the pottery downstairs. He nodded. She turned her attention to the pictures. "All yours?" There must have been twenty or more hung round the walls. Unspectacular landscapes, in the main.

"I've given up painting for pottery. I'm better at decorating it." She was inclined to agree. She followed him into a tiny kitchen where he had laid out an array of vegetables cut into squares. He took a piece of foil and wrapped the food up, then placed it in the fridge. "I thought we'd go to The Sow for that drink first."

They walked down the road side by side. She told him about her new job. About their hopes that the Hall would be open by this time next year. Of her pleasure at discovering him. They went through the revolving doors into the dark interior of The Sow and climbed onto high stools at the bar. Colin greeted the landlord like an old friend. "Hello, George."

"Sorry to hear about your father," said George Falconer addressing Cassie. "Awkward business, that. Awkward. What'll you have?" He picked up a damp cloth and adopting a businesslike air in the way one does when the subject is an embarrassment, wiped the bar.

"Gin and tonic, please." Cassie looked down at her hands, thinking, yes, everyone knows everything about the concerns of the Hall. Even as far away as Flyford they're being careful not to take sides. An awkward business, as the landlord said. They were sorry that Gerald Neilson had been in an accident, but all the same they didn't want him making trouble.

Time to put the community at ease. She said, "My parents are going to move into the Hall. The earl has given them a sort of grace-and-favour apartment – I mean, flat."

He smiled, knowing she had been in America, then swung away to pour the drinks.

"What were you and George going on about? What's this awkward business?" Colin asked as they walked back later.

"You'll hear soon enough. Nobody has any secrets round here."

"You're going to live at the Hall?"

"For the moment, yes. But we're not going to talk about me tonight. We're going to devote the entire evening to how we can sell your work at the Hall when it opens to the public."

Cassie stood around with a wine glass in her hand while Colin cooked the meal. They discussed logos; boxes; wrapping; prices; commission. They grew enthusiastic. She had a feeling of moving ahead on solid ground and relaxed for the first time since her return. It was ten-thirty when Colin, glancing at the time, said he had to take some pots out of the kiln. Cassie pushed back her chair and surveyed the remains of the supper, the salad, tired now and wilting in its dressing, the white grains of rice strewn round their plates, the dregs of brown coffee in cups decorated with Colin's distinctive designs. "I'll clear up," she said.

"No, you won't. But if you wait until I've done this little job I'll escort you," he replied. "It's pretty dark out there."

She said she wouldn't dream of bothering him. "The car's close by."

She went off up the lane feeling warm and satisfied with her night's work. As she came through the turnstile she saw in the faint light of the moon that her car stood alone. The

118

rest of the park was empty. With a sense of foreboding she crossed the tarmac, walking towards the gate. It was barred. She ducked underneath. A large sign, facing the street, announced, CLOSED. Open 8 a.m.–8 p.m.

Now what was she going to do? She couldn't go back and ask Colin, busy with his firing, to drive her. Besides, she didn't know if he owned a car. She would have to ring for a taxi. She knew there was a telephone box not far away. The street was eerily empty. She ran, nervously aware of the clatter of her own footsteps on the pavement. Inside the box she could not see the street, only her own reflection in the glass. Her nervousness increased. She realised then she did not know the name of a taxi company. She would have to ring Leila. Damn! So I am a dependent daughter after all, she thought wryly.

"Stuck in a car park?" Leila echoed in astonishment on the other end of the line.

Cassie explained. Leila said something she did not catch as though she was speaking to someone else standing nearby. Then she recognised Jonathan's voice, "Go back to the restaurant," he said. "I'll pick you up there. What's the name of it?"

"I haven't been to a restaurant." Startled by his presence in the cottage and made to feel guilty by his anger, Cassie spoke sharply, "I had dinner with a friend at his flat."

"Friend," said Jonathan in a hard voice and she knew with exasperation that Leila had told him she was having a meal with a stranger. "Go back to the car park and lock yourself in the car," he said. "I'll be there as quickly as I can."

"You're very kind," she managed, but he had already hung up.

She returned to the park, crept under the barrier, unlocked

the car and climbed in. She leaned back and after a while, feeling safe in the darkness, she closed her eyes.

It seemed only a moment later the door opened and she looked up with a shock into Jonathan's angry eyes. "Of all the stupid—" He broke off as though choked by his own exasperation. "You haven't even locked the door! My God! Don't you know what's going on in England now? Don't you read the papers?"

She blinked at him, bewildered by his anger. "Yes. Yes, of course. I'm sorry." She was aware of the silliness of apologising for putting her own life in danger.

"Not to mention accepting a dinner invitation from a complete stranger. Are you mad?"

"It was business."

"Business with strangers is conducted in the daytime. Get out." She did so, scrambling, dropping her handbag and keys on the ground. Jonathan knelt down, scrabbled round in the darkness and found them, locked the car then gave her a rough little push in the direction of the gate.

"You don't have the right to take over my life just because I work for you," she said angrily. "What were you doing at the cottage? Checking on me?"

"You had disappeared."

"I went to see some upholsterers. It's part of my job," she said. "Do you expect me to clock in and out? Must I leave notes telling you exactly what I'm doing?"

"No. Of course not. But Tom brought a car brochure for you to look at. Forgive me for interfering," he said with a touch of sarcasm, "but I thought your transport was a priority. I took it over to the cottage to get your opinion."

Brochure! They bent down to pass under the rail and came out into the High Street. His red BMW was parked on a double yellow line. She slid into the passenger seat, smothering an automatic desire to apologise, trying to come to terms with the dichotomy of his economising on her mother's kitchen, and then buying her a new car. He started the engine and roared away, swinging dangerously round in the middle of the road.

"You don't have to kill us both," she said, jolted out of her confusion by his careless disregard for safety rules, telling herself to remember how he had hit her father, perhaps driving just this way with his hands hard on the wheel. He slowed but did not reply.

"What brochure?" she asked, feeling some interest was expected of her.

"I thought a 940 Torslanda Volvo would be the best value. Volvos are reliable. And you'll need the space, as you said, for transporting stuff around."

"It doesn't have to be new," she said.

"Tom hasn't got time to spare for messing around mending and fixing. You'll be totally responsible for this car. And he'll expect you to look after it."

She felt crushed by his anger. "You didn't have to come for me," she said in a small voice. "Leila could have sent a taxi." He didn't answer. They drove in silence right up to the front door of the cottage. "I'll pick you up at eight in the morning," he said then, "and run you in to collect the Rover."

"Thank you, Jonathan. For all your trouble." In the lights from the dashboard she saw his face had softened just a little, but he did not smile.

"You'll find the brochure on the hall table."

"Thank you. Good night."

"Good night."

She carried it upstairs. Her mother's bedroom light was on, the door open.

"Are you all right, dear?" she called.

"Of course I'm all right." Standing in the doorway she said, smiling to soften the implied criticism, "I survived all those years you weren't there to look after me."

A shadow crossed her mother's face and she could see that some of the bitterness had come through.

The kitchen designers came, offered a plan and tendered a quote. Cassie showed it to Jonathan.

"Does it need to be as fancy as this?" he asked, standing feet apart, hands in pockets, looking down at the plans, glaring at the total.

"You haven't spent much of your life in kitchens," she said in that brisk way she had adopted when matters were in the balance. "You're not especially qualified to judge." She tried to soften her approach, smiling at him encouragingly. "Why don't we take the plans along and look at it together? Something has got to be done."

"Okay." But he looked less than enthusiastic as he turned towards the door. She took the key from her desk drawer. He walked beside her along the long corridors, beside her but not with her. An uncomfortable reminder of the expensive car he proposed giving her jumped into the forefront of her mind. She cast it aside. She told herself her mother shouldn't have to tolerate a dreadful kitchen in exchange for her daughter's unasked-for luxuries.

They entered the flat and went to stand together in the doorway. Jonathan's hands were in his pockets, rattling some coins. It was one of those things he did when he was not at ease. He stared round the scruffy little room, his face expressionless. His eyes lifted to take in the stained ceiling; went to the broken linoleum on the floor; flicked over the untidy cupboard doors.

"No," he said categorically. "It's an unwarranted expense to call in kitchen designers. It's not as though your mother's going to cook for a household. Or throw parties. Forget your Americanisation, Cassie," he said. "This kitchen could be transformed with a lick of paint and a bit of tidying up. Bart could help you there. He's good with a hammer and screwdriver."

"Jonathan, look at the floor!"

"Get yourself some new linoleum." He turned towards the door. When he spoke again, standing in the little vestibule, his words had lost their former edge. Almost, he seemed to be pleading. "I'm not a millionaire, Cassie."

She wanted to tell him he might have economised on the car but some sense of betrayal was involved. The car had begun to take on the symbolic shape of apology and gratitude. She was afraid to talk about it.

"I'd just like to remind you that you haven't spent a penny on them," she said, tight-lipped. "It's no skin off your nose to furnish the flat with pieces that would otherwise be under dust sheets." Then she remembered he had paid for the drapes for Leila's four-poster. She waited to see if he would point this out. He didn't.

"I'm bending over backwards to help your parents," he said. "Neither they nor I need you weighing in. If you don't mind my saying so, Cassie, I'm not certain you're on their wavelength."

Her heart was beating rapidly with anger. "You've convinced my mother this kitchen will do?"

"I haven't mentioned it to her. Nor she to me."

They went back towards Lady Selena's room in silence. Cassie felt crushed and angry. As she turned the corner into the passage that would take them to Lady Selena's room she realised Jonathan was no longer behind her. She shrugged, thinking he had shot off down a branch corridor or one of the little back staircases.

The beautiful Lady Selena was looking down at her from the wall. She thought there was sympathy in her eyes and a certain knowing. "He'll be all right when he marries the rich Miss Montcalm," she said to the portrait and realised she was spitting like a hurt kitten. "He won't have to worry about money, then."

"Sorry?"

She swung round, startled. Mrs Bachelor had come in carrying a tea tray. "Who was you talking to, dear?"

"Myself." Cassie glanced at the tray. "You can take that extra cup back, Mrs B. I'm on my own."

"I met young Jonathan downstairs. He said you had a lot to discuss and I was to bring his tea in here."

"Our discussion is over."

The woman put the cup down anyway. Cassie went to the window and stood looking down the drive. You knew it wasn't going to be easy, she said to herself as she had said a number of times before. She glanced back at Lady Selena and thought she saw the beginnings of a smile. Of encouragement? Of mockery? Certainly it was not a smile of sympathy. She shook her shoulders back, crossed the room and picked up her tea cup.

At that moment Jonathan came through the door. "So what's next in the way of trouble?" he asked, pulling out the extra chair and seating himself on the opposite side of the desk, giving her that enchanting smile as though the incident of the kitchen had never occurred. "What, no biscuits!"

She did not smile back. She put her cup down and went to the filing cabinet. "I've got an inventory of the furniture."

"You've what? Already?"

"With a certain amount of help from your mother in identifying pieces. And with the aid of your reference books. And the chalk." She lifted the file from the cabinet and handed it to him.

He stared at the sheets, turned them over. "You typed all that?"

"On that horrible typewriter. Yes, I did. It was a long, slow job. I finished at midnight," she told him, deliberately paving the way for what had to be said.

"Midnight!"

"You told me I am being paid for a twenty-four-hour day." She looked directly at him, standing her ground.

"Cass!" His expression held a mixture of dismay and respect.

"I've made an effort to come to terms with that type-writer," she said. "I know you considered it adequate, but you didn't use it much. And possibly you typed with one finger."

"Two."

"You wouldn't have typed that inventory."

"Er – it didn't arise."

"It should have arisen," said Cassie sternly. "You should have had an inventory. Well, it's done now."

"Thank you." Jonathan looked suitably subdued. Was it pretence?

"It cost me a lot in effort and anguish," she said. She did not take her eyes from his face.

"You want a new electric?" he asked. "Is that what you're saying? That you want a new electric typewriter?"

"No."

He was clearly uneasy. "A word processor?"

She steeled herself to tell him he was an amateur with the wrong priorities, but in the end could not. "I would like you to provide me with a computer. I cannot do this job with a typewriter. A word processor, yes, but in the end, when we're in business, you're going to find a word processor will prove inadequate."

He put his teacup down. "How much would it cost?"

"I'll have to make enquiries. I don't know about English prices. But I do know what I want. If I can get the software I used in LA I won't have to spend valuable time familiarising myself with it."

"All right," he said.

She wanted to leap out of her chair and hug him. Instead she said gravely, "Thank you, Jonathan. I think you'll come to see it as a wise move."

Later, as she stood in the middle of the kitchen in her parents' flat she thought, you lose some, you win some. She gazed round the drab walls, looked down at the hole in the linoleum, eyed the crooked cupboards and felt herself slipping out of her American skin.

I have to agree that in English terms, she considered to herself, there's nothing really the matter that can't be fixed by a pot of paint and a bit of linoleum. She glanced across at the vast utility sink. That certainly had to go. She decided she would buy a new one with her own money.

She went round the room opening one cupboard door after another. The storage space was adequate but the hinges were worn, and weak. The wood was good solid oak. If she were to rub it down, get some advice on how to treat it, buy some of those antique-type hinges that were featured in the kitchen she had tentatively chosen in the shop in Flyford and fix them to the doors, might they not look really rather elegant?

She went back to her office, took out the Yellow Pages and looked up C for Computers.

Chapter Eight

THAT week the computer came. Indoor and outdoor staff trooped into Lady Selena's room to view it. Even Lord Haldane came.

"Hrmp," he said, gazing suspiciously at the screen. "What will they think of next?"

Lady Haldane was fascinated. She sat quietly behind Cassie's chair for an hour. "Do you think I could get a little one?"

"A laptop?"

"Is that what they're called? I could take the book off your hands if I had a computer of my own."

Before she could stop herself Cassie snapped, "I thought you were going to the south of France."

"Not immediately." She rose and went out of the room.

Cassie watched her back thinking how frail was her standing here. How easily her rights could be snatched away. She looked up at Lady Selena on the wall. "It wasn't her idea," she said giving vent to her indignation. "It was mine."

Lady Selena looked back at her enigmatically.

Cassie found the Bevington Hall insurance file. She was horrified at the inadequacy of the cover. "Your treasures will have to be reassessed," she told Jonathan. "Even my

128

inexpert eyes can see everything's desperately undervalued. Your loss in the event of a burglary would be immense." She reminded him again of the fact that once they were open anyone could buy a ticket and come in. "I'm quite sure the insurers are going to require you to install an alarm system."

He looked depressed. She felt deep indignation that his father should be opting out and leaving him with so many problems. "You could make the Hall secure at far less cost than a villa in the south of France," she said. Jonathan did not reply but she felt her comment had struck home. "Do you want me to go ahead with arranging for valuations?"

Jonathan stood across the desk rattling coins in his pockets in that way he had. "What about guard dogs? A couple of Alsatians or Dobermans."

"Oh, that it should be so easy."

"Okay." Jonathan sounded tired. "Get the assessors in if you feel you must."

"I really do," she said sympathetically. "It may be a real shot in the arm to you to see how much you're worth on paper."

He smiled faintly. "Of course, one does know, but a Rembrandt on the wall doesn't pay wages and that's what we've opted for – paintings on the walls."

It was on the tip of her tongue to say he didn't have to have paintings on the walls but she stopped herself, remembering how, on her first day back, she had lectured him on the importance of retaining his heritage.

The next day Tom brought Cassie's car round. It was dark blue, sleek and beautiful. Holding her guilt at bay she allowed herself to fall in love with it. But all the same she made a protest. "A new car drops a large percentage of its value in the first year," she said to the chauffeur. "I'm sure you could have found me one a year or so old."

"It's what he ordered," Tom replied and she recognised in his lack of criticism the same rock-like loyalty of her parents.

"Would you like to try it out, Miss?"

They climbed in together. It was a wonderful car. Comfortable, with smooth leather seats and plenty of legroom. The engine purred like a contented cat. She drove down to the gate and back. "You're okay," Tom said as he climbed out. "You'll enjoy this car. She's a beauty." He added with a twinkle, "Just remember we drive on the left."

She laughed ruefully, realising he must have watched her going down the drive in her parents' Rover. She had often reached the gate before realising she was driving on the right.

She ran into Bart crossing the stable yard as she made her way to the side door of the flat. "I've got my pick-up truck," she said cheerily. "I'm going in to Flyford to get some chairs upholstered and I'll pick up the lino for the kitchen."

"Some pick-up truck," he said, giving her an old-fashioned look.

"It wasn't my choice," she said quickly. The staff should know she had not stood out for this luxury, though why it was their business she hadn't considered.

"It wasn't? Oh well, I dare say he looks on it as an investment," Bart said. "And it's part of the shop window, isn't it?"

"You think Jonathan might not want want his comptroller to be seen running around in an old van?" She hadn't thought she might be expected to help maintain the dignity of the Hall.

"Could be."

She told him she had decided to do the kitchen herself. "If I pick up some foam-backed lino, would you lay it for me?"

"Sure."

"I'm going up to measure the floor now."

"I'll come with you," he offered. "I might be better at it than you."

"Me, a mere woman?"

He grinned.

Cassie produced the vast key and held it out for him to see. "Can anything be done about this?"

"Not really. It's a mighty thick door."

"And what about plumbing? If I bring back a sink, could you fit it?"

"I dare say."

"You're a jack-of-all-trades?" She smiled at him with her head on one side.

"No. I'm a gardener. But I'm not grumbling. You have to muck in round here. And there'll be more of it when the public start pouring in."

"I suppose you wouldn't like to help me carry out four chairs that need upholstering?"

"Why not?"

Bart went down on his knees to measure the kitchen floor. Cassie put the details in her notebook then they went through to one of the disused rooms and between them transferred the chairs to the Volvo. She started up the engine reciting, "Paint. Linoleum. Curtain samples. Steel sink."

That night she showed the curtain samples to her mother. "You have to choose now because the assistant loaned them to me under duress. And even then, only when I tossed in the magic name, Bevington Hall. Such clout it has!" Leila looked proud, as though some of the Hall's fame had rubbed off on her. "I've promised to have them back first thing tomorrow. There's plenty to choose from." There were trailing vines; elegant roses lifting from prickly stems; stripes.

"I really don't know how I can make up my mind," Leila said when she had been through the swatches. She sat back with the air of one whose cup is full to the brim.

Cassie suggested she shut her eyes and poke a finger. "Would you like to make the curtains up? It's quite a lot of work, but I'm sure you'd want to keep the cost down. I'm hoping Jonathan will pay for the material." Leila protested, but Cassie reminded her, "You wouldn't have been replacing curtains if he wasn't putting you out of the cottage. He doesn't know yours wouldn't fit those huge windows."

"He will when you point it out to him."

Cassie laughed. "You're bright this evening. Yes, I'm willing to point it out to him."

"I shall be very happy to make them up," Leila said. "I'm sorry if you don't think Jonathan has been generous."

"I would have counted it as generous if he had thought of it himself. He's loaned us all that beautiful furniture yet ignored the curtains that were cheap and dull in the first place, and certainly never intended to last thirty years."

"A man wouldn't think about curtains. Don't be so hard on him, Cassie."

She remembered then that she had invited the insurance assessors in. Jonathan was going to be in for a hefty shock. Perhaps, after all, they should pay for the curtains themselves.

That week Bart removed all the cupboard doors in the kitchen and rubbed them down, then put them back with the new hinges Cassie had bought. "I'm glad you didn't want to put in one of them fancy kitchens," he said. "It would be a pity to waste such lovely old oak." He surveyed his handiwork with pride. Cassie felt subdued when the retainers talked this way.

Now that Leila had her car back and Cassie didn't have to pick her up from the hospital, she was free to go to the flat in the evenings immediately she finished work. She painted the kitchen walls a pale primrose to attract the light and put the coating of varnish that Bart recommended on the cupboard doors. Bart also came one evening and plumbed in the sink, then laid the new lino. Sometimes she felt the old house was gently levering her into her place in the natural order of things.

During the day now the Hall was peopled by efficient-looking men wearing spectacles and carrying portfolios. The countess seemed to enjoy the new life that had been injected into the house but the earl grew cantankerous. Cassie found him one morning hiding behind *The Times* in the 'snug' with the dog asleep beside him.

"A man can't get a bit of peace anywhere," he grumbled. "The place is like Piccadilly Circus. Who are they?"

"I thought you were going off to a villa in the south of France," Cassie said. "It would be a lot more peaceful there."

He put the paper down and sat forward, glowering at her. "What do you mean, young lady? Are you trying to get rid of me?"

"Of course not." She smiled at him. "I just want you to be comfortable."

His eyes remained steadily on her face. "There are things going on here I'm not sure I want to turn my back on," he muttered, fixing her with a gimlet eye.

"What, for instance?"

But it seemed he didn't want to answer that for he disappeared behind his paper again.

"I'll try to ensure you're not bothered too much," she said addressing the back of the paper and left the room, closing the door quietly behind her.

Where was Jonathan? Lady Haldane told her, looking pleased, "He's staying with the Montcalms for a few days." She added, looking unaccustomedly vague, "They've business dealings."

Cassie went back to her office feeling depressed. "Do you suppose Lord Montcalm is offering a dowry?" she asked, looking up at Lady Selena on the wall. The blue eyes gazed back at her, saying what? Sometimes she thought Lady Selena's expression was subtly changing; that there was veiled interest behind those heretofore limpid blue eyes.

A voice from the doorway said in surprise, "Oh! You are alone. I thought I heard voices."

"Talking to myself," said Cassie wryly. The stranger came forward into the room. No, she wasn't a stranger. Cassie looked at her hard, trying to place her. She had the stalwart outdoor look, the china blue eyes and the vaguely untidy air of a young Lady Haldane. And she was dressed like Lady Haldane in an ill-fitting tweed skirt, sensible shoes and woollen tights.

"I'm Tessa Copeland," she said holding out her hand. "You must remember me."

Ah, yes. Jonathan's sister. A distant figure in her childhood.

"I'm glad Jon's snaffled you," she said bluntly, dropping uninvited into the spare revolving chair, her useful-looking hands gripping the arms. An untidy drift of hair lay across her forehead. She sat with her sturdy legs apart, her back consciously straight. Her eyes were very direct. "It's quite a coup. Continuity, that's what these old houses need, more than anything. That's what's wrong with the National Trust. All those strangers taking over. The house stops being a house and then it's a blasted museum. I was desperately afraid, when Father got this crazy south of France idea, that was where the Hall was going to end up. With the National Trust."

"Maybe he won't go, after all," Cassie ventured, thinking with hope of the money that would be saved if he didn't buy a villa. She went round the desk to her own chair and sat down.

"And nor should he. God! South of France! That's so old hat." Lady Tessa thumped the desk with a show of irritation. "He hasn't thought it out. The Caribbean, now. That's more like it, except it's hardly their scene. What do you think?"

"He talks about his aches and pains. A warm climate might suit him."

"Nonsense," Lady Tessa broke in robustly. "He hasn't got enough to do. He could be one of the attractions on open days, bumbling around among the visitors. You know how snobbish people are. They'd love to have a word with him. And he likes people, really. He's a homely old boy at heart, don't you think?"

Likes people! He could have fooled me, Cassie thought. And homely! Jonathan's sister was still looking at her in that absorbed way. When she didn't answer Lady Tessa turned her attention to the new computer. "That must have cost a packet," she said critically.

"Less than a villa in the south of France," Cassie retorted, stung. "You don't organise a venture like this with stone-age equipment."

Lady Tessa smiled faintly. "How's your father?"

"Getting better. He's coming out of hospital next week."

"I hope you're not harbouring any grudges," Jonathan's sister went on in her straightforward way. "It was a fool thing to do. Nobody walks along an unlit lane at night these days unless they've got one of those yellow things on their back that car lights can pick up."

"I suppose so."

"I'd better get on." Lady Tessa rose, gave Cassie a thoughtful look and added in her blunt way, "You're the best thing that's happened round here for a long time. Don't do anything silly and spoil things."

Cassie flushed. Was she referring to the accident, or to her past? After her visitor had gone she looked up at the portrait on the wall and could have sworn Lady Selena winked at her.

Zoe seemed to be spending an inordinate amount of time at the Hall. Cassie, with her view over the drive, would see her coming in, sometimes in the morning for lunch, sometimes for tea. Sometimes Jonathan and she drove off in the afternoon in his car. Where did they go? It was none of her business, Cassie told herself. She stopped going to the private apartments when Zoe was there. Nobody commented on the change but when Jonathan or Lady Haldane wanted to talk to her they came to Lady Selena's room.

One evening Cassie realised with dismay that if she didn't

attend to the mail in her in-tray a number of important projects were going to be held up. She asked Cook to provide a salad, then telephoned her mother to say she would be late. "Don't stay up. I don't know what time I'll finish. How's Gerald?"

"Much better."

"Is he coming out next week?"

"Most probably, yes."

That meant she was going to have to take time off to clear out the cottage and arrange for the furniture to go to auction. Eddie, Bart and Sid had volunteered their services as removal men. "If you hire a van," Bart said, "we'll do the rest. It'll cost you a lot less than getting the removals people in."

"Oh golly you are kind."

Bart grinned. "It's not what they do in America?"

"I think they'd expect to be paid." A light of something like triumph flickered in his eyes. She was becoming aware that they were mysteriously jealous of her LA connection. They liked to rub home the fact that her roots lay in the soil of Flyford where all their ancestors had been born, hers and theirs.

And yet, they did not treat her as an equal. Neither did they call her Miss Neilson. They somehow managed to get by without calling her anything. Edward, the new arrival, didn't call her Cassie either. So he had talked to someone! Who? And what was explained?

"You'll fix it up, will you, the van?" Sid asked.

"Yes. Have you checked with Jonathan that it's okay for you to take time off?"

"We're going to do it in working hours. His orders."

Momentarily, Cassie felt uncomfortable, then she reminded

herself that it was Jonathan who had forced the move. She made a note to thank him.

It was nearly eleven that evening when she rose from her chair. She yawned, stretched and decided to call it a day. Rain was washing across the windows. She drew the curtains, turned off the lights and was stepping into the passageway when she remembered she had left the kitchen windows open in the flat in order to get rid of the smell of paint. This rain, coming as it was from the east, would be driving in.

Leaving her handbag on the desk, she took to her heels and ran soft-footedly along the carpeted corridors until she reached the west wing. Sure enough, the rain was lashing in across the new sink and Formica worktop. There was a puddle on the linoleum. She grasped the catch and was drawing the window shut when in a flash of lightning that lit up the courtyard below she saw two men bent half double under a large piece of furniture as they propelled it through the archway. What on earth was going on? The staff didn't move furniture in the middle of the night!

She ran all the way back to Lady Selena's room, picked up the telephone and rang 999. Now what to do? She had seen Jonathan disappear with Zoe in the late afternoon. Was he home yet? She sped down the passage leading to the private apartments and knocked on his door. When there was no reply she opened it, groped for the light switch and turned it on.

"Jonathan!" The room was empty, the bed made up. Should she wake the earl and countess? To what purpose? They could do nothing, and turning on lights could alert the thieves to make a quick getaway. But there was something she could do. She could close the gates.

She ran downstairs, flung open the door that led to the lobby and the flower room, turned on the light and jerked out the top drawer of the desk. There was the gate key and by its side a torch. She snatched them both up, ran to the front door, hauled back the bolts, extinguished the lights and slipped out.

Rain was spattering noisily on the gravel. Surely too noisily for rain! Wasn't that hail? As she exited from the portico and headed blindly down the drive the hard little hailstones hit her cheeks, her nose, her chin. She shuddered as she felt them slide down inside her jumper. Blackness everywhere. She switched on the torch, then swiftly turned it off again. How stupid of her not to realise a light would be spotted. How cold it was! She was already wet through. Why had she not thought to pick up an anorak?

Keep the gravel underfoot. On the grass you'll be lost.

She stumbled, regained her balance and felt soft turf beneath her feet. "Damn! Where's the drive?" She ran back and forth distractedly, her sopping wet hair slapping her in the face. Was that gravel beneath her feet? Yes, it was. She couldn't hear a crunch but she could feel its rough texture through the thin soles of her shoes. Now, in which direction was the gate?

"If I keep the grass on my right I have to be okay." She forged on. "But how will I know the verge is there unless I kick it?" She did so and sprawled full length. The torch and key went flying.

She struggled to her knees, groping around on the wet grass. Her fingers slid coldly into little banks of hailstones. Ah! Her numb fingers struck something hard. The key! Where was the torch? She floundered round on her knees then gave up. She would have to manage without. Anyway, hadn't she already decided the light was unsafe?

She proceeded in little hops, touching the grass verge with her right foot at every move. The wind, miraculously, dropped.

She lost track of time and distance. The wind whipped up again. She turned her head away, whimpering with the cold, lost her balance and fell forward on the gravel. It cut painfully into her knees. She scrambled once more to her feet, cast a panicky look behind and hurried on. At least she would see the lights when they came for no vehicle would be able to keep to the drive without them.

Suddenly, painfully, she came up against iron. A searing pain shot through her head. She dropped the key and rocked backwards and forwards, moaning. Inside her head a voice was saying 'Hurry! Hurry!' but she could not, she could only rock, moaning. It was another aggressive rush of hail that brought her to her senses. She cast another panicky look back the way she had come. Still there were no lights. She felt her way to the outside rim of the right hand gate. There must be a hook or clip here to hold it against the wall.

Ah! A chain! One end was attached to the wall, the other hooked into a horizontal bar on the gate. She released it, set her feet against the wall, took hold of the central bar, leaned back and pulled with all her might. The gate would not budge. She tried again. And again. She took a deep breath and gathering up all the strength she possessed, she gave the gate a tremendous wrench. The hinges shrieked and she felt it begin reluctantly to move. She pulled again and it gave a few more inches.

There was now a small space between the gate and the wall. She squeezed herself in, set her feet against

the wrought iron and pushed with all her might. Slowly
and jerkily, squealing on its unoiled hinges, the big frame
inched outwards. She cast a frightened look up across the
park. There were still no headlights but in the back of her
mind a fear that she had kept at bay was growing, that
the burglars might indeed find their way down the drive
without lights.

Inch by inch she forced the gate forward and at last it
came level with the wall. Again she looked round fearfully
for car lights, squinting against the rain. Still the park was
in darkness. She squelched across the gravel, and carefully
feeling in the darkness, located the other half of the gate,
felt her way along it, undid the chain and pulled. This one
screamed more loudly but it moved more easily. At last she
had the two parts together. Now for the key. She felt around
for the lock. Oh for the lost torch! She found the keyhole
but the key refused to go in.

Oh no! Oh no! After all that effort, it can't happen!
Sobbing with frustration she stabbed and pushed with her
right hand, intermittently missing the lock and hitting her
left, gritting her teeth against the pain. Of course it would
be full of rust! It hadn't been used since goodness knows
when. "I am going to make you work," she muttered and
pushed with the strength of desperation.

The key shot in.

"Oh thank you!" Cassie sobbed, addressing no one in
particular. "Thank you." Gripping the key between finger
and thumb she twisted it with all her might and at last
with a groan and a screech it turned. The gates were
locked! But the key wouldn't come out. She placed both
feet against the base of the gate, and tugged. "Come out
you devil! Come out!" A moment later she was on her

back on the gravel and the key had flown out of her hand.

She rolled over and scrambled to her knees, wincing as again the sharp little pieces of gravel dug into the soft flesh of her palms and knees. Her fingers struck the cold metal of the key. She snatched it up and staggered to her feet, wiping away a fan of hair that had clamped itself wetly across her eyes.

Now, what to do? Where were the police? How long had she been battling with the gate? How long finding her way here in the darkness? Still there were no approaching lights. She thought fearfully the burglars might even now be close by and that her life could be in danger.

She stepped onto the grass and began to run diagonally back towards the house, staggering because her soaked skirt was clinging round her knees, clutching the key tightly in her fist. It was almost with relief, then, that in front and out to her right she saw the glow of dimmed headlights moving down the side of the Hall between the stables and the orangery. They rounded the corner and entered the driveway.

She hurtled off the gravel onto the grass and ran blindly, looking for the chestnut trees that were dotted randomly through the park. But how would she find a tree in this darkness except by running into it?

The lights remained dimmed as the vehicle advanced, but still, might it not be possible to pick her up if, nearing the gate, they risked putting them on a long beam? She threw herself down on the grass. A ridge of hailstones, built up by the wind, struck her chest. The cold was unbearable but she lay still, suffering.

The lights were level now, perhaps a hundred yards away. They moved on, the idling engine silent behind the rush of wind and rain. They passed her. She could see the glow of the tail lights now. She struggled to her knees, brushing the matted hail from her jumper. Would they be able to break the lock? Burglars were bound to carry tools. Oh, where were the police? Flyford wasn't that far away. What on earth was keeping them?

At that moment a cry came faintly through the beat of the rain. "Turn the lights up! Holy shit! It's bloody locked!"

A moment later the lights of the vehicle went on full beam and two men were silhouetted in their glare. A panicky voice shouted, "We're trapped!"

Another voice, "Get the jemmy! Quick!"

They were going to get away! Cassie crouched with both hands over her face, listening to the sound of clanging metal, agonising because all her work was going to be wasted. She forgot about the wet and the cold. Minutes went by like hours. She shut her eyes and entreated the lock, Don't give way. Please don't give way!

And then, in the distance, she heard the eery, insistent wail of a police siren.

She staggered to her feet. Powerful lights swept along the road and swung in, exposing the huge gates and the two men standing behind. They took to their heels and disappeared into the darkness. The car lights swept through the rain, spread out across the park. They picked up the runaways, three of them now, arms and legs going like pistons. Another siren sounded. Another car swung in. Two policemen slipped briefly into the arc of light, then disappeared.

Clutching her key in her hand, holding her impeding skirt high with the other, Cassie raced for the gates, tripped on uneven turf and fell headlong into a pool of rainwater.

Soaked and frozen she picked herself up and dashed on, taking her direction from the car lights. Two of the policemen were examining the lock. She splashed across a puddle in the gravel calling through the driving rain, "I've got the key!"

"Good God!" They swung round and stared at her.

"If you want to get your car in . . ." she began breathlessly.

"Give it to me and get out of the way."

Between them the policemen hurled the gates back. "Look out!" Numbed as she was by the cold she was not quick enough. The rim of the gate hit her, sending her sprawling. Someone shouted, "Are you all right?"

"Yes." She staggered to her feet, hoping she was all right, not at all certain. She felt bruised and half drowned.

The police cars edged carefully round the van then raced off across the park. With the powerful searchlights gone, darkness closed in. Cassie dragged her way to the van, opened the driver's door and removed the ignition key from the lock.

In the distance she could hear threatening shouts. A scream. Car lights zig-zagged. She watched them, fearful and at the same time fascinated, as they caught the fugitives in their glare, lost them, caught them again. Then all at once it was over. In the distance three figures stood silhouetted in a yellow glow, holding up their hands.

She began to make her way back towards the Hall. Now that there was no hurry she could drag one leg easily along the grass verge and keep direction without losing her balance. She was so cold she had lost all feeling in hands and feet. Her teeth were chattering. The grass verge veered to the left. The building must be in front of her now.

She blinked, narrowed her eyes and thought she saw a

dark shadow. She approached carefully, reached out and touched the hard surface of stone. Using the wall as a guide she felt her way and came to the first column. She slid a hand round it and followed the inner wall. Inside the central portico the silence and stillness was a shock. It was like entering another world.

She came to the big front door. She felt her way inside and switched on a light. What to do now? She looked down at herself, at the jumper and skirt clinging with unbearable cold to her body and dripping a pool of water onto the floor. She squeezed water out of her hair and kicked off her soaking shoes. Here on the marble floor it didn't matter but she couldn't drip her way up the beautiful staircarpet and along the passageway to Lady Selena's room to collect her handbag and car keys. She could go naked. But then she would have to get back into her soaked garments in order to drive home.

No. There must be a better solution.

She crossed the marble hall, uncaring of the puddles she was leaving at every step, and made her way down the passage towards the kitchen. On her right now were the cupboards where linen was kept. She opened them one after another. Table cloths, table napkins, tiny kitchen handtowels. In a frenzy of shivering she shook out the little hand towels and rubbed at her dripping hair and her soaking clothes.

Suddenly she remembered the dreary little suite of rooms she had briefly considered taking for her own accommodation. There was a bathroom! Hot water! But had it been cut off? The rooms hadn't been used for ages. She snatched a handful of the little towels and padded off down the passage to investigate.

The door was unlocked. She went in and pushed open the bathroom door. The bath was furred with the fluffy non-dust that is a product of disuse. She turned on one of the enormous brass taps. An aggressive spurt of boiling water choked and coughed its way dementedly into the bath. Steam clouded through the tiny room. She ran the cold tap. Brown water came out. She turned it full on and gradually the colour cleared.

She rinsed the bath, wiped it with one of the handtowels, put the plug in and turned both taps on. She didn't wait for the bath to fill up. With numb and shaking fingers she removed her clothes, dropped them on the floor and stepped in. At first she felt nothing, then gradually the feeling came back to her limbs and she relaxed. As the bath filled up she lay back with her hair swirling round her head. She didn't care that there was no way of drying herself afterwards, nor that anyway she had no clothes. She felt she could lie here for ever. When the bath had filled to the brim she closed her eyes, feeling sleepy and content.

Chapter Nine

"CASSIE!"

She started up out of her warm trance, sending a wave of water over the top of the bath. Jonathan's voice! "I'm here!" she called.

"Yes," he said dryly, speaking now from right outside the bathroom. "I gathered that from the puddles. I followed them across the hall and down the passage. What on earth are you doing?"

"I'm stuck in the bath."

"What do you mean you're stuck in the bath? What are you doing having a bath in – Cassie, was it you locked the gates?"

"Yes, and I got wet. And I haven't got any clothes." She was going to cry again. "Or a towel. Only some little handtowels and they're no use now because the water has gone over onto the floor and they're floating." Tears of weakness and relief rained down her face. For the first time she wondered what she had been going to do for the next five or six hours until the house came alive and she could call for help. But Jonathan had come.

"Oh Cassie!" A moment's silence, then Jonathan said in a subdued voice, "The police want to talk to you."

She sank back into the warmth, sending another wave

over the rim of the bath onto the floor, not caring, crying because Jonathan was there.

She heard the door close. Minutes later it opened again and Jonathan's voice said, "There's a towel hanging on the door knob. I've put some clothes in the next room. They won't fit but they'll make you decent. You'll find us in the small library."

She wiped her wet face with the back of her wet hand and hooked a toe round the plug chain. The water rushed noisily into the down pipe. The towel Jonathan had brought was enormous. She wrapped herself in it and padded wetly through to the dingy little living room.

Jonathan had brought her some of his own clothes. A pair of jeans, a Viyella shirt and a thick Arran sweater; a pair of cosy felt slippers and some blue socks. He had also thoughtfully provided a belt. She folded the excess material of the jeans across her front, fixed them in place with the belt and rolled up the trouser legs.

There was no way she could get her hair dry without some heat, and the bath towel was too big to wrap round her head. She rubbed it hard, taking out the excess water, then shuffled out into the passage in her over-large footwear and made her way up the stairs to Lady Selena's room. Her slippers fell off so she carried them until she reached the landing then put them on again. She found a rubber band in her desk, a comb in her handbag, combed her hair, fixed it in a knot on the crown of her head, then carrying her handbag under her arm, shuffled back downstairs and along the passage to the library.

The door was open. The men rose to their feet. The two policemen looked at her with intense curiosity.

Jonathan introduced her. Superintendent Howard was a

148

stocky, middle-aged man with sandy hair cut so short he could have passed for a convict, and pale eyebrows. PC Cook was tall and slim, with a shock of black curls.

"She's normally better dressed than that," said Jonathan casually and the policemen laughed. She went to the sofa and sat down.

"So, tell us what happened." Superintendent Howard sat forward in his chair, hands on his knees.

She felt weak and spent now, scarcely able to hold herself up. She leaned on the sofa arm. PC Cook scribbled in his notebook. Jonathan said there was a problem of the van standing at the gates, packed with the booty, and no ignition keys. Another man had been left to guard it. Her hand flew to her mouth. What had she done with the keys?

"In your pocket?" Jonathan asked looking at her quizzically.

"I didn't have a pocket. Maybe they're with my clothes, on the bathroom floor."

Jonathan went to look for them. "I have to congratulate you," said the superintendent. "It was a brave thing to do."

"Anyone would have done it."

"Not anyone," said the younger man and they both looked at her with respect. It occurred to her then that Jonathan had not thanked her for her part, and again she wanted to cry.

"You could say it was my responsibility," she said, and wiped a tear away. "I work here."

Howard said gruffly, "I hope they're grateful. And I hope you don't catch cold."

Jonathan came back with the keys to the van. "I found them lying among a pile of wet towels on the floor outside the linen cupboard."

"Oh – yes. I had a go at drying myself with table napkins

and tray cloths." She added wryly, "I'll be in trouble with the kitchen staff."

"You probably will."

They discussed what to do with the van.

"I suggest we lock it in with the Rolls," Jonathan said. "That garage is tight as a drum." He turned to Cassie, "Now, what about you?"

"I'll get a hot drink, then take myself home."

He looked uncertain. "I won't be long." At the door he turned and said again, "I won't be long."

When the two policemen had gone she thought about the hot drink, but she hadn't the energy. She lifted her feet onto the sofa and sank limply against the arm. Jonathan's slippers fell with a plop onto the floor. She didn't feel like driving home. She didn't think she could move from where she was. And as to going out into the rain again . . . She closed her eyes and felt herself drifting.

She wakened to a sound, soft and insistent. Was someone calling her name? She opened her eyes with a start. Jonathan was standing looking down at her. She rolled drunkenly into a sitting position. "Sorry. I must have gone to sleep."

He knelt on the floor beside her. "Your hair's wet," he said and felt it with his hands.

"It's too thick to dry with a towel. I don't suppose you've got a dryer?" She spoke in a panicky voice, frightened by his nearness and his unaccustomed gentleness.

He wasn't listening. "Cassie," he said, "you did something tremendous tonight." His hands were on either side of her face. He was looking into her eyes.

"Jonathan! Don't! Please don't!" She tried to pull away. She nearly said, 'Nothing can come of it', but he knew that. Hadn't he been out tonight with Zoe Montcalm?

"You can't go home."

"I can. I meant to. Really. I don't know how I came to go to sleep. I was going . . . I . . ." She broke off, floundering for words.

"It's raining cats and dogs out there."

She couldn't go home. He was right. "Please—" She cast around for a way out of the dilemma. "I could stay here – on this sofa. I'd be perfectly comfortable, if you could bring me a rug."

"No," he said, still in that gentle voice. "You can't sleep here." He pulled her to her feet.

She was too weak, too nervous, too emotional to argue. "There are dozens of beds," she said.

"Yes."

She shuffled along beside him, gripping the slippers with her toes. She lost them as they went up the stairs. Jonathan went back and picked them up. She continued with bare feet that had grown cold again.

He stopped at the door of his room. Hadn't she known that was where they were going? He switched on the light. "I'll get that towel," he said and hurried out again.

She huddled on the edge of the bed, shivering. He came back with the towel. She undid the rubber band with trembling fingers. Her heavy hair fell down onto her shoulders. "I'm dreadfully cold," she said and wiped away a teardrop.

"I dare say reaction has set in." He had begun to rub her hair. "You'd better get quickly into bed. This hair does need a blower, but it might dry in the night if I wrap the towel round it. I'll see what I can do." He wound the towel round her head and she tucked in the ends. His hands slipped down onto her shoulders.

Cassie thought afterwards that that was the moment she allowed herself to recognise that there was – had been ever since her return from Los Angeles – a slow ticking bomb hidden in her.

"I love you," whispered Jonathan with his lips against her ear. "You know that, don't you?"

Yes. She knew about his love. A self-indulgence for him. A trap for her. She didn't want to think about the fact that what she was about to do could mean, would unquestionably mean, her swift departure, to London this time, with the staff sniggering.

"I love you, too," she whispered, moving into another world where treachery did not exist. A quite unnerving happiness spread through her. She had a sense of deliverance from the past. Of being poised on the edge of a clifftop with the sun beating down on her. Jonathan turned out the light. She closed her eyes. And then she was naked and he naked beside her. She caught her breath.

"Don't talk," he said, his lips on hers. "Don't say anything."

Her arms tightened round him, binding him to her. But there was something she had to say. Wanted to say. "I love you, Jonathan. I love you. I love you." She said the words softly, frenziedly, wanting to put them into the ether where they would be imprinted on time. All the longing of the missing years slipped away as she held him.

They made love, joyfully, physically, sensually. He was hers and she was his. Afterwards when they lay in each other's arms she said, "Jonathan . . ."

He put a finger to her lips. "We're not going to talk tonight. Only make love. Oh Cassie, I need you so." His arms tightened. "I have always needed you."

She heard the words as a cry from his heart. As a fear and a warning. But because she was shining inside she also heard them as a promise. She tightened her arms round him, felt their hearts beating together. And after a while they drifted off to sleep. To nirvana.

She wakened in darkness. For a moment she lay still, holding the night around her. Then she saw a sliver of light showing through the heavy curtains. Day! She jerked upright. Jonathan's side of the bed was empty. She squinted at her watch. Ten o'clock! She leaped out of bed, drew the curtains aside.

The rain had washed the sky clean. The chestnut trees had lost their stark outlines. She saw them with new eyes. Everything looked fresh and beautiful. She folded her arms across her breasts, holding in the memory of Jonathan's caresses; cherishing the new-old belonging. "I love you, Jonathan," she whispered. And he had said he loved her. That he needed her.

Jonathan's clothes that she had worn last night were draped across a small sofa. She stood looking down at them, still dreaming, not yet ready to face the fact that somehow she had to get out of here. Crabapple Cottage, even her own desk in Lady Selena's room where she should be at this moment, was a world away. She stood there naked, savouring the dream. Dreaming. She lifted the sleeve of her love's Arran sweater and held it against her cheek. "I love you, Jonathan." She whispered the words from her heart.

The door opened. She swung round, her face lighting up. But it was not Jonathan. Zoe stood there, her face set in a dreamy smile, a zip bag in her hand. She saw Cassie and the smile froze. Her eyes glazed over. The bag dropped with a thud to the floor. For a breathless moment the two women

153

stared at each other. Cassie saw her nakedness reflected in
the shock of Zoe's eyes and dazedly moved a hand across
her front.

Zoe was impeccably dressed in an expensive cashmere
jumper, lavender-coloured, with a soft woollen skirt that
fell in folds. "You bitch!" Her face was twisted and ugly.
"You scheming whore!"

In the same moment that Cassie snatched up Jonathan's
jumper and held it across her nakedness she recognised
the soft zipped bag Zoe was carrying. "Thank you for
bringing my clothes," she managed, her voice high-pitched
and wretched.

"Your—? Oh, it's yours?" Zoe looked down in surprise.
Her eyes came back to meet Cassie's. "What a cheap tart
you are!" she said. "You've been thrown out once. Didn't
that teach you anything?"

Cassie trembled with the effort of keeping her temper
in control. She advanced towards the bag. With a deft
movement of one foot Zoe slid it behind her.

"What do you think you're going to get out of this?" she
asked, enunciating her words precisely, sharp as cut glass.
The girls were approximately the same height. Zoe raised
her head so that she had an air of looking down on Cassie
in her bare feet.

She clutched at the jumper now spread across her body.
"You must know what happened last night," Cassie said,
making a tremendous effort to sound reasonable, as though
being naked in Jonathan's bedroom was a perfectly normal
happening. "I got wet. Jonathan very kindly loaned me
his bed."

"Loaned you his bed, did he?" Zoe's voice was scathing.
"Any woman can lure a man into bed," she said, spitting

the words out like tacks. "That's not very clever. Cold, were you? Cold and wet?" she went on sarcastically while Cassie hovered before her, eyeing the bag, wondering if she dared pounce. "And what did you expect to get out of it? We're not supposed to guess, are we. But everyone knows. Trollop from one of the servants' cottages to lady of the house? That's what it's about, isn't it? Oh yes, the bed's a great stepping-stone," said Zoe scathingly. "The middle classes might get away with it, but not the offspring of servants."

"If you don't mind," said Cassie, biting back the dangerous rejoinder that rose to her lips, "I'd like to get dressed." She took a tentative step towards the door, though knowing that short of attacking Zoe she was not going to get the bag.

"You want this job, don't you?" Zoe's eyes were narrow, cold and cruel.

"I've already got the job and I don't propose to discuss it with you," Cassie retorted.

"You may have to. I suppose you think you're indispensable, but you're not. There are plenty of people who could do what you're doing. You don't know a damn thing about country houses. How could you, you've been in America for years. And you don't know anything about antiques. Her ladyship tells me you're having to learn it all from books," Zoe said, as though that was the ultimate sin. She came a step nearer. "Let me tell you I could replace you just so easily." She clicked her fingers together and smiled coldly, triumphantly. "You are so very unimportant. There are dozens of people who've had experience of setting up stately homes. People with the right background who know their antiques and *objets d'art.*"

"I'll be happy to discuss it with you another time when I'm dressed," Cassie said. "Hand over my bag, please."

She might not have spoken for all the notice Zoe took. "Don't you know that my father has offered to finance the opening of the Hall? Maybe Jonathan hasn't told you – there's no reason why he should – that they can't go ahead without the stake my family is putting in?"

"I don't think Jonathan is the kind of man who can be bought," said Cassie, her eyes on the bag that was now partially concealed behind Zoe's pretty, flowing skirt, clutching Jonathan's jumper against her front, trying to sound confident, feeling desperately at a disadvantage in her nakedness. What did she know about the family's finances? Or to what lengths a man might go when desperate to keep his heritage?

"No," said Zoe, showing by her harsh rejoinder and cold glare that Cassie had hit a sore spot. "And he can't be tricked, either. Everyone's watching you. Don't you see everyone watching you? Do you think anyone has forgotten you were banished for seducing the heir? People don't forget these things. And maybe you've forgotten how the village thinks," she went on, still in that spitting voice. "They don't want the gardener's granddaughter as lady of the great Hall. They want things as they've always been. They expect Jonathan to take a bride from a good family. You know this very well, of course, but just in case you've forgotten while you were living in America let me remind you, the locals won't have it. Get that into your scheming head, Cassandra Neilson. You may be good in bed but you're not going to be allowed into the family."

She paused, only long enough to savour with satisfaction the anguish on Cassie's face, then swung round, picked up the bag, deliberately kicked the door wide open so that anyone passing would see her in her nakedness, and disappeared along the corridor.

There was nothing for it now but to get back into Jonathan's clothes and make her escape. Before she could move, Spicer appeared in the doorway and trotted over to her.

"Oh Spicer dear," sobbed Cassie, cracking up under the warmth of the dog's devotion, "you do seem to know when I need comfort." She knelt down on the floor and put her arms round the dog. Spicer delicately licked her forehead. Cassie put a hand to the spot and felt a lump that was painful to the touch. "That was the gate," she said to the dog. "Oh, you are such a comfort. But I have to go."

She stood up and began to haul Jonathan's clothes on – shirt, jumper, jeans. She rolled up the sleeves of the jumper and the legs of the jeans. In the mirror she looked tousled and ridiculous, rather like one of those circus clowns who come into the ring in garments many sizes too big. She dragged the comb through her hair, picked up her handbag, opened the door cautiously and looked to right and left. There was no one about.

"Don't follow me, Spicer darling," she said. "You go back to your master, there's a good chap."

Spicer obediently settled on his haunches. She blew him a kiss, waited another moment, listening, then sped down the passage towards the back of the house. It ended in a narrow oak staircase. She ran nimbly down, paused to hitch up a trouser leg and looked round, getting her bearings. She knew where she was. Not far ahead there was another little staircase that would lead her to the long gallery. Beyond that lay her parents' flat and the steep stairs from which she could escape to the stable yard and her car.

She ran lightly on bare feet. The trouser legs fell down. She had to stop to roll them up. Was that a footstep? Keep running. She came to the stairs and hurried down, clutching her bag under one arm.

The door key was missing. Heart in mouth, she ran back to the flat. It had to be here! She couldn't risk going out of the front door. Nor the back door, which led into the garden where Eddie, Bart or Sid, at least one of them, would be working. She found the key lying on the kitchen bench, snatched it up and fled down the stairs again bent double, holding on to her trouser legs that were refusing to stay up.

At the bottom she opened the door very, very carefully. There was no one in sight. She slipped out, pushed it shut behind her and turned the key. The Volvo stood in the stable yard where she had left it. She hobbled across the gravel, wincing as the small stones cut into the soles of her bare feet.

The engine purred into life. She cast another apprehensive look to right and left then edged out of the stable yard. As she entered the drive she kept her eyes straight ahead. The muscles in her shoulders and the back of her neck were tight, her breathing quick and shallow. She was nervously aware of being exposed to the view of anyone standing in the portico or looking out of windows on this side of the Hall. She felt she couldn't afford to be seen running away. In order to diminish the sound of the engine she kept her foot very lightly on the accelerator. The car quietly gathered speed. As she came level with the front of the Hall she saw a police car parked near the front door.

The gates were still open. She realised then, and her heart jolted with the shock, that they would probably have been locked when the police left and that had she come earlier she would have been trapped. No doubt Jonathan had opened them this morning to let the police car in. She sped through, turned left into the road, dashed round the park and with a great sigh of relief nosed in at the gateway to Crabapple Cottage. It was then that the full impact of Zoe's words hit her. She slumped in her seat, staring blankly into space with the insults darting through her brain. Cheap tart. Bitch. Trollop from a servant's cottage.

"Cassie!"

She started. Leila was standing at the front door, a puzzled expression on her face. She slipped out of the driver's seat and went up the steps.

"What on earth!" Leila gazed at her in consternation, at the long baggy jeans hanging over her bare feet, at the jumper many sizes too big with the sleeves hanging over her wrists. "I sent your clothes. What happened to them?"

There hadn't been time to think about what she would say to her mother. "Hang on a minute," she said, brushing past her. "I'll talk to you later. I'm going to change."

"But your clothes!" persisted Leila, following her to the bottom of the stairs. "Jonathan came and collected them. What are you doing in . . ."

"Yes, well. I don't know," Cassie said distractedly. "I need some breakfast." Clutching the trouser legs, hauling them over her feet, she ran up the stairs to her room.

She did not think of an explanation. It did not come to her. She could only think, I am going to be sacked. I've blown it. I've lost my lovely job. She looked in the wardrobe and without considering took out an old pair of jeans. As she

159

slipped into them her thoughts darted frenziedly hither and thither. Of course I'm going to lose my job. Zoe isn't going to marry Jonathan while his lover lives on the premises and works with him.

Cassie pulled an old jumper over her head. Her feet were cold. She was cold all over, now. The cold came from fear. Would she be easily replaced, as Zoe had suggested? She had no way of knowing whether Zoe was right, that there were plenty of people who could do what she was doing, and very much better.

She found some socks and a pair of slippers, brushed her hair and looked at herself in the mirror. Her face was pale and frightened. She felt with despair that she was correctly dressed for an easy ride down the slippery slope. There might be less of a thump when the granddaughter of the head gardener got the sack than if a dignified and correctly dressed comptroller was deposed.

'A month's pay in lieu of notice.' She could imagine Lady Haldane, châtelaine of the stately Hall, saying that, commenting sardonically perhaps that the experiment in classlessness had not worked. She wondered if Zoe would dare call her a tart in front of Lord and Lady Haldane.

Any woman can lure a man into bed. Zoe had said that was not very clever. She recognised that she was not without blame. Hadn't she known what would happen when she left the library with Jonathan's arm round her waist? At the very least she had been guilty of making her mind a blank.

Their love had been beautiful, yet Zoe's indictment had made it appear shameful. She saw what had happened through the eyes of others. Saw how easily it could be reduced to a tawdry escapade. She saw herself as undeserving of the responsible job that they had thrust upon her, she an Americanised descendant of the servant class who knew nothing of antiques!

Her mind went dizzily over and over the possibilities, seeing it from different angles, hearing different words. Maybe Lord and Lady Haldane would blame themselves. A proper comptroller of such a prestigious set-up, as Zoe said, a woman from the right background who knew antiques, would know how to behave. She felt small, foolish, and frightened.

If Zoe walked out, would she take the Montcalm loan with her? Was it a loan? Or a dowry? She had to recognise that Jonathan belonged to Zoe Montcalm. He could never be hers.

Lady Haldane's voice once more burst into her thoughts. 'We shouldn't have allowed Jonathan to talk us into this.' And then magnanimously, 'It's our fault, Haldane.' She would be thinking of a young man's appetites, the moral weakness of the servant class. Oh God!

The telephone rang downstairs. Leila called, "Jonathan's on the line." She stood with the receiver in her hand looking up at Cassie with a puzzled expression as she came slowly down the stairs.

Cassie took the receiver from her. "Hello." She stared glassily at the wall. Her voice was scarcely audible. She cleared her throat and said it again. "Hello."

"Are you all right?" He did not sound like the lover of the night before. He was formal. Businesslike. A man who had taken what he wanted and was now getting on with more important things.

"I'm all right," she said, knowing she was not.

"The police are here. They want to talk to you."

She caught her breath. "I talked to them last night."

161

"Yes, well, they want to go over it again."

"I haven't had breakfast." She didn't need breakfast, but she needed time.

"Don't be too long then," said Jonathan in the kind of voice she imagined he would use when talking to staff. Then he put the receiver down.

Any woman can lure a man into bed, Zoe had said. Was that the tone a man would use, she wondered with fear and bitterness, the morning after he had been lured into bed?

It occurred to her then that she need not wait around to be sacked. She could save Jonathan the trouble by resigning. And come to think of it, save her own dignity at the same time. 'We disagreed,' she would say. 'He wouldn't go along with my American ideas.' All faces saved.

Leila was back in the kitchen. Cassie could smell toast. She went and stood in the doorway. Leila was tipping some scrambled egg out of a pan. She looked up. "Are you all right?"

"A bit shaken." She swallowed over a great lump in her throat and blinked tears out of her eyes.

"I'm not surprised. Jonathan told me a bit about what happened. And it was on local radio."

Local radio! Was that what had brought Zoe? "Instant fame!" she said lightly. She looked at the toast, smelled the egg and felt she could not put food into a stomach that had become queasy with nerves.

"They mentioned you," said Leila. "Not by name, though. A member of the staff, they said, foiled the burglars by locking the main gates. I'm dying to hear the whole story. You are so clever." She put the pan down and turned to smile proudly at her.

Cassie sat at the table. Leila put the coffee percolator

on. "I can't imagine what happened to your clothes," she said, still worrying. "Jonathan was so anxious to get them to you. He said yours got soaked last night. Those were his clothes you were wearing, weren't they? How did you get hold of them?"

Cassie by-passed the question. "I haven't seen Jonathan. I've got to go up to the Hall and talk to the police now." She looked down at the egg. "I don't think I can eat this."

"You must, dear. Try a little. Please. Before it gets cold."

Cassie picked up her fork. Leila stood watching her. "Why are you dressed in jeans, dear?"

"I didn't think I'd be working."

Leila looked indulgent. "I dare say you're right. As the heroine of the hour you may be given the day off. Where did you sleep?"

"They found me a bed." She swiftly put a forkful of egg into her mouth and choked. Coughing, she pushed the plate away. Leila put a cup of coffee down in front of her, then thumped her on the back. Cassie thought, I cannot face the police. I cannot face Jonathan.

"Do try to eat, dear." Leila was very concerned. "It will give you strength. And you'd better hurry. Better not keep the police waiting."

Cassie thought, Zoe is right. She wiped a tear away. We are the kind of people who wouldn't want to keep the police waiting. She thought Zoe, with her self assurance, would ask them to make an appointment to see her. You could do that if you came from a background like hers. She recognised that Zoe had stripped her of the little confidence she had. Such a small amount it must have been to be so easily swept away.

163

She said, "I'm going to do some clearing up this afternoon. If Gerald comes out of hospital next week you're going to have to be in the flat. We don't want to move him here then move him out again. I'll start on the garage. It has to be done sometime. Are you ready to move? Have you sorted out what pieces of furniture you want to take, if any?"

She was already distancing herself from them in her mind. She would have to get them settled before she went to London. They would be all right. Nobody would hold them responsible for her misdemeanours. Nobody would point the finger at them and whisper that they were the parents of the upstart who had tried to get off with Jonathan Tarrant.

"I could make up a list quite quickly," Leila said. "You'd like to take the contents of your room, wouldn't you?"

Cassie felt panic rising. Saw the complications that were going to arise. She would have to break the news to them that she would not now be moving into the flat as they had hoped. "I don't know," she said. "I can't put my mind to it at the moment." She pushed back her chair. "I'd better go. As you say, I'd better not keep the police waiting."

Chapter Ten

THE POLICE car was standing outside the front door. Edward Harding the young butler was hovering in the hall. He smiled at Cassie in a friendly, suitably detached way. So the news had not yet got through to the staff! He said she would find Jonathan with the policemen in the library. "I believe you're to be congratulated, Miss Neilson," he said, looking pleased.

"Cassie," she corrected him, thinking the staff wouldn't have too much trouble calling her by her christian name when they heard she had once more fallen from grace. "Thank you, Edward. It was quite a night."

"You've got a lump on your forehead."

She fingered it gingerly. "I got a few bumps. I haven't had time to think about them, yet." Out of the corner of her eye she saw a movement on the staircase. She looked up. His lordship was beginning to descend the staircase with Spicer at his heels. He had reached the second or third tread when he saw her. Their eyes met briefly then he turned and stumped swiftly back to the landing. The dog came running on down, went straight to Cassie and lifted his head for a pat. Lord Haldane did not call him.

"What's the matter with him?" Edward asked, his frowning eyes following his lordship's figure as it disappeared into the upstairs corridor.

"You'd better go back to your master, Spicer," Cassie said, smoothing the dog's head, not wanting to answer the butler's question. Spicer wagged his tail.

"You'll have to take him, Miss Neilson," Edward said. "He won't follow me when you're around."

She sighed and set off down the passage. His lordship would no doubt find his way back to his 'snug' by another route. Spicer accompanied her. The door was ajar. She pointed. Regretfully but obediently he nosed it wider and went in. She heard the familiar voice of Lady Haldane say, "Hello, Spicer. Nice of you to visit us."

Us! Was Zoe closeted there with her hostess? Cassie hurried past.

"Good morning," said Jonathan formally as she came into the room. There was nothing in his expression to show her he was thinking of what had passed between himself and Zoe in the past hour and a quarter. Nor, indeed, what had passed between the two of them in the night. "How did you sleep?"

"Good morning," she replied. "I slept very well. Thank you for collecting my clothes."

Jonathan slapped a hand to his head and in that moment became human again. "I forgot. I left them in the hall. You got them anyway. Somebody— Is that a lump on your forehead?"

"I had a collision with the gate. Yes, somebody picked my clothes up," she said and experienced again the anguish Zoe's arrival had brought. Bitch. Tart. She turned to the two men who were hovering beside their chairs. Her hands were trembling. She put them behind her and twined her fingers tightly together. "Good morning, Superintendent." There was another man present whom Jonathan introduced as McKenzie. She sat down opposite them. They went over the night's events again. The thieves had come in the back way, through the garden. They had broken a window directly under her parents' flat. Jonathan had a list of the valuables that had been found in the van. "A good many thousand pounds worth," he said.

There were several pictures in exquisite frames that had been designed by Robert Adam. A bust of an eighteenth-century Countess Haldane by Louis Roubiliac. "Easy enough to sell on the Continent," said Jonathan. "A sixteenth-century Tudor chest. A bureau bookcase and a set of Hepplewhite chairs. A – er – tapestry." He hesitated. Cassie noticed beads of perspiration standing out on his forehead. He took a handkerchief from his pocket and wiped them away. "We've had a narrow escape," he said. She wondered if his gesture was due to a guilty realisation that he should have dealt with the insurance and the alarm long since.

"The report's due any day from the valuers," she said, feeling distanced from what had to be done. "When that arrives we'll know what treasures to rehouse within the alarm system."

Jonathan turned with a frown to the two policemen. "I'm afraid we've been a bit naive. Miss Neilson has been on to me about an alarm. But the problem has been – there's so much of the Hall. And we've never had a burglary. But Miss Neilson has made a suggestion." His nod to Cassie was an invitation to explain.

"My idea is to have a system covering only part of the building," said Cassie, thinking it was none of her business any more, wondering why she was allowing herself to be led on. "The cost of wiring the whole lot would be prohibitive. But we—" she swiftly corrected herself, "they – can cover the part that's on show to the public. The most valuable pieces will be there. As for the rest . . . All those surplus treasures," she looked directly at Jonathan, "why not send them to auction?"

Jonathan's face closed.

"Of course it's none of my business," she continued, speaking her thoughts out loud, "but if I were you I'd get the alarm technicians in tomorrow. There's a list of local companies on my desk. We've got the visitors' route mapped out now. You can go right ahead."

"You do know," said Jonathan, as though he hadn't heard a word she had spoken, "that most of the stuff you're consigning to auction will have been in the family for hundreds of years. We can't put everything on the visitors' route."

"They'll be bought by people who can afford to look after them. Some may go to museums. That's better than keeping them under dust sheets where nobody sees them." She was conscious of wanting to hurt him for the hurt that had been done to her.

The policemen both looked uncomfortable. The inspector cleared his throat, "I'm afraid you'll have to appear in court when these fellows are charged, Miss Neilson."

She nodded. "I'm prepared to do that. May I go now?"

Jonathan opened the door for her. She hurried out without looking at him and made her way towards the kitchen. As she emerged from the passage into the hall Lady Haldane was crossing to the stairs. She half turned, presumably at the sound of Cassie's footsteps, then swung instantly back and went swiftly up to the first floor.

Well, what did she expect? Cassie was glad she had run away. Jonathan's mother was the last person she wanted to talk to this morning. Although, she said to herself bitterly, her superior ladyship might have had the grace to thank me for saving the family a small fortune.

She told herself she mustn't get bitter. Where was her sense of humour? Go on, laugh. She couldn't. She made her way down the passage to the kitchen. It was all over. She must get her clothes, go home and that would be the end of it. She told herself she was glad she had put in that jab about selling the stately treasures.

So if she was glad why was she not laughing? Why did she feel shredded with guilt? A lump came up in her throat. Oh dear, she was going to cry. She sped past the kitchen door and found refuge in the little suite of rooms where she had lain in the bath last night. Tears rained down her cheeks. She wiped them away, but still they came. She collapsed onto the dreary little sofa and gave herself up to her misery.

Afterwards she went into the bathroom to wash her face. Somebody had removed the floating linen from the floor and mopped up the flood. A dry towel lay neatly folded over the edge of the bath. Surely they didn't think midnight baths were going to become a feature of her life! She forced herself to smile about it. Holding the smile on her face she opened the door and crossed to the kitchen.

The room was warm, steamy and smelled sweetly citric. Cook was making marmalade. She was greeted with cries of delight.

"We wondered what had happened to you."

"Are you all right? Is that a lump on your forehead?"

"I fell over once or twice getting down the drive," Cassie explained. "I've got a few bruises."

They were full of sympathy.

169

"I found your wet clothes. I've rinsed them out and hung them in the drying room." That was Janet Chadwick, one of the dailies from the village. "By the way, my sister wants to know, in case you're taking on more cleaning staff, if she could have a job?"

Cassie felt a surge of panic. She recognised she must say something. "Yes, cleaners will be needed."

"I can tell her?"

"Better not, for the moment." She must go home. She must keep out of sight until . . . She said in a bright, bright voice, holding that smile, "I only came over to talk to the police. I'm going back to the cottage now. I'll take my clothes with me."

Janet said, "Won't be a minute," and hurried out of the door.

Cassie sneezed.

The staff were concerned. "You haven't caught a cold, have you?" They offered aspirin, a glass of orange juice, advice. "Keep warm."

"It was freezing last night," said Mrs Bachelor. "I had to have an extra blanket. Just fancy, hailstones in April!"

"Go to bed, won't you dear?"

"You must be tired, anyway. You must have been up half the night."

She looked at them with sadness, thinking this was the last time she would see these good people who were her friends. She went to the door to wait for Janet, took the clothes, thanked her, and made her way down the passage towards the back of the house.

As she went up the narrow staircase that would take her via some convoluted corridors to the flat's side entrance, she looked round her, thinking that if she never came this way again at least she had had a rich experience that would stay with her all her life.

At the second staircase, just below the gallery, she became aware that something was different. She paused, looking round. Now she knew what it was. On this bare wall there had been a small but rather beautiful tapestry depicting knights in armour. Was it the one Jonathan mentioned in front of the police? She remembered the shine of perspiration on his brow. Was the tapestry extremely valuable? She was certain it hadn't featured on the insurance list.

She took the route through the long gallery, looking up at the pictures that she had planned to have cleaned, thinking how much more beautiful they would be when restored to their original bright colours. Then she climbed the stairs to the little tower room, opened a window, and leaning on the sill, looked out over the park for the last time, feeling the tears in her heart now, too heavy to shed.

Crabapple Cottage was empty. Leila had gone to the hospital. A little bit of manual labour is what you need, Cassie said to herself. That sneezing was nerves. And the weeping, mere self-pity. Hard labour's good for both. She decided to clean out the garage. She could feel the bruises, now. One on her shoulder, and a very painful one on her knee. She thought, trying to be philosophical, that she couldn't expect to get out of that lot unscathed.

She found some wooden boxes and packed away spanners, a hammer, two windscreen de-icers, jars of nails, slug-killer pellets. What was the slug-killer doing here? She was reminded that she would also have to clear out the garden shed. There was an axe in a corner behind some bean poles. Would Gerald want to keep it? A couple of saws. She laid them lengthwise across the wheelbarrow. Replacement tiles for the roof. She wondered if the new owner would like to buy it all as a job lot.

She stacked everything neatly and swept the floor with a garden broom. She discovered to her astonishment it was two o'clock. She went inside and made herself a tomato sandwich. She thought about Leila and Gerald sitting on their Hepplewhite chairs at the beautiful Georgian table in the flat and felt her nerves tighten again. Would they really be safe in the flat after she had been banished?

Leila walked in swinging her keys. At sight of Cassie she pulled up in surprise. "What are you doing here?"

"I came home to clear up." At her mother's startled reaction she reminded her that Gerald was to come out of hospital next week. "You did agree that he shouldn't have to move twice."

"Yes, of course."

They both went to the window and stood looking out. All over the garden lay a golden haze where the fat buds of the daffodils were bursting through their green casings. Leila heaved a huge sigh. Cassie gingerly fingered the lump on her forehead.

Leila exclaimed, "You're hurt!"

"I'm hurting all over."

Leila gave her a sharp look and Cassie turned away.

She went round the house with a pad and ballpoint pen, making an inventory. In one column she listed articles Leila might want to keep, in the other the furniture that would certainly go to auction. In a third column she listed carpets, curtains and pieces of furniture that were on their last legs and should be sent to the tip.

172

"Go through it carefully and make your decisions," Cassie told her mother. "Those columns are only suggestions."

Leila put the list down on the hall table as though it was burning her fingers.

"Don't you want to go?" She suddenly saw what had happened to her as a way out for her parents.

"I'll look at it after supper," Leila said. "And yes, I have faced up to going and that's what I want. Why should you think I've changed my mind?"

Cassie gave her a tense, uncertain smile. Leila's smile in return was uncertain too, but her eyes were very direct. "We're going to be happy at the Hall," her mother said.

Sick with apprehension, Cassie turned away.

They prepared supper together. Afterwards, Leila wandered from room to room saying, "It didn't seem real until now." And, "Do you realise, we've been here nearly all our married lives?" Cassie remembered that they had been living in a flat over the school. Then her grandmother died. "We moved in to look after Grandad because he wouldn't come to us. He wouldn't leave his garden."

Cassie jabbed a fork into one of the pork chops. "All good things come to an end," she said and wiped a tear away.

"Cassie, dear, are you crying?"

"No. I'm tired. And I might have got a chill. I'm going to have an early night."

She lay awake for hours. Had Jonathan departed for his London pad? History, as she well knew, had a habit of repeating itself. She weighed herself up against the Montcalm millions and felt a terrible despair.

Was everyone really – who was everyone? the village? the staff? the Haldanes' friends? – watching her, as Zoe had said? She thought of kind Mrs Bachelor. Of Edward.

Of the gardeners, the boys, whom she had thought were her friends. Had they been stealthily watching her all the time? Eventually, her mind and body tired out with speculation, she fell asleep.

She wakened the next morning with a sore throat and a streaming nose. It was almost a relief to know that the emotional muddle she had been in yesterday had after all a respectable root.

"You can't go to work," Leila said, dismayed. "I'll ring Jonathan."

"No. I'll ring him." She knew she had to talk to her mother some time. But not now. She returned thankfully to bed.

Leila called from the kitchen, "There's only one orange. I'll go out and get some more. And some juice, too."

Cassie went back to sleep. When she wakened, her pyjamas were soaked with sweat. Leila returned from shopping and wanted to telephone the doctor. Cassie refused to have him. "It's only a chill," she croaked. "All I need is rest, an aspirin or two, and lots of orange and lemon drinks."

Leila demurred but allowed herself to be persuaded. She did not go to the hospital that day or the next. "Jonathan must be worried," she said. "Shall I give him another ring?"

Cassie croaked, "You rang him?"

"No, dear," her mother replied. "You said you would. Did you not?"

She sneezed and that got her out of replying.

"There's one thing for certain," Leila said. "We can't move while you're in this state and neither can we bring Gerald back."

"No. But I'll be better soon."

It was in fact several days before Cassie began to feel anything like herself. Jonathan still hadn't rung. Why? What did they think she was doing for four days? It did occur to her that the staff could have told him she looked as though she might be going down with a cold.

Leila went off to the hospital. "Now promise me you'll stay in bed."

"I'm really feeling better," Cassie told her, meaning the chill had lost its grip, but her nerves were tight as violin strings. She wasn't certain lying in bed was the answer, now. With nothing to do there was too much time to think about the fact that she was a scheming bitch, ill-educated in the arts; a conniving whore from the servant classes. She put her head under the pillow in a useless endeavour to suffocate the whispers.

Leila hadn't been gone more than an hour when the telephone rang. The pillow failed to keep the ringing out as it had failed to keep the whispers out. The ringing stopped then started again. She put one foot out of bed. It could be that Leila was in trouble. The car might have broken down. Gerald might have taken a turn. She pulled her dressing-gown on and hurried down the stairs.

It was Colin Darcy on the other end of the line. "They told me at the Hall where to find you," he said. "Working at home, are you?"

"I'm confined to bed with a chill."

"Damn!"

"What's the matter?"

"I don't want to disturb you if you're ill," he told her. "The reason I'm ringing is because I've done some new designs and I'm having a crisis of confidence. I need your opinion. How ill are you? Could I possibly look in for a moment and leave the drawings with you? I won't stay long," he said, entreatingly. "Truly."

"I've probably got germs."

"You can get germs in the supermarket. I do quite desperately want your opinion, Cassie," he pleaded. "I've got a mental block. I know from past experience it's something that can be cured by getting another viewpoint."

She felt sorry for him. She had put him to a good deal of trouble. He was going to be disappointed if she said now she had no authority to commission his work. On the other hand, might not that well-born person, educated in the arts, whom Zoe would find to take her place, be enchanted by Colin's designs? She/he might be willing to carry on where Cassie left off. She recognised she, too, needed someone to talk to. The voices in her head – Zoe's voice in her head – was driving her mad.

"All right," she said. "I'll leave the front door on the latch. Walk in and up the stairs. I've promised my mother I'll stay in bed so you'll have to bring the designs to my room."

She trailed back. She was weaker than she had anticipated. One step, two steps, three steps, four. What on earth was she going to say to Colin? She shouldn't have allowed him to come. She should be packing up to get on the next train to London. If it was good enough for Jonathan to disappear it was good enough for her. It was 1989 all over again.

She crawled back into bed.

He climbed the stairs whistling. "Which way, left or right?"

"Left." She sat up, pulling her dressing-gown round her shoulders.

He stood in the doorway with a folder under one arm and a box under the other. "What a pretty place!" he said genially, looking up at the old oak beams in the ceiling, the diamond window panes, the uneven walls. "How I love old houses!"

She told him that it had been her grandfather's grace-and-favour dwelling. "He came to work as gardener's boy at the age of fourteen in 1913." She felt it was important to place herself. She felt she was writing the words in blood.

"Really?"

"Yes, really. I'm proof of the social mobility of the working classes."

He chuckled. "You say that as though you consider it a sin."

"Do you think it's a sin?" she asked, holding her breath, suddenly desperate for his opinion.

"I hadn't thought about it," he said. "It could be a subject for discussion over a pint in The Sow."

She joined in his laughter, glad that she had allowed him to come, bringing his good humour and his good common sense. She felt her nerves relaxing.

"Can I spread out my papers on the duvet?" He put the box down.

"Sure."

He opened the folder. She picked up the designs one by one and examined them. They were beautiful. She longed to show her enthusiasm. All she dared say was, "They're very nice," carefully keeping her response low-key. "What's in the box?"

He lifted the lid, took out some tissue paper and then, very carefully, a bowl. "Close your eyes." She obeyed. "Now open them to slits." He held the bowl up to the light. "What do you see?"

"Foxes?"

He was delighted. "That's what I wanted to know. If you could see foxes. And what else?"

"Towers? But they could also be . . . bells?"

177

His narrow, ascetic face widened into a delighted smile. "The important thing now is, do you like them? Do you think you could sell this kind of thing? You know what I've done, don't you?" And without waiting for an answer, "I've designed them specifically as a product of the Hall. The towers. The country conjured up by the suggestion of a hunt. I tried to make the designs as personal – I mean personal to the Hall – as I could." His dark eyes were eager.

She was full of anguish. She looked at his bright, hopeful face and looked away.

"Would you like me to go ahead?" His dark eyes were pleading. She could see how much this commission meant to him.

"I can't give you a firm order," she said. "I haven't discussed the idea with Jonathan, or sorted out space for a shop or an exhibition . . ."

The hope went out of his face. His shoulders slumped.

"You didn't mention business when you rang," she said, accusing in her despair. "You told me you had a crisis of confidence. You wanted to know if I liked the designs."

Downstairs the doorbell rang. He said heavily, "You've got another visitor. Shall I see who it is?" He left the drawings on the bed.

Footsteps on the stairs. A familiar voice. Cassie sank back against the pillows, quivering.

Jonathan came into the room first, half a head taller than the potter. He wore an air of being in charge. As though this was his house, and he had a right to be here. He said, glaring at her, "If you're well enough to be entertaining, I should think you'd better be at work."

"I'm afraid it's my fault," apologised Colin, gathering up his sketches and hurriedly putting the bowl back in its box. "I wanted her to see some designs I'd done for the pottery."

"Pottery?"

"I did tell you," muttered Cassie.

"Yes. You did mention it. But we hadn't discussed taking it on." Jonathan turned his attention to Colin, making no effort to hide the fact that he was waiting for the potter to go.

Colin, deeply embarrassed, tied the tapes, put the folio under his arm and said, "I was going, anyway." He backed towards the door.

"Thanks for coming." Cassie gave him a wan little smile. "I'll be in touch."

Jonathan stood as still as a statue until they heard the bang of the front door. Then he said, "I'd like to know what that fellow was doing here, since you're so sick you can't go to work."

"I told you. He wanted to show me his designs."

"He's got a pretty funny way of doing business. First, over dinner in his flat. And you'd only known him about a minute and a half. Now he comes to your house when you're alone and in bed."

"You're here when I'm alone and in bed," she flared. "How dare you tell me what I can and can't do?"

Without bothering to reply he reached into an inside pocket in his jacket and brought out a fold of thick paper tied with tape. "I've brought your contract," he said, speaking formally. "I want you to sign it. Both copies, please."

She gathered up all her courage. "Isn't there a problem?" she asked, not daring to speak Zoe's name out loud.

"You gave me your word."

"Jonathan . . ." Now was the moment to say that she had

no intention of being his 'bit on the side'. That anyway, no wife worth her salt would tolerate him having it off with his comptroller under the dust sheets on one of the many spare beds. She said, "Jonathan . . ." again, and stopped. She couldn't bear the way he was looking at her. She flared, "You'd no right to throw a visitor of mine out like that. And you'd no right—"

"Yes?"

"To walk in here."

"They told me you were ill. You hadn't bothered to let me know. I had to get the news from Mrs Bachelor that you might be ill. Might," he repeated. "Only because you sneezed in her presence. For a person in your position it's pretty irresponsible."

She collapsed against the pillows, deflated, realising they had been quarrelling like a couple of children.

A voice from the hall called, "I'm home, Cassie. How are you?"

Jonathan tossed the paper down on the duvet and went to the door. "She's in bed, Mrs Neilson. She's fine. I just dropped in to do a bit of business. I won't stay long enough to tire her."

A moment later Leila appeared in the doorway looking pleased. "Well," she said complacently, "you're obviously better, dear. Rosy cheeks again!" she exclaimed, misreading the colour in Cassie's face. "I'm so glad. I'll just take my things off." She disappeared to her own room.

Jonathan came back to stand by the bed. "I've got a pen," he said, and put a hand into an inner pocket of his jacket. "We need to have things on a proper footing."

"Jonathan—"

"Sign here," he said, speaking politely but firmly.

180

She took the pen in a hand that trembled. "I need to read it first."

Leila called from the stairs, "Come down to the kitchen, Jonathan, when you're ready, and I'll pour you a drink. Or would you rather have a cup of tea?"

He raised his voice, "A cup of tea would go down very well." Without a backward glance at Cassie he went through the door and down the stairs. After a moment or two laughter and chatter floated up from the kitchen.

Cassie looked down at the contract. How could she go back to the Hall? She thought of his lordship appearing at the top of the stairs then turning to run. She remembered Lady Haldane walking past her, looking straight ahead. And then there was Zoe, whom Jonathan had to marry in order to replenish the family coffers – as Leila had said, in the time-honoured way of the old families.

This is his way of holding me, Cassie thought. He thinks that he'll get away with having his cake and eating it. That I'll be his mistress. That one night stand was only the beginning of it. She sat staring into space, hearing without listening to the happy laughter and chatter that was floating through the house.

Ten minutes later Jonathan appeared in the doorway, smiling, as though there had never been a quarrel. "Right," he said confidently, "all complete?"

She wanted to throw the contract at him. She wanted to shout at him to go away. Then he gave her his endearing smile. "Jonathan," she beseeched him, "how can I go back?"

"Easily," he said. "You'll find things a bit sticky for a while, of course. But, yes, easy. You can handle anything, if you put your mind to it." He came right up to the bed, and bending down, kissed her firmly on the mouth. Then he picked up the pen that had slipped through her fingers and was lying on the duvet. He frowned down at the contract. "You haven't signed?" He handed her the pen. "Put your signature here. And there. There's no real reason why you should read it. It's quite straightforward. You need something to press on." He took a book from the bedside table and set it in front of her with the contract on top. "It merely says you're obliged to stay until the house is open to the public. And it mentions your salary. But we've agreed on that."

"Jonathan—"

"Sign," he ordered.

Numbly, Cassie obeyed.

"I'll get your mother's signature as witness." He went to the door and stood looking back at her, smiling.

"Thank you," he said.

Chapter Eleven

CASSIE wakened the next morning feeling different, knowing something had changed. And then she remembered she was contracted to work at the Hall with Jonathan until April next year. She gazed at the beamed ceiling, not seeing it, luxuriating in a new kind of contentment.

She went to the wardrobe and took out one of her newly acquired blouses, a cream silk that matched any one of the three skirts she had bought in Flyford. She slipped into the blue one, added a warmly lined paisley waistcoat, combed her hair out and after a moment's consideration left it free.

In the kitchen Leila was plugging in the electric kettle. She looked up with the lid in one hand. "You've made a miraculous recovery," she said, pleased and at the same time puzzled.

"I can't afford to be ill. There's too much to do." Cassie said briskly, "I'm going to get hold of the boys and move us into the flat, now."

"Cassie," Leila protested, "are you up to it? You've been ill."

"Huh? Well, it was mainly psychosomatic, you know. Must've been, or I wouldn't have made this miraculous recovery."

"Psychosomatic! You had a chill," protested her mother,

reaching for the coffee percolator. Cassie gave her a warm hug. "Look out! You could get scalded!" Leila put the jug down.

"By the way, I'm transferring the entire contents of my room to that spare room in the flat."

"Spare room? I like to think of it as your room, dear."

"Not my room. No. I'm not going to be with you forever. But while I'm here I may as well have my own furniture."

Leila said diffidently, "It's going to look a bit shabby beside – I mean—"

"Hardly up to the standard of the four-poster and the sitting room carpet? It won't be seen in juxtaposition with the glories of the sitting room," Cassie said, roughly quoting Jonathan on the kitchen. She crossed to the toaster and dropped in a slice of bread. "And by the way," she looked at her mother with her head on one side, "how does it happen that you always wanted a four-poster bed and I never knew?"

"Why should you know? It wasn't a possibility. But Jonathan has a way of getting things out of one." She admitted, looking embarrassed, "I've sometimes been surprised at what I've told him."

"He twists you round his little finger, doesn't he?"

Leila coloured. "If you want me to clear up here I'd better ring the hospital and tell them I won't be in today."

"You do that." Cassie whipped out the toast and began to butter it. "I'll get a skip sent round for the junk that's to be thrown out and I'll come back early to deal with it. And I'll order the van for the day after tomorrow, if that's okay with you."

Leila said bravely, "Yes. The day after tomorrow."

Cassie jumped into the Volvo and drove fast to the Hall.

184

There was no one around. She went straight to Lady Selena's room and began her telephone calls. First the skip to be sent to Crabapple Cottage. Next, she had to arrange for the hire of the van to transport the cottage furniture to the flat. She made a note to advise the boys, and another note for herself to remember she would be driving one of them in to Flyford to collect the van. Now, the security firm. She consulted the Yellow Pages.

The post arrived. There was a large envelope from the insurance assessors. She put it aside. Jonathan should be here when she opened it. All morning as she worked she kept glancing across at it, then away. She had said he might be surprised to see how much he was worth. She wanted to see his face when he looked at the total.

Nobody came to Lady Selena's room. Sometimes when she was talking on the telephone and making her notes she heard voices in the distance but none she could identify. She thought they probably belonged to staff. When Janet arrived with her mid-morning coffee her newly found confidence was ebbing.

"Has everyone left home, Janet?" she asked. "I haven't seen a soul this morning."

The daily put the tray down on a corner of the desk. Cassie noted immediately that there was only one cup.

"They're all in the small drawing room," Janet said. "What they call the 'snug'. They've been there all morning. Lady Tessa's there with her husband and those ill-tempered spaniels of hers. They're upsetting poor old Spicer no end. He's not himself at all. And how are you, dear? You've been poorly, and not surprising, after what happened."

After what happened? Cassie kept herself from looking at the woman's face, fearful that there might be a knowing look in her eyes. "I'm better, thank you Janet. Why don't you discreetly leave some doors open? Spicer might take the opportunity to get up here." She longed to ask if Zoe was there also at this family gathering.

"He does like you and no mistake," the woman said. "I'll see what I can do. I could tell Edward. He'll be taking their coffee in. Now drink yours while it's hot, dear."

Cassie picked up her mug, went to the window and stood looking down into the drive. There was no sign of Zoe's little car but an ancient Daimler was parked in front of the portico. She guessed it belonged to Jonathan's sister and brother-in-law. She finished her coffee and continued with her work.

She made telephone calls, checked lists, put letters up on the computer screen. There was a formal proposal to Susan Pannington whom she hoped might take on the teas. Mrs Pannington of the village cake shop had supplied her with her daughter's address.

She must also give Colin a firm commitment on his pottery. She made a note to search out Flora Barnard's hand-made chocolates shop next time she was in Flyford. Now, how did one go about getting a coat of arms on gift-wrapping? She added that question to the list she was making for Colin. And she would have to find a small copy of the Bevington coat of arms for him to work with.

She saved the text on the screen and sat back in her chair, frowning. Time to talk to Jonathan. But how could she get hold of him without walking into the lion's den? Edward, again. She found him cleaning silver in the butler's pantry.

"I'll give him your message," Edward said. "I'm going in to collect their coffee tray as soon as I've done with buffing up this jug. And I'm supposed to leave the door open for Spicer?" He gave her what her mother would call an old-fashioned look.

"Discreetly, Edward." Speaking very casually, she asked, "Is Miss Montcalm here?"

"No."

She turned hurriedly in case he should see the relief in her face.

Spicer wandered in to Lady Selena's room and laid his chin on Cassie's thigh. She fondled his silky head. "You are a clever dog, aren't you?" Spicer wagged his tail. "Now go and lie down there," she said, pointing, "while I get on with my work." Spicer ambled over to the window, flopped down on the carpet and closed his eyes.

When Jonathan came, the dog climbed to his feet and uttered a low 'Woof!' Cassie, who had been dialling, put the telephone down.

"Hey!" said Jonathan addressing the setter, pretending to be outraged. "Since when did you become my comptroller's guard dog?"

Spicer's head drooped and his tail moved uncertainly.

"Don't embarrass him," scolded Cassie. "He's hiding. Janet said your sister's dogs were giving him hell."

"So they were." They smiled at each other. "I'm glad to see you're on your feet again."

"It was the contract that did it. Thank you, Jonathan."

He came and stood beside the desk, looking down at her. His face was gentle. "It works both ways," he said. "I don't want to lie awake at night worrying that one day things will get too much for you."

"I promised," she said indignantly.

"And I know you were sincere. But promises aren't stone walls. Even if they were, life can throw up a battering ram

187

if it's a mind to." He became businesslike. "Edward said you wanted to see me."

She told him the final decision regarding the visitors' route was a matter of urgency. "I've made three plans. They vary only slightly. I want you to walk over the three routes with me."

"Cassie! Didn't I tell you that you were to decide?"

"You did, but I didn't accept it. I've got to have your agreement today or tomorrow because the security people are coming tomorrow to look around and give us an estimate. And I'd also like your mother's agreement because one of the variations takes in the private apartments."

"Private apartments?" Jonathan's brows rose.

"Why not? There's voyeurism in seeing where the owners actually sleep. If they'd agree I think it would add a certain cosiness, as well. That kind of thing is good for custom."

Jonathan took in a quick breath and expelled it slowly. "You think this is going to appeal to my mother?" he asked incredulously.

"No, I don't. I'm hoping you can talk her into it."

"You wouldn't like to try?"

"I don't think her ladyship's in the right mood to discuss it with me," she said, ignoring the mischief in his eyes, and looking down at her hands. "I think it would come better from you. Slippers by the bed. Perhaps a coat slung over a sofa – or, if she feels daring, her dressing-gown? By the way, were you conceived in the bed they're sleeping in? That would be great for tabloid publicity."

"Hell's bells! Come off it, Cass." Jonathan dropped his tall frame into the spare swivel chair and looked at her with an expression that was a mixture of awe and admiration.

"I mean it. We're going to be different. It's the little

differences that can put a house at the top of the list. For instance, your father, who's everybody's idea of an eccentric aristo, always being around. They're not going abroad. That's definite, isn't it?"

"Yes. They're not."

Somehow, she had known it would become a certainty. Known, since the night she had spent in Jonathan's bed, that they wouldn't dare turn their backs, now.

Jonathan rubbed a hand across his brow in that way he had. "Right. You're the boss. I just work here. I'll have a go at his lordship, but not the conception stuff. Neither of them would wear that. What's next?"

She picked up the envelope that was still lying on the desk. "I've got the valuations here. After we've made a firm decision about the visitors' route I want you to look at them. You've got to come to terms with the fact that something of value has to go to auction."

"No," said Jonathan.

She shrugged, pretending she didn't care that he preferred to take the Montcalm money with its attached strings.

"You said yourself—"

"I didn't know the extent of your difficulties. You haven't taken me into your confidence."

There was a pregnant silence. Then he said, "Let's go and inspect this route." He put the envelope from the assessors into his jacket pocket. "Where are your three plans?"

So she wasn't going to see the expression on his face when he saw how much he was worth! Cassie picked up the plans and handed them to him. He examined them thoroughly then without comment rose to his feet. "Let's go."

Spicer also rose to follow them. Jonathan paused in the

doorway. "You realise, don't you, that dog's attachment to you is going to cause serious trouble."

"Shall we send him back? What about those cruel spaniels your sister brought?"

"Oh heck, all right. We can take him with us."

She thought Lord Haldane was unlikely to come looking for his dog in any part of the house where he might cross her path.

Afterwards, Jonathan went off to the dungeon to read the valuations. He came to Lady Selena's room an hour later and laid them out on Cassie's desk. "I'm sick at the thought of the insurance," he said.

"No," she retorted. "You're delighted to see how much you're worth."

"The amount of money that's short at the moment is temporary. We can get over it. We'll never recover from the sale of precious items that have been in our possession for hundreds of years. Don't you see, Cassie," he said earnestly, "I'm in a pass-the-parcel situation. These treasures aren't mine to sell. I'm their temporary custodian. If I cash in I start a precedent. My son, and his son, will see a quick sale as an easy way out. And in the end Bevington Hall will be a shell. Stone walls and roof tiles. Don't you see?"

Yes, she did see that marrying into the rich Montcalm family was the way out of this fix. She again reminded herself of what her mother had said, that it was the time-honoured way aristocrats had, for centuries, been getting out of their difficulties.

"Let's go through the list," she said briskly, "and decide what we're going to move into the alarmed area."

It was late afternoon when the job was done. Bart and Eddie had been brought in to carry furniture from previously closed rooms. "It looks positively cluttered," Jonathan muttered, looking down the length of the long gallery that had acquired three more sofas, half a dozen small tables, two enormous – priceless, according to the valuers – vases of the Ming Dynasty which Cassie had positioned centrally on either side of the fireplace.

"I think I now know what you meant when you said you needed me to use my outside eye," Cassie told him. "It doesn't look cluttered to me. I thought it was – austere?" She turned the word over her tongue then discarded it. "Not quite that, but lacking in warmth."

"Warmth?" Jonathan repeated the word wryly, rubbing his chin, "I never thought of the long gallery as having warmth. Or any part of the house, for that matter."

She smiled, for she knew the love he had for the house. And now she knew that his father, in spite of what he said about draughts and the costs of upkeep, loved it too.

She was glad money wasn't going out of the coffers to pay for that expensive villa in the sun. And she was glad, in spite of the discomfort of their disapproval, that Jonathan's parents would be here when the Hall opened. A testy old earl and a countess in cashmere and tweeds was perhaps corny, but it was real.

That evening she returned early to Crabapple Cottage, needing an extra daylight hour to carry out the unwanted junk. She found a metamorphosis had taken place. Leila was seated on the old sofa in the living room looking spent.

Cassie scolded her. "You didn't have to do all this." The windows were bare of curtains. Unwanted rugs had been carried outside and put in the tip. She said exasperatedly, "I should have known I couldn't trust you to leave it to me."

"You've been in bed for days," Leila reminded her.

"I'm young and strong. But you're still getting over your accident. You've no right to do it, Leila," Cassie said severely.

"I wish you'd call me Mother," Leila complained.

"Sorry. When I finish this job I'll go back to calling you Mother. But not just now."

"Why not?"

"Because I'm living at home."

"Sometimes I don't understand you, Cassie."

"Yes, well, you're tired," she said, "and I've been away for a long time. You put your feet up and watch TV while I cook supper." Leila had been so busy she had forgotten to go shopping. Cassie took a chicken out of the freezer, decided it would take too long to defrost, and chose another frozen meal, more easily cooked. "What you need is a microwave," she said.

"I don't fancy a microwave." Leila sat down on a kitchen chair and obediently lifted her feet onto a hassock. "You never know what those scientists are putting into us in the way of damaging rays."

"I'll take my chances" She wished she could talk to her mother as a friend. Was that why she called her by her christian name? Because she now had no real friends? Real friends called each other by their christian names.

Next morning she found a note on her desk. "Very, very reluctant approval for the private apartments to be shown, but none the less, approval. So go ahead."

She looked up involuntarily at the portrait of Lady Selena on the wall. "Do you think that one day I'll have them eating out of my hand?" Lady Selena looked back at her with a secret smile.

By ten o'clock the security engineers had arrived with

their wires and cables, stepladders and interesting looking boxes. Cassie dealt with them, made sure they understood the map, then went to find the gardeners. She didn't want to approach Colin until she had established that her plan for a showroom in the stables would work.

She met the boys in the passage on their way to morning coffee. She joined them in the kitchen and outlined her plan to route the visitors through the archway on their way to view the gardens. "I want to see if it's possible to set up a showroom, even a working pottery, that they have to walk through. If the exhibits are right in their way there's always a chance people will be tempted to buy."

"I'll get the keys," Bart said in his obliging way, "and we'll go out now. I'll show you what's there and you can decide if you can use it."

An hour later she knew her plan was not going to be possible to implement without knocking a doorway out of the back of one of the stalls. "I don't see why not," said Bart. "It's not a mammoth job."

She glanced at her watch. "I'm going to see the potter now. I'll have to know how deeply he wants to get involved before we ask permission to mess around with the structure."

She drove into Flyford with a stop-over at Crabapple Cottage to ensure her mother was resting. There was a car parked outside the gate. A middle-aged couple were standing just inside the drive looking up at the cottage. They looked sheepish as they stepped out of the way. Cassie lowered the window. "Can I help you?"

"I'm very sorry," apologised the woman. "We've heard the cottage is for sale. We thought we'd come and have a look. Is it yours?"

Cassie told them it was not yet for sale. "But it will be." She told them it belonged to Lord Haldane and advised them to get in touch with him. "Are you local?"

The man produced a card. She looked down at it and switched the engine off. "Darcy?" She looked at them hard. The woman had the same narrow face and fair hair as Colin. "I'm Cassandra Neilson. I work at the Hall. Do you have a son who's a potter?"

Their faces lit up. "You know him?"

Cassie told them she was on her way to talk to him. "I'm hoping to sell his work."

They were delighted. Mrs Darcy said, "It was Colin who told us about the cottage. We want to move near to him so that I can help him."

It was on the tip of her tongue to ask how Colin knew the cottage was to be sold, then she remembered she had told him her parents were moving. They thanked her and said goodbye. She went on up the drive. Leila was not at home.

Cassie drove into Flyford and parked in the lane outside Colin's pottery. The door to the workroom was open but Colin was not there. She was about to make her way through the archway when he appeared, dressed in a big apron. He scowled.

"I'm sorry about what happened," she said in a rush. "You mustn't blame me. It wasn't my fault. You know I was sick."

"Sick!" he repeated, wiping the clay off his hands. "You were scared witless and who could blame you? Who the hell does he think he is?"

Cassie said solemnly, "He thinks he's the heir to Bevington Hall."

"Arrogant bastard. Does he own you, too?"

"I've said I'm sorry it happened. Let's go down to the pub and have a sandwich. I want to talk about selling your pottery."

"I think there are better ways to sell my pottery," Colin retorted, "than by getting involved with him."

"Like using your mother as a saleswoman?" She looked at him with her head on one side.

"Come again?"

"I met them looking at Crabapple Cottage. I think your mother might be the answer to the problem of your not being able to take time off to come up to the Hall to sell your work."

Colin looked wary.

"Come on, clean yourself up and let's go down to the pub. I want us to make some firm decisions before I put anything in writing."

"I got the impression you didn't have the authority." He looked at her with suspicion.

"I didn't. But I have now. Come on. Let's spread a bit of gossip round the public bar. It won't hurt you to have it known you've been taken up by the Hall. You may not realise it but it's going to be the biggest thing round here when it gets going."

"That's what they say."

"So, wouldn't you like to be involved?"

He didn't answer, but he had begun to undo the ties of his apron.

She thought, when he had run off upstairs to change, that family ties and village ties being the strength of this venture, how very nice it would be if Colin's parents bought Crabapple Cottage. Already the idea of the sale had taken on a different slant. A city man with money to spend on it, as Lord Haldane had said, conveyed a very different picture from that of the parents of the potter who was to sell his work on open days. She crossed her fingers and put a wish into the air that they would be able to afford the price.

Chapter Twelve

THE THREE gardeners went to Crabapple Cottage in the van and transported the Neilson belongings up to the Hall. Cassie whipped round the flat with a duster. Mrs Bachelor, unasked, appeared with furniture polish and cloths. "Not that they need much, even after having been under dust sheets for years," she remarked, looking admiringly at the lovely Georgian dining table. "Them housemaids from years ago knew how to polish and no mistake. Mind you, they had a housekeeper breathing down their necks, I've no doubt. And plenty of time and plenty of housemaids to share the work. His lordship can't afford them now, he says, and where would you find them, anyway?"

Cassie's narrow bed, the chest of drawers with its chipped paint and the old carpet looked like poor relations in the surrounding grandeur of the flat. "Can't they produce—" began Sid but she cut him off.

"I'm attached to my bedroom furniture," she said.

Leila fetched Gerald from the hospital next day. Cassie saw them from Lady Selena's room but she couldn't run down immediately because she had some important work running through the printer. When she managed to get downstairs he was crossing the portico between the great stone columns, leaning heavily on a stick.

"So here I am," he said jovially. "In at the front door as you advised."

"Quite right," she said, taking his arm. "Back stairs are for nocturnal, clandestine meetings or skulduggery."

"I'm long past the former and was never into the latter." He stood looking round the impressive and beautiful hall, at the scagliola columns, the curved staircase swinging up to either side of the landing, at the gilt-framed portraits of the family. "Now, do I have to climb those stairs?"

Cassie had no intention of telling him he could reach the flat via the kitchen passage and a narrow stairway at the end that would bring him out near the tower. "We'll help you," she said. They went to the foot of the staircase. She took his stick and she and her mother positioned themselves on either side of him, holding his forearms. It was a slow climb.

Cassie said, as they made the landing, "I'm going back to work. I can't spare the time to escort you any further. Will you be all right?" She wanted to leave them alone in their new premises. Gerald, for all he had been warned, was going to be somewhat taken aback by the flat's grandeur. She thought they should be alone while he came to terms with it.

Jonathan appeared soon after she returned to her desk. "Somebody called Darcy has put in an offer for Crabapple Cottage," he said, frowning. "Is it that fellow?"

"No," said Cassie. "Not 'that fellow', who by the way makes the most beautiful pottery." She nearly said he would have seen one of Colin's bowls if he hadn't been concentrating on throwing him out the day they were both at the cottage. She thought better of it. "According to the contract I signed, I have the authority to sell it here at the Hall on open days."

Jonathan grunted.

"That sounded like your father. Are you going to be like him when you're growing old?" Heavens! The confidence that contract had given her!

Jonathan glared at her. "Now, about this Darcy."

"The offer for the cottage would have been made by his parents." Cassie told him how she had met them viewing the building from the gateway.

"They've inspected it now."

"I do hope you'll accept their offer because Mrs Darcy could be an asset. She could sell the pottery in one of the loose boxes under Tom's old flat."

"Loose box into pottery showroom? Come off it, Cassie."

"You're paying me for my expertise," she reminded him. "I see a tarted up loose box as a quaint background for the pottery. And by the way his name's Colin. He'd like you to call him that, I'm sure. I'll need to have a doorway knocked in the wall at the back so people can walk through on their way to the gardens."

"Walk through the stables? What's wrong with the drive? We don't have to knock a hole in that."

"Because to take people straight down the drive would be false economy. I want them to walk past the pottery and be seduced by Colin's beautiful pots. We're going to get a percentage of the sales. And come to think of it, if his mother's working for him, as I believe she might, we won't need to pay her."

"What a sharp businesswoman you are!"

"I'm here to make you money, remember?"

He straightened. "So, that's great. Yes, it's quite a good offer this chap's parents—"

"Colin's parents."

"Colin's parents," he intoned the name dutifully, but his eyes were smiling, now, "have made for the cottage." He stood looking down at her for a moment then said gravely, "I'm sorry, Cassie. I didn't realise – I'd have got the contract drawn up before if I'd known you were—"

"Scared," she said. "That's the right word."

He seemed bemused. For a moment she thought he was going to say something important, or at least significant. She waited. He turned abruptly and went out of the room.

That afternoon she went to the cottage with Bart and Sid. While she cleared out the remaining rubbish they loaded the discarded furniture into the van and drove off to the storage unit attached to the Flyford auction rooms. Cassie walked through the empty cottage feeling nostalgic and inevitably, sad. The rooms that she had known since childhood looked lonely and strange. There were squares of unfaded paper on the walls where pictures had hung. She noted that someone had swept the floors and hoped Leila had not done it.

So, it was not to be, she said to herself, remembering how she had rushed home from Los Angeles to fight for this, her parents' home. "That's life," she said out loud. She squared her shoulders. "You win some, you lose some." Cassie recalled herself saying that when she had lost the battle for an updated kitchen in the flat, and thought maybe that would be her motto for the future. She looked at her watch. There were several matters to attend to in Flyford. She would see Colin at the same time.

She locked the cottage and drove into the town.

"Go on with your work," she said, finding Colin in his big apron at the potter's wheel. "I only came to tell you I'm definitely going ahead with the pottery and I'm going to set up your showroom in the stables. So it's up to you to pile up the stock between now and April next. Have you asked your mother if she'd take over the selling?"

He nodded. "She's keen to do it. In fact, it's her dream come true. You know how mothers are with sons?"

Cassie didn't like to think about that. "I'm glad," she said. "Your family will be taken to the hearts of the locals if you and they get involved with the Hall." She was amused and astonished at herself. At the confidence in her.

Colin stood back from his wheel, looking at her quizzically. "You're a different person today."

Yes. She had been different ever since signing the contract; ever since knowing there would be no repeat of 1989.

"Would you like to meet me at The Sow tonight?"

"Love to," said Cassie, "but today my parents moved in. They're my priority for this evening."

"Tomorrow?"

She hesitated.

"I get the message. The Honourable Jonathan says 'hands off'. That's it, isn't it?"

"I believe," said Cassie stiffly, making herself say it, though every word hurt, "that he's to be married. To a woman called Zoe Montcalm. You may have heard of Lord Montcalm. He's very rich," she said pronouncing the words distinctly. "It would be a great help to him, of course, to have some of those millions." There, it was out. Another hurdle jumped. And her new confident persona had survived.

"If he's going to be that rich, why is he opening to the public?"

Cassie stared at him.

"Let it pass," said Colin.

Driving back to the Hall Cassie thought, Indeed, why should they open the Hall if Zoe has a dowry sufficient to pay for its upkeep? She tried to put the question into the back of her mind but it wouldn't go away.

That evening she finished work early and went straight along to the flat. The outer door was ajar and opened to her touch. She found her parents in the big drawing room. It had taken on a mix'n'match look. Leila had kept her little tables and footstools. They didn't, after all, look incongruous. The sheepskin pouffe she had picked up on a holiday in Portugal years ago and was now shedding its stuffing stood against the grand Knole sofa wearing an apologetic air. Familiar pictures were on the walls. Two watercolour scenes of the Lake District that Cassie had bought on a school trip. Some unpretentious prints. Only the curtains seemed out of place. They looked what they were, good enough for the nursery thirty years ago.

"I don't dare take them down to wash them," Leila said. "I suspect they'd fall to pieces. When will the new material be here?"

"Any day now. Are you up to getting out your sewing machine?"

"She's dead anxious to get to work," said Gerald. Leila picked up his hand and kissed it.

"Good for you. I'm going to unload all kinds of jobs onto you when the curtains are done."

"I'm delighted to be involved."

The door to her parents' bedroom was standing open. The four-poster in its Colefax and Fowler drapes dominated the room so that you scarcely noticed the rest. Her eyes roved over the old sofa, the elegant kneehole dressing table, and standing before it the piano stool that Leila had bought in a sale; the oak chest where she stored miscellaneous woollens in the summer. Cassie scarcely saw any of these. The bed dominated. Queen Elizabeth could have slept here.

Next door she might have stepped into her old room at Crabapple Cottage, except that the windows were more than twice the size. Here, there were no curtains. That wouldn't worry her. Summer was coming and no one was going to look in except the birds. Nothing had changed in the bathroom. Back in the drawing room she told her mother, "I'll paint it one day when I get the time."

"I'll paint it," retorted Gerald when she told him. "There's no hurry."

So, after all, it was only the dining room that was grand and they would get used to that. They agreed they had reached a reasonable compromise.

Spring was merging into summer. All over the park the huge chestnut trees were coming into leaf. From the window of Lady Selina's room Cassie would see her parents emerge from the portico to stroll round to the gardens or the park. She persuaded Bart to transport a garden seat to the shade of one of the big trees so that Gerald could rest before the slow trek home.

Rather to her surprise she was enjoying having her parents on the premises. She found it conveninet to run along to the flat and fix herself a sandwich for lunch. She could check that Gerald was all right when Leila was out shopping or at a Women's Institute meeting in the village.

One evening when she was peeling the potatoes for supper she thought she heard a scratching at the door. She opened it to find Spicer sitting on the mat. The old dog trotted in.

"Now I'm going to be in trouble," Cassie addressed him ruefully. "You really mustn't do this." She led him back into the passage and told him to go home. He squatted on his haunches, panting up at her, his old eyes shining. It was no good. He had no intention of returning to his owner. Cassie removed her apron and walked with him.

Halfway down the stairs it occurred to her that perhaps this was meant to happen. The rift between herself and Jonathan's parents had to be mended. It was ridiculous that they should continue to avoid her. She experienced a moment of sheer terror as she came close to the door of the small drawing room. But I'm in charge, she reminded herself. I'm the boss. They can't do a damn thing to me; I've got a contract. She drew a deep breath, lifted her head high, then knocked. Spicer nosed the door open and wandered in. Cassie followed. Lord and Lady Haldane were sitting at a card table, the cards fanned in their hands. They looked round, their faces rigid with disbelief.

"I've come to bring Spicer back," Cassie said in a voice that was higher than she would have chosen to use. "He was scratching at the door to the flat. He wouldn't go of his own accord."

"You encourage him." Lord Haldane put his cards down and glared at her.

"Please believe me, I don't."

He picked up a card and stared at it.

Cassie pulled in another deep breath and went on, "I want to say that I find it very uncomfortable working here with your disapproval. Since our paths are bound to cross I'd like to be on good terms with you."

"You've got a nerve," said the earl, looking up again.

Cassie noticed with a tremor of apprehension that the card he held in his hand was an ace.

"I'm sorry if you disapprove of me," she said, "but I'm contracted to put the Hall on its feet. I'm going to be here at least into next April."

Her ladyship snapped, as though this was the cause of the dissension, "I am not willing to have the public peering into my bedroom."

"And where do you think I'm going to lie down if I want a rest after lunch?" Lord Haldane glared at her.

"You don't have to give permission—"

"Jonathan said you didn't need my permission. You make the decisions." Lady Haldane glared in her turn.

Cassie lifted her shoulders, held her hands palm up. "What can I say?" When they made no attempt to reply she added, "It was my understanding that the more money I can pull in the better pleased you'd be. I do know what attracts people. But if you don't want—"

"And rock concerts!" burst in Lord Haldane. "Do we have to descend to that?"

"If you want to make real money, yes."

There was a long silence, then, "Just leave my dog alone," Lord Haldane muttered and returned his attention to the cards.

Cassie backed through the door, closing it quietly behind her. She was thoughtful as she made her way back up the staircase and along to the flat. I believe those two sillies were waiting for me to make the first move, she said to herself. Hell's bells, I don't know what's come over me. I never thought I'd be talking to the noble lord like that. She took a little dancing step, and then another. Are they actually scared of me? Me, the gardener's granddaughter?

Suddenly it seemed extremely funny that she, whom they now accepted as being in charge, should once have been the gardener's granddaughter!

The old setter continued to wander into Lady Selena's room. "You're not my dog, Spicer," she said again one morning, sitting on the floor with her arms round his neck, nuzzling her face into his soft coat. "You know that. Now, why don't you go back and keep that grumpy old earl company?"

Spicer licked her forehead and wriggled up against her shoulder. It was then she became aware of another presence and looked up to see her ladyship in the doorway. Cassie clambered to her feet. Deliberately ignoring the dog Lady Haldane said, "I've been doing some research, as you know. I've found a recipe headed Lady Alicia's Fudge." She indicated a sheet of parchment she held in her hand. "Lady Alicia was the wife of the ninth earl. I've consulted Cook who tells me she isn't a great expert on fudge, but all the same she seems to think it may be interesting. She's going to try it out this afternoon. Had you thought of selling fudge?"

Cassie smiled at her. Lady Haldane did not smile in return. Her head was high, her face expressionless. She put the recipe down on the desk and Cassie, recognising it less as a recipe than as an olive branch, read it through. "I think it would be lovely," she told her, "though perhaps expensive to make with all that cream going in. It may mean we'd have to charge too high a price. Unless, of course, we could get the cream at a discount. Do you think one of your local farmers would cooperate?"

"You'll remember the Sheldrake family."

"Yes. I went to school with the children."

"They've leased Home Farm."

"How very convenient," said Cassie. "If the recipe proves outstanding we could get away with charging a high price for it. People will always pay for quality. Lifted out of the range of ordinary fudges, it could become famous." Her mind was already racing ahead. She could see tins, or boxes, with a wrapper designed by Colin incorporating the Haldane coat of arms. Or, instead of the coat of arms, a cameo picture of the Lady Alicia?

"I'll ask her to bring some of it up as soon as it's set," said Lady Haldane in a not unfriendly voice. She turned her attention to the dog. "Come on, Spicer," she said. Spicer stood up and reluctantly followed her out of the room.

Cassie looked at the open doorway and felt laughter bubbling up inside her. "Lucky old you," she muttered. "You've got a village girl with all the right contacts."

During the afternoon she drove in to Flyford and sought out Flora Barnard's chocolates shop. If they were going to sell Lady Alicia's fudge, then the same wrappers and boxes, or nearly the same, could be used for Flora's hand-made chocolates.

Flora, delighted to be involved, took Cassie into the back of the premises and showed her trays of chocolates hardening. "I can't tell you how pleased everyone is that you've taken over." She was a pretty girl with long dark hair that was today caught up in a white cap. "Hygiene," she said wryly. "I look a bit of a guy in this but I have to wear it while I'm working. Regulations. I'd be simply thrilled to have my chocs go out with the Haldane coat of arms."

"Could you supply enough for us, and still keep your shop going? I'd have to be sure of sufficient stock. There's a lot

207

of word of mouth in this business. If people come looking for chocs and we've run out they don't hand the word on. And what's more, they leave disappointed. I can't afford that." It was one of her shibboleths. Nobody, whatever they came for, should ever leave disappointed.

"I'm nothing if not responsible now, Cassie. You're remembering I was a bit wild when we were growing up," Flora said. "But then, so were you." She looked at Cassie with a knowing twinkle, waiting for her to react.

Cassie saw the intimacy not as a jibe but as a reminder of why she had gone to America. It was the first time anyone had referred to it as directly. She recognised, with a sharp little jolt to the senses, that in the position she had taken on she could not afford the intimacy of 'all village girls together'. She said, "We all grow up. I'm glad you've made a success, Flora. I'll be in touch."

She thought, as she walked back up the High Street to talk to Colin about wrapper designs, that in answering Flora's knowing smirk she had reacted a little like Lady Haldane. I'm learning, she thought. But I mustn't get haughty. There had to be a middle way for someone who was no longer a village girl and yet who had not been integrated into the life of the Hall.

The first wave of loneliness swept over her.

Chapter Thirteen

THE LONELINESS grew. Cassie guessed Spicer was under careful surveillance for he did not again appear in Lady Selena's room. She missed Jonathan's calling in. Where was he? She knew that sometimes he went to London. At other times, when he disappeared with Zoe, she had to recognise that he must be spending the night at the seat of the Montcalms – Lethbridge Place. And why not she would ask herself, if he's going to be their son-in-law?

When she had had no contact with him for some days she was glad to go to the flat in the evenings and chat with her parents. Wrong again, she admitted wryly. But she did miss the company of young people. The older village folk treated her as they always had, with kindness, but the young avoided her.

The fudge recipe was tried and pronounced unanimously the most tasty, the richest, the best fudge ever. Cassie talked to Owen Sheldrake at Home Farm and persuaded him to give her a small discount on cream. She was going to have to charge a little over the top if she kept faithfully to the recipe. She decided to try it for a month and see how sales went. If the customers were frightened away by the price she would just have to offer a meaner product. She reminded herself of what she had told Lady Haldane, that quality usually won.

And why not produce a tiny booklet, no more than two inches square, with a gold cover and two little pages revealing a potted biography of Lady Alicia herself? Was there anything about Lady Alicia that was interesting? She wondered how much Lady Haldane knew about her, or if she could find out about her, and if so, would she be willing to write a hundred words for the booklet?

Several times, in the evenings, she went to the pub with Colin. His parents were moving into Crabapple Cottage within weeks, as soon as the contract was signed. One night he said musingly, sitting across the little oak table from her in the saloon bar of The Sow, "I never expected to be designing chocolate and fudge wrappers. I'm not sure you're good for my career, Cassie, but at least I can now see my way to paying the butcher and baker."

"I'm glad," she told him, eyes twinkling. "Sometimes we have to compromise."

He regarded her thoughtfully, fingering his glass. "That's what you've done, haven't you, compromised?"

"What do you mean?"

"It's an odd life you're living up there at the Hall," Colin said. "Do you ever go out with village people? Some of them must be old friends. I know you went to the village school."

She wondered what else he knew. "No one has asked me out," she said lightly, glancing up at people coming in through the door, hoping to divert him by not taking his question seriously. But he was not to be diverted.

"I can understand that," he said. "I can imagine you don't fit in, you with your big Volvo."

"It's not my car. It belongs to the estate."

"Nevertheless, you're the only one who drives it. Anyone

could be forgiven for thinking it was yours. That, and the fact that you're living at the Hall, hand in glove with the noble lord. You're neither fish, fowl, nor good red herring, are you?" His eyes were shrewd as he waited for her to answer. "You're a curiosity, did you know that? I'll bet the staff talk about you non-stop."

She looked down into her glass. "I'm sure they've got more interesting matters to concentrate on."

"I listen to gossip."

"Then you shouldn't," she retorted sharply.

"Oh, I don't know. Gossip's the breath of life. If you reckon I've got it wrong you could put me right." When she didn't reply he went on, "You see, I'm still sweating from my encounter with the Honourable Jonathan. So, in view of the way he threw me out, I'm inclined to believe the gossip. There's something between you two, isn't there?"

"Purely business," Cassie responded, putting on her brisk voice, wishing she hadn't come.

"I'm not going to believe that," Colin said. "I think the answer to your lack of social life is that people know you're tied up with him. And nobody's going to tread on the toes of the heir to the Hall. True or false?"

"People know no such thing," she answered hotly. Then she drew a calm expression onto her face and using a carefully controlled voice added, "I've already told you he's to marry the daughter of Lord Montcalm."

"Yes. I know about that, too. But he wants you. That's the gossip." Colin leaned across the table, touched her wrist and added, "Come clean, Cassie. You may as well. It's said you were hauled off and sent to America. If that's so, what are you doing back again, in the heart of the cauldron, so to speak?" There was just a touch of dangerous malice in Colin's eyes.

She said carefully, "I'm sorry Jonathan upset you. But he was understandably concerned about me. He wanted me back on the job. He felt that if I was well enough to be entertaining you I was well enough to be at my desk. Look here, Colin, you're going to do work for the Hall. Let's be friends." She was feeling desperately vulnerable. She felt he had peeled away some of her outer protective skin, and he had no business to.

He was thoughtful for a moment. Then he said, "You haven't answered my question."

"It was asked for the wrong reasons. I'll admit you had a bad start, but you'll like Jonathan when you know him."

He peered into her glass. "Have some more wine?"

"Thank you. But it's my turn." She reached into her handbag, gave him some coins and he went off to the bar. She didn't really want any more to drink. She was afraid it might lower her defences, but she needed space while she got herself in hand.

Zoe's little car was more and more often in the driveway. Sometimes she arrived in the morning and stayed all day.

The date of the burglars' trial was fixed. Cassie was summoned to give evidence. One morning there was a brisk tap on the door. Advancing into the room, Jonathan's mother said in a businesslike voice, "About your court appearance. It may be a little bit of an ordeal, going into the witness box and facing those rogues. I shall come with you. I've arranged for Tom to drive us."

Cassie was so astonished at her offer that she could only look at her blankly.

"The least I can do," said Lady Haldane, "is to accompany you."

It was on the tip of Cassie's tongue to offer her thanks and add that she was quite happy to drive herself. "Thank you m'lady," she said instead. "You're very kind." Now, there was something she could do in return. "By the way, there's a portrait of you in one of the disused rooms. I'd like to put it on the visitors' route."

"Whatever for?"

Cassie found it easy to smile at her. "Personal touches are so important. People like to be able to say, 'Ah! That's Lady Haldane. I saw her in the garden.' "

Her ladyship said brusquely, "I doubt if they'd recognise it. It was painted a long time ago." But she looked pleased.

When she had gone Cassie sat there bemused. They don't like being beholden to me, but they're grateful. I suppose that's the message. And escorting me to court in the Rolls is, in their opinion, a way they can show it.

Jonathan's sister was now turning up frequently at the Hall. Was she showing support? Or was she keeping watch? She arrived one warm summer's day in Lady Selena's room preceded by Edward carrying a tray bearing a china teapot and pretty cups. In spite of the balmy air she was wearing a hacking jacket over an ill-fitting and rather ancient skirt, with, incongruously, a very elegant and obviously brand new buttercup yellow blouse. "May I join you?" she asked and without waiting for permission sat down in the seat on the other side of the desk.

"Mind if I pour?" She proceeded to fill Cassie's cup. "You don't object to my being frank?" With the teapot held dangerously in the air she looked straight at Cassie with candid eyes.

"Feel free," Cassie said. In the pit of her stomach a trembling began.

"Forgive my interfering. That's how I am. A bit of an interferer." The tiniest flicker of a smile. "You do know, don't you, that if Jonathan doesn't get this money from Lord Montcalm you can't go ahead?"

Cassie stopped with her teacup halfway to her lips.

"I want to put one or two things into the front of your mind," Lady Tessa went on, without waiting for Cassie to reply. "There are people here who think you're after power. And others who say you're here for revenge. I'm not asking you for an answer. It's not the kind of thing one expects an honest answer to. I'm just telling you what people are saying."

So, Colin was right. People were talking. She was exploding inside yet even as she cried, "That's outrageous!" she was remembering having asked herself that very question on her first day back.

Tessa let a moment go by. She handed the plate of biscuits to Cassie, taking one for herself on the way. She bit into it thoughtfully, chewed, then looked up again. "Frankly, I wouldn't marry a man who had his comptroller on the premises and felt free to bed her. There are, after all, a great many beds in the Hall. Very tempting, that."

After the first moment of renewed shock Cassie's mind went into overdrive. She decided to be blunt, too. "You're saying he has to marry Zoe in order to get the money?" When Tessa did not immediately answer, only looking at her thoughtfully, she added, "They're holding a gun to his head?"

Tessa picked up a pen from the desk and began to doodle on a small notepad that lay beside the computer.

Cassie could see from her deliberately absorbed air that she wasn't going to answer, so instead she said, "Zoe doesn't feel confident with me in the house? There's a problem here, Lady Tessa—"

Without looking up from her doodling Jonathan's sister said in a voice that was both sharp and brusque, "Tessa, please."

"Tessa, I have a contract binding me until April next year."

"The contract is rather a problem," Tessa conceded speculatively. Then, with an air of tossing the problem into the ring she went on, "Jonathan seems to have burned his bridges."

"I suppose he has. Is this what you're saying – he can't get his hands on the Montcalm money until next April when I go? And he needs it now?"

Tessa picked up another biscuit and ate it thoughtfully. She drank her tea. Cassie waited. After a long silence Tessa pushed her chair back and stood up, smoothing her hacking jacket over her considerable bottom. Speaking down at Cassie from her superior height she said, "We're very grateful to you for what you did in foiling the burglars. I hope you will understand that my parents find it difficult—"

"Anyone can say thank you," said Cassie lifting her head.

"Not anyone," said Tessa. When Cassie thought she was going to refer to the Neilsons' standing compared to her own she surprised her by adding, "Not people who feel under threat." She moved to the door then turned and added, not at all as an afterthought but as though this might really be what she had come for, "That was a bloody silly thing to do, to get into my brother's bed." Then she left and Cassie could hear her heavy footsteps going down the passage.

So Jonathan couldn't marry Zoe while she was on the premises. And he couldn't get the Montcalm money until he married her.

What a fix!

Again that telling remark of Colin's came into her head. 'If he's going to be that rich, why is he opening to the public?'

Why, indeed!

I'll have to talk to Jonathan about money, she said to herself. One thing I haven't done is treat this as a normal job. And I know why. I haven't asked for a budget because Lord Montcalm and his daughter have been in the way.

Things were moving ahead fast. The boys, between them, had made plans for a show garden. Eddie brought them in for Cassie to vet. There was to be an area given over to spring bulbs and backed with azaleas and rhododendrons. There was to be an autumn garden designed to take shrubs whose leaves made a late blaze as they changed colour. And in between them, the summer garden would be planted with annuals.

"You're in charge here," she had said, handing the plans back to Eddie, smiling at him as he stood on the other side of the desk. "Gardens are not my field."

"There's a lot of plants to be bought."

She experienced a quick intake of breath. "Of course," she

said, speaking, she hoped, as though there was no problem about money. "Have you got an estimate?"

Eddie produced a list. "It's just an idea," he said diffidently and Cassie knew that something had been showing in her face. "The gardens are perfectly all right as they are. We can cut those yews that are threatening to block out the Florentine statues and make an impressive walkway. The white gardens are still thriving."

She noticed that his voice faded away on the final words. She said, "You mean all right for the family but perhaps not impressive enough for paying visitors?"

"Got it in one." Eddie gave her a mournful grin. "I did get the impression when I talked to you about opening the gardens that there'd be money going for plants."

She remembered saying, 'We either do nothing about them or we spend money and make them worth the cost we must charge for a visit.' There hadn't been a discussion since.

"I think we must spend on them," she said now. "Since you plan to make them seasonal, people will very likely come to see the house once and the gardens two or three times. I think it's a good idea." She looked down at the formidable list, turned the sheet over and carefully hiding her dismay at sight of the total said, "I'll need a little time. I'll get back to you as soon as I can."

Wandering along the visitors' route as she did daily, Cassie saw a stain on the wall of the narrow stairway that people would use after visiting the chapel. She frowned, trying to recall if she had seen it before. She didn't think she had, but then there were so many stains on walls. This one would have to be dealt with.

She remembered the small tapestry hanging on the wall

of a staircase, the one that she had assumed, by watching Jonathan's reaction when reading out his list of the items nearly stolen, must be valuable. Should it not, then, be included on the route? She went to investigate. Yes, the tapestry was back in place.

She examined it closely. It couldn't be valuable, for it had not been on the list given to her by the insurance assessors. Knights in armour, war horses, a forest, high stone walls. The colours were beautiful. Forest greens and the soft grey of stone. When her tea was brought that afternoon she asked Mrs Bachelor to send Bart up.

She took him to the stained wall and showed him what she wanted done. Then she showed him the tapestry. "I'll have to get my stepladder," he said.

"I'll wait here for you."

Between them they took it down. "It's more frail than it looks," Bart said. "It may be very old."

She carried it carefully. Bart followed with his stepladder and between them they hung it so that it covered the mark on the wall.

Cassie thanked him and went back to her office. That night it rained, and all the next day. The following morning Jonathan appeared in the doorway to Lady Selena's room looking distressed. Without pausing to greet her he exploded, "Did you move that Crusaders tapestry?"

"Crusaders? Oh, you mean the one on the stair wall above the chapel. I did. I found a stain on the wall. It didn't look very nice. And besides, that's such a fine tapestry I thought it ought to be on show."

Jonathan looked at her with angry eyes. "Don't you know what a stain on a wall means?" Taken aback by his anger she could not immediately reply. He went on, "It means damp has begun to come through. Last night's deluge brought water trickling down the wall and the tapestry was soaked. That tapestry is very valuable."

"Oh-h-h!"

"It shows the storming of Jerusalem in 1099." His words emerged as though they were searing his throat. "It's been in the family for God knows how long. Christie's man couldn't date it."

She gazed at him, appalled. "I'm sorry," she managed. "Terribly sorry." There was no point in saying it hadn't occurred to her that the stain was dried out damp. "I'm just terribly sorry," she repeated. "What can I do? Who can I take it to?"

"My mother's already dealing with it." He half turned away, as though he could not bear to look at her.

"I'll apologise to your parents, of course." Her confidence that had been so high for so long now hit rock bottom. The carefully built up relationship with Lady Haldane would be destroyed. Zoe's callous indictment darted into her mind, 'You don't know anything about antiques.'

"If a tapestry as valuable as that one is ruined," said Jonathan, "an apology isn't going to go very far to putting things right. I'd advise you to keep your distance." He added, "I thought you had a feeling for the house."

She couldn't bear his condemnation, and more than that, his blame. Her temper flared. "If you had a feeling for the house you would have investigated that stain. You're not being fair. If it's so valuable, what was it doing on a back stairway? Why wasn't it put on the visitors' route?"

"Because I've had it in mind to sell it." Jonathan spoke slowly and heavily. "But I've never put the idea to my parents. It's our oldest possession and the most valuable."

219

"Why wasn't it on the valuation list?" Cassie asked sharply.

"Because I didn't want it there until I'd sorted things out. The insurance would have skyrocketed."

"So you took a chance on its being stolen and losing it altogether?"

Jonathan looked at her as though he hated her.

"That's the tapestry the thieves tried to get away with, isn't it?" Cassie looked down at the desk because she could not bear to see the expression in his eyes.

"Yes," he said.

"Dear lord! You were walking a tightrope."

"What else do you do with something that's priceless if you can't afford the insurance?"

"Pretend it isn't there? Oh Jonathan!" Cassie's hands went to her face.

When she looked up he had gone. She heard his slow footsteps going towards the stairs.

She put in a miserable day. That night after supper she slipped out of the side door. The sky was cold and clear, the moon almost full. She wished she had someone to talk to, to whom she could safely let off steam. It was true what Colin said, she was isolated. She didn't belong anywhere, now. Not in Los Angeles because she had become Anglicised again. Not with her parents because she had grown up. Not in the village because, as Colin so truly said, she was neither fish, fowl, nor good red herring.

She walked slowly across the park, feeling the damp from the grass coming through her light shoes, not caring. She hugged her arms across her front, getting some relief from the punishing cold. Why had Jonathan not told her about

the tapestry? She was baffled by what he had done. Why
had his parents never mentioned it?

Her mind ran round and round until, after a while, little
points began to show themselves. Lord and Lady Haldane
wanted Jonathan to marry Zoe. Again, that comment of
Colin's came into her mind, 'If he's going to be that rich
why is he opening to the public?'

Money invested gives control, she said to herself. Was it
control that Lord Montcalm wanted? Control of Bevington
Hall for himself, and for Zoe? She already knew Jonathan
was more of a country gentleman than a businessman. He
would know that, too.

Did the sale of the tapestry represent his freedom?

She walked to the edge of the park and leaned over the
fence looking into the garden of Crabapple Cottage that her
grandfather had built up with such love and care. She felt the
ties of the distant past tugging at her. She thought of how
generations of her family had shown not only allegiance
to the incumbents of the Hall, but genuine affection. And
she thought about how the Haldanes had looked after her
ancestors. As Jonathan had said, it was not given to many
to be allowed to go on working until their souls were ready
to depart.

She thought, I have been so wrong. So prejudiced, so
hurt. All right, she would admit that now. I have been so
unbearably hurt that I've allowed the scars to show, and
not only that, I've allowed them to influence me. Was
Tessa right when she suggested I was out for revenge?
Cassie wasn't at all sure, now. When your heart has gone
to a forbidden place there is no knowing what the mind
will do.

She lifted her head, looked up at the sky, pricked now by

stars, and made her vows. Together we will get out of this. Somehow. Goodness knows how, but we will. We will not sell the tapestry. We will put it on the wall and advertise it. We will use it to lure the connoisseurs in. We will invest in the gardens and lure the gardeners in. We will put on rock concerts and lure the young people in. She straightened her shoulders. We will start the way we mean to go on. We will impress people with Lady Alicia's fudge and we will not cut down on the cream.

Zoe? To hell with Zoe. She said it out loud, "To hell with Zoe and the Montcalm money. We will manage without it."

She slowly circled the park once more, then turned again towards the Hall. As she came to the edge of the drive she heard a scuffle in the gravel and suddenly Spicer was there in front of her, jumping up, pounding her chest with his paws in an ecstasy of welcome.

"Hello, old boy," she said. She pushed him back onto all fours and went down on her haunches to hug him. Spicer licked her hands, her face, her hair. "This is what I need," she told him. "A bit of love."

"Spicer! Come here, boy."

Cassie leapt to her feet and turned to run. Spicer made to race with her. "Go to your master," she whispered, but Spicer, tongue lolling, only gazed into her face, muscles tensed, ready to move after her.

"Spicer you devil, come here!" shouted Lord Haldane.

Cassie streaked for the side of the Hall. Spicer bounded along at her side. She stopped, protesting. "Go back, you naughty dog." He gazed up into her face and wagged his tail. Reluctantly, she retraced her steps. "He's here," she called.

His lordship did not answer, but as she came closer he said grumpily, "What are you doing out here at this hour young lady?"

"I needed a walk."

He peered at her in the dim light of the moon. "What's the matter with you?"

She saw the chance meeting as a heaven-sent opportunity to apologise. "I'm very sorry about the tapestry, Lord Haldane," she said. "I really am." As though he knew this was a portentous moment Spicer leaned up against her thigh.

"Why should you be sorry?" his lordship asked gruffly. "You can't take responsibility for what that fool boy does."

Cassie opened her mouth to protest that it was not Jonathan who had moved the tapestry, then closed it again. So that was why he didn't want her to apologise! She experienced a moment of shock.

"What do you know about it?" Lord Haldane asked.

"Nothing."

"I thought you were studying the history of the house."

"I am doing my best. I can't learn everything in a few months."

"Hrrmp!" said the earl. He poked his stick several times into the gravel, giving it all his attention. "It was made at a convent in Belgium for one of my early ancestors. It shows the Knights Templar, among whom were my ancestors," he said at last as though after some thought he had decided to tell her. "It's an emblem of poverty. Two knights on a single horse. Their motto was: *Non nobis, Domine, non nobis, sed nomini tuo da gloriam.*"

Cassie lifted her head in that way she had learned from Lady Haldane. "I didn't take Latin at school, your lordship." A few weeks ago she would have apologised.

223

"Not unto us, O Lord, not unto us, but to thy name glory."

She thought he was talking obscurely about the Hall. About holding it in trust.

"Why have you and her ladyship changed your minds about going to live abroad?" she asked.

He thrust his face nearer to hers. "You want to know? I'll tell you. Because I can't trust that fool boy. That's why."

Can't trust him to marry into his own kind? Couldn't be confident that the house would go on, serene and safe, in the hands of people who could look into the heart of a tapestry and know it's story? He seemed to be waiting for her to say something. She said, "I'm glad you're not going. May I say that I would like to be your friend. I'm taking the Hall into the twenty-first century the best way I know. It's not proving easy, because I've felt I didn't have you and her ladyship behind me."

He scowled and she could see he had no intention of answering her. She wasn't important enough. The Neilsons hadn't sailed off to conquer on foreign shores; stood steadfast at the side of kings; hauled booty home from exotic lands to enrich their heritage. So what! She wanted to ask him what he had done in the way of glory. Better not. But she reckoned she was entitled to react in her own way.

"I'm surprised you didn't see this situation arising twenty or thirty years ago," she told him. "I'd have thought you'd have equipped yourself to meet rising costs." She wondered if he had been living on capital and that was the reason he had now to clutch at an heiress, taking the easy way out.

He glared at her. "I'd be grateful if you'd remember this is my dog," he said huffily. "If you want a dog get one of your own. Come with me, Spicer."

The dog shuffled towards him, then turned and gazed up into Cassie's face. "Go on, Spicer," she said, feeling sad and deflated after her outburst, "go home."

Spicer hesitated as though waiting for her to rescind the order. Then Lord Haldane snapped, "Come on boy."

Spicer went reluctantly off towards the front door with him.

Chapter Fourteen

CASSIE, good businesswoman, person-in-charge, comptroller, knew what to do. She would get Jonathan into Lady Selena's room and have a very serious talk with him. He had never offered to show her the books. She intended to ask to see them. Why had she not insisted on this before? She knew the answer to that question. Little Cassie Neilson hadn't the right to look into his lordship's personal affairs.

But the comptroller had that right.

She had lain awake half the night working out what she would say. She was going to be very professional, very businesslike and very firm. She intended to suggest he sell the farms that were now leased out. The Hall didn't need farms. It needed only its surrounding parkland, and the gardens.

And cash.

She was going to ask him to give up his flat in the Barbican. Jonathan's mind was attuned to possessions. He had probably never heard the old saying that was one of her father's maxims: 'Take care of the pence, for the pounds will take care of themselves.' Hadn't she known when she first saw the dungeon that serious business, as she understood it, lay at the bottom of his agenda? If only she had had the courage then to tackle the job in the style she normally adopted when working for strangers she would have saved herself a great deal of heartache.

There was money needed now to publicise the rock concert she planned to hold in September. The newly determined Cassie was ready to tell his parents, if they protested, that there wasn't much profit in dignity. A rock concert would put the Hall on the map, and she would be able to slip in publicity for the opening next April.

There wouldn't be a great deal of expense in the staging of the Elizabethan cricket match and it certainly wouldn't attract so many onlookers, but the novelty of it, she hoped, would establish in the mind of the public that variety was to be their aim. What could be more different from rock than cricket? She aimed to have people on their toes wondering what Bevington Hall was going to come up with next.

But where was Jonathan?

His mother came to Lady Selena's room bearing a file. She said formally, standing in the middle of the carpet, "I've brought you the notes I've made on the history of the family." She tapped them with two fingers. "I believe everything that's available is here."

Cassie could tell by the way Lady Haldane stood rigidly, looking at a spot slightly to the north of her left ear, that she was remembering she had offered to take over the booklet herself, and Cassie's negative reaction.

Time to show grace.

"I'm now so very busy," she said, smiling up at her visitor, "that I couldn't begin to think of collating the book until after the opening of the Hall. But I'd very much like to have it ready to sell on that day. You did offer to take it off my hands. Would you still like to do that? After all, it's you who's done all the research. And it would be a tremendous help to me if you would."

Lady Haldane, gracious in her turn, replied, "I'd be only too pleased. I'd like you to glance through the file, though. Just a quick vetting."

"Thank you." Never mind that it was going to take up her valuable time. She was building bridges. While booting up the computer Cassie opened the file and leafed swiftly through. There were letters from grandees. She didn't pause to read more than the names and addresses. A title to a property. A marriage certificate. A photograph of a group of men and women in Edwardian clothes, the men bearing guns. Dogs sitting on their haunches, looking alert. Was that King Edward VII with the beard? She swiftly flipped over page after page. Here was a recipe concocted by the eighth countess for the purification of the skin. A bath oil. More letters.

Lethbridge Place! She stopped dead, her fingers poised rigidly above the file while she stared at the address on the next letter. Lethbridge Place was the seat of the Montcalms. The date was almost indecipherable but it could be, at a guess, 6 May 1870. The letter was addressed to the Earl of Bevington. Her eyes skipped over the text. '. . . deem it an insult . . . refuse, in quite insulting terms . . . your daughter's hand in marriage . . . I will have you know, sir – not an upstart . . . earned my title and I am a gentleman'.

Cassie sat back in her chair, frowning down at the page, her heart beating rapidly. Could this be the reason, three generations later, that Zoe's father was getting himself dug in to Bevington Hall? Was it possible that Lord Montcalm wanted to avenge his ancestor? She closed the file and continued with her work but the text of the letter worried away at the back of her mind.

Insulting terms . . . Upstart . . .

After supper she went carefully through the entire file. There was no further reference to the Montcalms.

The next morning at eleven o'clock she went in the wake of the butler with his coffee tray to the small drawing room. Lady Haldane was working at her tapestry. She looked up over her glasses. "Thank you, Edward," she said. Cassie was gratified that neither she nor his lordship had slipped back into calling the butler by his surname.

"You were quick with that," she said, glancing at the file Cassie held in her hands.

"I knew you wanted to get on." She laid the file on the coffee table and took a deep breath. "There's a letter here from the first Lord Montcalm protesting that one of his lordship's ancestors turned down his offer of marriage to a daughter. Do you know why?"

"The twelfth earl," replied Lady Haldane screwing up her eyes as she threaded a strand of wool through her needle. Then she transferred her attention to Cassie. "That Montcalm was the first of the family to be enobled. The Johnny-come-latelys didn't get the best pickings. Poor Lady Althea. She went on to marry Lord Lippington and had a perfectly horrid time. Edward, why didn't you bring a cup for Miss Neilson?"

"No, please," said Cassie hurriedly. "Mine will have arrived in my room. Thank you all the same." She wanted to get away before Jonathan's mother could ask her why she needed to know. She went back thoughtfully to Lady Selena's room. It seemed inconceivable to her that a hundred years later the present Lord Montcalm should be striving to

229

get even for the slight to an ancestor. On the other hand, grand families were nothing if not proud. She conceded it had been nice of Lady Haldane to invite her to coffee.

She had an early supper that night then, unable to settle, she returned to Lady Selena's room. Around eight o'clock there was a discreet knock at the door.

"Who is it?"

"Delivery man," replied a cockney voice.

A delivery man at eight at night! "Come in."

The door opened and Jonathan appeared wearing a wide, schoolboyish grin. In his hands he held a square basket. "Parcel for yer, Ma'am," he said, touching his forelock.

Cassie suppressed a titter. "What on earth . . . ?"

He lowered the basket to the floor, lifted the lid and turned it gently on its side. There was a wild scuffling and two fluffy pups, one tricoloured, one toffee, bounced out onto the carpet then stopped dead, looking round in wide-eyed amazement. They saw Cassie and hurled themselves across the room, slid to a stop at her feet, then with yearning squeals of affection tried to scramble up her legs.

"Two half-pint guard dogs for you," said Jonathan. "We can't afford to have such a valuable asset as a burglar-foiler unguarded."

"Oh Jonathan!" She bent down and gathered the pups into her arms. They scrambled across her chest, snatching mouthfuls of her hair in a frenzy of love.

"Oh Cassie!" he mimicked her, grinning.

"You shouldn't have! Really! They must have cost—"

"Nothing. Tessa's involved with the corgi rescue service. The pups' owner died suddenly. The rescue people didn't want them separated. Tessa wondered if, as an act of charity, you might like to take them on. By the way, the tricolour's called Puck and the other one's Goldie. They're five months old and housetrained. Well, to a point. You'll need to keep your wits about you. But you're nifty on your feet. I'm sure you won't let them pee on the Aubusson."

She lay back in the chair. The pups stretched their long bodies out straight on her chest with their noses tucked into her neck.

Jonathan came and stood over her. His face was gentle. She felt emotional, overwhelmed by his kindness.

There was a tap at the door. "That'll be Edward." He turned. "Come in." She stayed where she was, her mind in a turmoil, a huge lump in her throat, tears in her eyes. Edward entered carrying a cushioned basket and a blanket.

"I found it in the stables and gave it a clean up, Miss," Edward said. "And I'll bring up a bowl for their water. Start as you mean to go on, I'd say. Put them in this basket tonight."

"He means not on the end of the bed, don't you Edward?"

The butler nodded, amused, then left.

Jonathan came back and stood looking down at Cassie. Just when she thought he was going to kiss her he said, "I'll be on my way," and turning went out the door.

She looked after him in consternation. A moment later he was back. She struggled into a sitting position. The pups fell over each other. "I haven't thanked you," she managed.

He looked at her with those gentle eyes and said, "I was running away from myself, not you. I wanted to ask you to come to my room tonight."

Her heart turned over. "And you thought it was too much like asking for your pound of flesh?"

"Isn't it?"

"No," she whispered. "I want to come but this is where I

231

have a problem. You thought it was a good idea for me to live with my parents."

"Would they know if you weren't in your own bed?"

"Mothers, in my experience," said Cassie dryly, speaking over the thump of her heart, "tend to be half awake until they've been reassured their children haven't been involved in a car accident."

"You couldn't tell them the truth?"

"You know the answer to that." But did he? At that moment she lost her grip on the pups. Rather than let them fall she slipped out of her chair and sank to her knees on the floor. "We'd better give them a run before bedtime." She struggled to her feet with one pup tucked under each arm and carried them to their basket. "Righto, you two," she said pretending nothing at all had gone wrong, "we'll go down to the courtyard."

Jonathan didn't move. She looked at him mutely for a moment then overcome with emotion she flared, "I'm not going to blame my parents. They may not be so old-fashioned, but they would be very distressed if they knew I was in bed with a man who intended to marry someone more suitable."

He took a step towards her then stopped. "Cassie, don't say such things. You know I love you."

"Yes," she replied bitterly. "I do know that." What was the point of holding the truth back? She may as well clear the air between them. "But you're going to marry Zoe Montcalm." Suddenly, she saw the truth and added, "If you have to. If you can't get her father's money any other way." She picked up the basket and hurried through the door then ran along the passage that would take her to the flat.

*   *   *

The pups were a great success. Cook wanted them in the kitchen. Her mother wanted them in the flat. They preferred to follow Cassie every waking hour. In the end, everyone compromised. The basket travelled between the flat, the kitchen and Lady Selena's room. The setter came up to visit and stayed to play. The pups pulled his tail. He lay down and they jumped on him. They teased him unmercifully. Spicer loved it. He opened his jaws and held their little heads delicately between his teeth, pretending he was going to bite them off. He shed his years and became a puppy again.

"I thought Goldie and Puck were intended to keep Spicer in his rightful place," Mrs Bachelor remarked, standing with Cassie's tea mug in one hand, smilingly watching the boisterous game that was being played out on the floor. "I thought young Jonathan was being clever, bringing them like to take your mind off his lordship's dog."

"They're a thank-you present for my part in catching the burglars."

"Oh yes." Mrs Bachelor put the tea down and stood with hands on hips watching the dogs, apparently absorbed. Cassie waited for her to elaborate but she left after a moment or two without saying anything more.

The arrival of the pups, Jonathan's generosity (for she did not wholly believe the story of Tessa finding them at the rescue house) and Cassie's outburst, had created an impasse. That's life, she thought resignedly. Just when you get everything sorted out some natural force comes in like a bolt of lightning and destroys the lot.

Jonathan came and went about his affairs. They were polite to each other. Cassie had lost the courage to tackle him about the finances. Maybe he truly loved Zoe . . .

Maybe he loved both of them . . . Maybe he was angry with her for exposing the truth.

She went doggedly on with her work. Janis Lawson, the daughter of the woman who owned Jane's Boutique in Flyford, came up to inspect the stables. They weren't going to make a fortune out of commission on the sale of her gowns, but Cassie felt it would add to the attractions. Cassie wondered if eventually she might make the entire stable block into a little shopping mall. New ideas flew daily through her mind.

Susan Pannington finished her catering course and came up to work out details of space for the urns and tea tables in the old barn.

The restaurant was going to have to be shelved until they could give time to working out how it might be run. The best restaurants are run by the owner," Cassie said.

"No way," retorted Jonathan.

She might have laughed about that but the laughter between them had stopped.

Colin agreed to have his designs on tea towels. "I never expected to be this commercial," he remarked, looking quizzical.

"What people will do for money!" She could still laugh with Colin.

"I've noticed that," he said. "By the way, I've talked to him. He's not a bad chap. We're on quite good terms now."

"Him? Jonathan? I'm glad." Jonathan hadn't mentioned the fact to her. She experienced the loneliness again.

"Are you coming down to the pub for a drink?"

"Sorry. No time. I really am working very hard."

"That's why you need relaxation."

Cassie knew that might be true, but when she relaxed her heart began yearning. She needed to work hard.

Who would have thought it would be a combination of the tapestry and the dogs that would bring the two of them back on an even footing? One morning Jonathan arrived with a bounce in his step and a smile on his face. The three dogs were playing quietly on the floor by Cassie's desk.

"The tapestry has made a full recovery."

"Thank God!" Cassie collapsed into her seat, emotional with relief. The next moment the door was flung open and Lord Haldane appeared. Standing with feet apart and thumbs in the pockets of his old tweed jacket he looked from Jonathan to Cassie, back with some uncertainty to Jonathan, then down at the warring animals on the carpet.

"What's this? A damned kennels?" he shouted.

Jonathan said gravely, "Cassie doesn't invite Spicer. He's got a problem. He likes girls. And pups."

His father gave him a black look, then addressed the dog loudly and with considerable authority. "Come here, Spicer!"

Spicer climbed to his feet and with head drooping crossed the floor to his master. Lord Haldane stumped off down the passage with Spicer in his wake. The pups raced after them, yelping. "That'll teach her." His words, carrying a grim kind of satisfaction, found their way back.

Cassie and Jonathan looked at each other and stifled a burst of laughter. "Problem solved?"

"Tit for tat." Jonathan pulled out the spare chair and settled in, elbows on the arms, fingers steepled. The laughter had gone from his eyes. "We now have to talk," he said.

"About selling the tapestry?"

235

"About the fact that it's once more available for sale."

"You don't want to sell it. And nor do I. But it's a way out of your dilemma?"

He looked at her tiredly. "Have you a better plan?"

She recognised that at last the moment had come. "If I could see your books – if you would be totally open with me about the state of your finances – I might come up with a plan."

He brushed a hand across his forehead in that way he had. "We've come to the end of the road," he stated.

"I see the sacrifice of the tapestry as a wish to be free of Lord Montcalm," she said gently. "I'm not asking about Zoe. I'm asking about your freedom."

Jonathan's forehead creased in a frown. "It's a mess," he sighed.

"You could tell me about it."

"All right," he said at last. "I will. When Montcalm first offered the money there were no strings attached. That's the crux of the matter. That's why I took him up. Then Zoe moved in and the balance shifted. Nothing was said outright, but it began to be more and more clear that the money was to come with the daughter attached." Jonathan added bitterly, "Mother doesn't help by referring to Zoe as 'part of the family'. Don't think I'm running Zoe down, she's a nice girl. But marriage wasn't in my mind. I'm not certain it was in her mind either, at the start. Anyhow, while I was worrying about how to get out of all of that, I realised that Montcalm wanted control of the Hall. I could see he never had any intention of handing over the cash on a legally binding loan." Again he brushed the hand across his brow. "I wake up in the night in a sweat, feeling the house slipping away."

"Oh Jonathan." She wanted to take him in her arms.

"He wants to give me money on what he calls a 'friendly basis'. I can't get him to discuss terms and interest. That's why I've been spending time over at Lethbridge Place. I've been trying to get a proper business deal. I can't prove it, and I can't put it to him, but it's there. I'll swear he wants control."

"Why should he want the Hall when he has a mansion of his own?"

"I don't know. Power's an insidious thing. That's why I decided to sell the tapestry. I recognise now it was a stupid way out but when you're desperate you lose track."

"Why sell your most valuable possession?"

He took a moment to answer. "I couldn't see that opening the house was going to work on a long-term basis. The sale of the Crusaders tapestry would be real money in the bank. It represented generations of safety for those who come after me."

She looked at him with sadness. "You didn't have faith in me."

"Oh Cassie! Do you know what it's like to be desperate?" Without waiting for her reply he went on, "All I could think was that I needed to get clear of Montcalm."

"Listen to this," Cassie said. She told him about the letter she had found in the file.

Jonathan's eyes dilated. For a long moment he didn't speak. "It makes sense," he said at last. "Yes, it makes sense."

Cassie sat up straight. She felt newly filled with confidence. "Let's see what we can do without selling the Crusaders tapestry, which after all is your family's greatest asset. I'm going to do something long-term with that, if we can hang on to it. I'm going to make it a showpiece, so connoisseurs will come from far and near to see it."

"You're full of ideas, aren't you?"

"Yes. And one of them is to cut my salary to what I reckon to be local rates. It's a small thing in the context, but important to me."

Jonathan opened his mouth to protest.

"I'm in charge. I make the decisions. What is this job all about if not your family's extravagance?"

"You," said Jonathan with a twinkle, "are my family's greatest asset, never mind the Crusaders tapestry."

"Nice of you to say so. I'm very glad I've got your confidence at last. And by the way," she went on using her brisk, businesslike voice, "if you're so hard up, why am I driving round in an impressive great Volvo?"

He took a long time to answer. Then he said, quietly but very, firmly, "The Volvo stays."

Chapter Fifteen

THEY CLOSETED themselves in Lady Selena's room for the best part of three days. They visited Jonathan's bank manager and arranged a loan with the Gauguin picture as collateral so that they could support a heavy programme of advertising for the rock concert. Cassie contacted a well-known group. The manager suggested she meet him in London. Cassie insisted he come down to Hampshire.

"Such power you have," said Jonathan, half teasing, half in awe.

"I want him to see the venue. If he's greatly impressed, as I'm sure he will be, I'll be in a better position to screw a higher fee out of him."

It was a wonderful summer's day. The park looked beautiful. Pheasants roved fearlessly among the chestnut trees. Squirrels scurried up and down the trunks as though trained for some film set. Cassie thought God must be on her side. When she drove the man back to Flyford to catch the train for London she felt she had him in the palm of her hand.

"I've arranged the most amazing fee with him," she confided to Jonathan that evening. "It's extortion, at least I thought it was extortion until I got him to admit how much they expect in takings. Next year, when all this work is done, and we've got time, we're going to hire the band and the seating ourselves. We're going to do all the work and take the entire profit."

Jonathan said, "His lordship's going to hate it."

"He hated me running off with his dog and look how that worked out. Things have a habit of falling into place."

Lady Haldane came with the news that she had unearthed some period costumes. "They're not in very good condition," she said, "but we might be able to do something with them if you're interested. I was thinking of glass cases just inside the front door."

"I think it's a good idea." Cassie made a note on her pad to look into the cost of glass casing.

Then Zoe came to stay. Cassie knew because, having a view of the drive from Lady Selena's room, she saw the car drive up; saw Edward go out and collect a suitcase.

Cassie had a visit from her the next day. She rapped sharply on the door then without waiting for a reply walked into Lady Selena's room wearing an air of immense confidence. She looked very pretty in a pink summer dress with cut-away shoes and her wealth of dark hair flowing over her shoulders.

Without offering Cassie the courtesy of a greeting, she said, "I've heard from Lady Haldane that she's unearthed some period costumes."

"She has."

"You're going to put them on show."

"I haven't decided. I haven't seen them but I believe they're not in very good condition. They need mending and possibly cleaning. They're not a priority for the moment."

"I've got an aunt in a grace-and-favour flat at Hampton Court Palace." Zoe waited for Cassie's reaction.

"Yes?" Cassie smiled, unsurprised that Zoe should have an aunt at Hampton Court.

"There are expert needlewomen working there all the time. I thought she might be able to have them attended to."

"That's very kind of you."

"I'll take them, then."

"No." Cassie shook her head.

Cassie noted that Zoe was not so pretty when wearing a hostile expression. She said angrily, "What right have you to say no."

"We're very busy at the moment. I haven't time to start on anything new."

"I've told you, I can deal with it."

"I'm sorry," said Cassie.

Zoe flounced out of the room saying she would talk to Lady Haldane. "And a fat lot of good that will do her," Cassie said to Lady Selena without looking up, not wanting to see if her expression had changed; if she disapproved of the gardener's granddaughter standing up to the daughter of a noble. Half an hour later Zoe stormed back and thrust a pair of mangled shoes across the desk. "Look what those beastly pups of yours have done!"

Cassie's heart sank. "I'm terribly sorry," she said. "I'll replace them. Would you like to buy a new pair and give me the bill?"

"*You*," she said enunciating the word with cut-glass precision, "replacing *my* shoes. You've got a nerve!" She swung round and marched out of the room.

Cassie shrugged. Now she did look up at Lady Selena. "She can afford them," she muttered. "And it's her own fault. If she hadn't left them lying around the pups wouldn't have found them."

Lady Selena had put on her enigmatic look again. It occurred to Cassie then that she was no longer afraid of Zoe. When she heard a car start up in the drive she did not look out of the window.

Later, Jonathan came in. She pushed her chair back, brushed her hair away from her forehead and said, "I'm sorry."

"Don't be sorry." He laughed softly. "Those pups are earning their keep." He pulled out the chair opposite and sat down. "Zoe says she won't come back until you go. And you can't go because you're tied by contract until next April. I'm going to have to follow her over to Lethbridge Place and tell his lordship . . ."

"Write a letter," snapped Cassie, allowing herself delayed reaction about the fact that she wasn't considered even a suitable person to replace Zoe's footwear.

He looked at her oddly, then said, "That's the businesslike way, but it's not the way I'm accustomed to do things. I'm not without fault in this. I should have pulled out immediately I suspected Zoe was involved. I should have realised I wasn't going to win."

How could he know? He was speaking with hindsight. But she recognised he wished to shoulder some of the blame.

"By the way," he said, "I've got a confession to make. I caught your mother using the back way through the servants' – sorry, staff – quarters. I'm afraid I rather upset her."

Hadn't she known Leila would find a way to avoid the front door?

"If you don't mind," Jonathan said, "I'd rather you didn't – um – could you possibly not – er – manage to go to the flat until I come back?"

"Were you very hard on her?"

"It's more complex than that." He rose, pushed his chair up against the kneehole and left.

Suppertime came and went. Cook made Cassie a sandwich. The pups, looking angelic, were asleep in their basket by the Aga.

"Them little darlings are in disgrace," said Cook cheerfully. "You heard about the shoes?"

Everyone knew about the shoes. The staff were smug. Watchful. Cassie felt their eyes following her. Zoe's abrupt going seemed to have let loose something in the atmosphere.

She hid in Lady Selena's room. As the light faded it was as though the lady stepped out of her portrait and became a mysterious centre of the room.

It was late when Jonathan came.

"You are here!" he exclaimed in surprise, looking round the door, blinking into the dimness. "What's the matter with the light?"

"You forbade me to go to the flat, remember? So, as I've finished all the work I want to do, I'm communing with my ghost."

Jonathan's eyes lifted to the ash blonde hair, the high curved bosom, the sloping shoulders. "What's she got to say?"

"Sometimes I think she's trying to tell me something."

He reached across the desk and took her hands. "I hope you're listening. I knew when I first asked her if you could bring your office in here, that she wanted you to stay."

"You talk to her, too?"

"I wander round the house in the night sometimes when everyone's gone. It's mine, then. Truly mine."

243

"Is it yours again?" she asked him softly. "Have you got rid of Lord Montcalm?"

His mouth turned up with a pleased smile. "Zoe made it easy for me when she said she wouldn't come back until you went. I told her you were going to stay forever. You didn't mind my jumping the gun, did you? I saw it as the only way to finish things quickly and cleanly."

When Cassie got her breath she asked softly, "Is that why you met me at Heathrow in the Rolls?"

"And why no one's allowed to call you Cassie."

"And why I drive that fancy car?"

"And why I've moved your parents into the Hall."

Suddenly everything fell into place.

"I had to build up a background for you, Cassie. I had to set a scene that would enable you to stand with dignity at my side."

She said in a small voice, "I'm very glad to know what it seems to me the staff and the village have already guessed. But my parents haven't. Mother's going to be shattered." She recognised with surprise that she had called Leila Mother.

Jonathan noticed it, too. "I thought you called her by her christian name."

"That was when I was a dependent daughter and needed to hold my own. As the wife of the Honourable Jonathan Tarrant I shall be happy to call her Mother."

He said, "I was going to LA to propose to you, marry you there if you'd have me, and present everyone with a fait accompli. Then the accident happened."

"It was better this way. It's always better not to shock people. It's been a rough road but yes, this was best. About your parents?"

"I think my father's ready, thanks to the miracle of the dogs. He's been cocky as the devil since the pups started following him. And Mother knows when she's beaten. She's always been a past master at compromise. Tessa will smooth out any problems."

Cassie remembered how sharp Jonathan's sister had been with her when she used her title. And the enigmatic nature of her visits to Lady Selena's room. Perhaps she, like the staff, had seen what was coming. "By the way," she said, trying to smile, feeling terribly emotional, "are you proposing? Is this the way heirs propose?"

"I could go down on one knee in the Elizabethan way."

"I'd like that," she said.

Much later Jonathan asked, "When can we get married?"

She dragged herself back from nirvana. "We're in no position to indulge ourselves with privacy. Why don't we get married right after the cricket, in the little chapel, the evening before we open to the public?"

"With the teams as guests?"

"In their Elizabethan costumes?"

"And have our reception in the tearoom?"

They rocked with laughter.

"I'll sell my life story first, with the headline, 'Gardener's Granddaughter to Lady of the Hall'. I'll offer it to a tabloid and ask a record fee. That'll bring in the television cameras. There's nothing the public likes more than a cinderella story. We'll have visitors fighting to get in. We could give the first fifty a bit of wedding cake."

Jonathan looked at her quizzically, "Are you joking, or not?"

"I'm not absolutely certain." Cassie's mouth twitched.

"Anyway, there's plenty of time to think about it. Why did you not want me to go to the flat until you got back?"

"I didn't want you to have to make excuses for my being sharp with your mother until you were in a position to say I can't have my mother-in-law using the servants' entrance."

"Staff. I remember to drive on the left. You remember to say staff."

Everything seemed incredibly funny. Again they rocked with laughter. Perhaps it was because it had been so long since they had anything to laugh about.

Jonathan's parents accepted the news without protest. Even with a certain grace. The countess produced a ruby ring, the stone surrounded by diamonds. "It was my great-grandmother's engagement ring," she said. She looked over her glasses at Cassie in a quite unmannerly way. "Ah well," she said, "there's no doubt you'll be a good helpmeet to my son."

Cassie was touched by her choice of the old-fashioned words.

Gerald said merely, "I felt it was always on the cards."

"You're glad?"

"Of course." His eyes twinkled. "I rather fancy myself as co-grandfather with his lordship to the next heir to Bevington Hall."

Leila looked nervous. "I cannot see myself—"

Cassie cut her off. "You'll manage very well," she said firmly. "Now, if you've had a good look at this ring I'll put it away in the office safe."

"Are you going to tell the staff?"

"Not yet. But they'll get it by osmosis, in the usual way."

*   *   *

The rock concert went ahead with a minimum of disruption for the Hall. Lord and Lady Haldane, to everyone's disbelief, preceded by Edward carrying their chairs, settled behind the back row and saw the concert through from start to finish.

"Who says folk can be too old to change?" Cassie felt smug as she banked the cheque.

"I feel myself growing more like Shylock every week," said Jonathan looking apologetic.

"You've got to learn to like making money."

There were lots of laughs these days.

Autumn came with its silvery evening mists creeping across the parkland, the big trees ghostlike in the expanse of gardens. Sometimes in the cool, silent evenings Cassie and Jonathan walked in the park, taking the dogs with them. Here they made their plans and dreamed.

Christmas was imminent.

"I think we might shelve moneymaking, just for the season," Cassie said. "Why don't we resurrect the carols and the tree ceremony and give little presents to everyone? We could have a dance in the Hall and invite every member of the present staff and all those who've contracted to work here once the Hall's open."

"Remember when I tried to give you the teddy bear?"

"I took the scar to LA and brought it back with me."

"It's gone now?"

"It went when you asked me to marry you."

In March she put a notice in the cricket pavilion asking for volunteers from the two local teams to play a match at the Hall in April. They were swiftly oversubscribed. Cassie asked the players to send up their measurements. Jonathan contacted the old boys of his school who had played at Bevington Hall all those years ago, and asked for theirs.

Cassie ushered the corgis into the back of the Volvo and sped off to meet the wardrobe mistress of the local amateur dramatic group. She collected long jerkins, shirts with embroidered sleeves, heeled shoes with wonderful buckles, doublets and triple ruffs. But there were not enough. She scoured the wardrobe of every group within twenty miles and at last was satisfied that with a little compromise, they could manage.

"You were teasing when you said you'd get married after the cricket, weren't you?" Leila asked tentatively one day.

"No. And by the way, I forgot to say that the player with the highest score is to be best man."

Her mother looked unnerved. "You are teasing."

"I'm not sure. I'm thinking of the television coverage we could get. Jonathan and I are part of a huge commercial enterprise, now."

"Are you going to be a bride?"

Cassie hugged her. "Sure, if it brings a smile to your face. Janis could fix me up with a glamorous gown from her boutique. It would be great publicity for her. We could exhibit the dress afterwards."

Gerald shook his head.

"If it's any comfort to you," Cassie said to him, laughing, "Jonathan's parents are bewildered, too. But you have to remember that whatever we do, we do in the interests of the Hall. It's ruling our lives, for the moment. Privacy and publicity don't go together."

"What about a honeymoon?"

"Next winter."

*   *   *

The village cricket team came to try on their costumes. The earl and countess joined in the fun. The young men strutted round the big entrance hall in doublet and hose with jaunty feathers in their hats, thoroughly enjoying themselves. The earl seated himself in a big Jacobean chair beneath the family coat of arms, teasing the corgis, criticising, handing out advice. A photographer and a journalist came from the local paper. The other team, who would arrive on the morning of the match, were going to have to take their chance on the fit of their costumes.

Everything was under control. The chapel was decked with flowers arranged by the women who were to be guides. The cream satin dress that Janis had designed was on its hanger in Cassie's bedroom. Lady Haldane's tiara had been cleaned. Unbelievably, she had kept it in the top of her wardrobe with some old hats.

Susan Pannington and her helpers were bustling round the decorated tearoom setting up tables for the evening reception. Cassie stood at the window of Lady Selena's room musing on the fact that she must surely be the first bride who ever went to a cricket match before her wedding. And the first to preside over the opening of a stately home the following day. She was remembering, too, Jonathan's twenty-first birthday when she had hidden in the rhododendrons that in those days bordered the drive, enviously watching the pretty girls and the handsome young men stepping out of cars.

How easily they had, after all, bridged the social gap. The tiny chapel would be bulging at the seams with the two immediate families, the two cricket teams, and the staff.

She turned as the door swung open.

As Jonathan came towards her he said, "A groom isn't supposed to see his bride before the wedding."

She gazed at him with love. "But it's no ordinary wedding. None of the usual rules apply."

He took her in his arms.

"This," she said, "is the day that has been waiting for me all my life."

"And me."

Over Jonathan's shoulder she saw the first of the television vans coming up the drive. She turned to look at the portrait of Lady Selena on the wall and saw that she was smiling.